Elske

❖—●—❖

Also by Cynthia Voigt

Bad, Badder, Baddest

Bad Girls

Bad Girls in Love

Building Blocks

The Callender Papers

Come a Stranger

David & Jonathan

Dicey's Song

Homecoming

It's Not Easy Being Bad

Izzy, Willy-Nilly

Jackaroo

On Fortune's Wheel

Orfe

The Runner

Seventeen Against the Dealer

A Solitary Blue

Sons from Afar

Tell Me if the Lovers Are Losers

Tree by Leaf

The Vandemark Mummy

When She Hollers

The Wings of a Falcon

Elske

＊—●—＊

CYNTHIA VOIGT

Simon Pulse
New York London Toronto Sydney Singapore

First Simon Pulse edition October 2003

SIMON PULSE
An imprint of Simon & Schuster Children's Publishing Division
1230 Avenue of the Americas
New York, NY 10020

Also available in an Atheneum Books for Young Readers hardcover edition and an Aladdin Paperbacks trade edition.

Designed by Ann Bobco
The text of this book was set in Goudy OlSt BT.

Printed in the United States of America

10 9 8 7 6 5 4 3 2 1

The Library of Congress has cataloged the hardcover edition as follows:
Voigt, Cynthia.
Elske / by Cynthia Voigt. —1st ed.
p.   cm.
"An Anne Schwartz Book"
Summary: Thirteen-year-old Elske escapes rape and certain death at the hands of the leaders of her barbaric society and later becomes handmaiden to a rebellious noblewoman whose rightful throne together they claim.
ISBN 0-689-82472-6 (hc.)
[1. Kings, queens, rulers, etc.—Fiction. 2. Fantasy.] I. Title.
PZ7.V874El   1999   [Fic]—dc21 98-50219
ISBN 0-689-84444-1 (Aladdin pbk.)
ISBN 0-689-86438-8 (Simon Pulse pbk.)

For Bob Fraser, in fond memory, and
for his beloved wife, Penny—
two halves of one

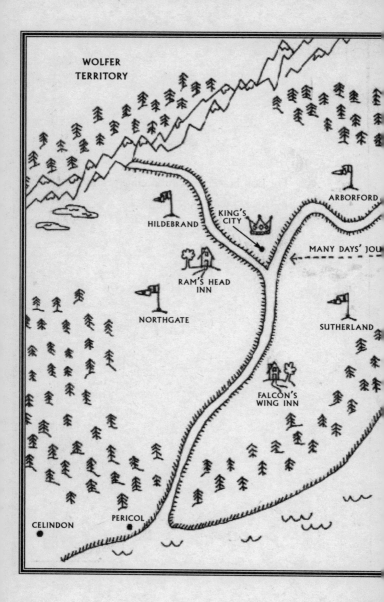

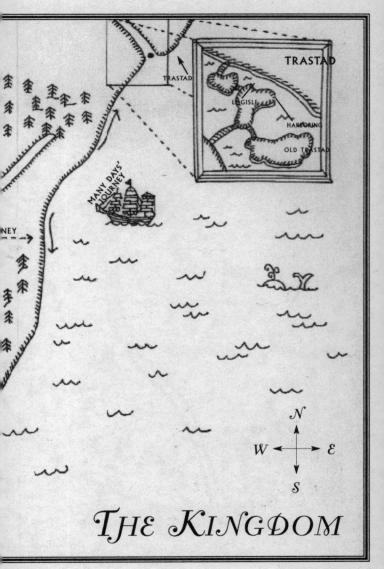

TRASTAD

LEGISLE

HARBORING

OLD TRASTAD

TRASTAD

MANY DAYS' JOURNEY

NEY

N

W ← → E

S

THE KINGDOM

map by Caitlin Van Dusen

Chapter 1

THE VOLKKING STRUGGLED, but his sickness attacked him both day and night, a war band giving the enemy no respite of sleep. From the longest day until harvest-time, the Volkking sickened, and as it was with the King, so was it with his land. Crops grew unnourished, unrained on, sickly. Streams sank back into their stony beds and fish died in the shallow water. Game was scarce and scrawny, the pelts thin. The people of the Volkaric, too, across that wasting summer, fell into a sickness of lethargy.

The days grew shorter, and still at each sunrise the Volkking came out to sit on his carved wooden throne. Each morning the wounds of the night's battle were visible on his whited face, and in his shaking hands—but still the Volkking kept his treasure under his eye. He counted the chests his warriors had filled for him with coins, golden jewelry, silver plates and goblets pillaged from the rich southern lands; he measured the piles of furs his hunters had gathered, wolf, bear and beaver, ermine; he counted his women and his sons. The Volkking kept his treasure close. His people he also kept close, as if he believed that all standing together might withstand Death's attack, or at least conceal their King from Death's cold eye.

The people of the Volkaric did not question him.

All the long days of his slow dying, the Volkking sat enthroned, and his eye measured his treasure and measured his people, and then he turned his face to the western distances, waiting to glimpse Death's approach.

His captains, too, awaited Death and the Strydd that came after. That captain who rose victor from the Strydd—dead comrades at his feet, vanquished comrades on their knees—became Volkking.

His women, too, awaited Death. They would then wash the Volkking's body one last time, dress him in the richest of his woven robes, and cover his face with pale, fine hair cut from their own heads. They knew that after the death feast and the death fire and the Strydd, some among them would be taken to give sons to the new Volkking.

The Death Maiden, chosen for her honey skin and dark grey eyes, picked out by the Volkking himself from among the girlchildren, when his previous choice started her moonly bleeding—the Death Maiden, too, awaited her day.

Elske was the chosen Death Maiden.

Even the ironhearted women of the Volkaric, who bore their children soundlessly and lost their men without an eyeblink for grief, would have wished some other girlchild for Death Maiden, even if this did make a good vengeance on Mirkele, that mansnarer, that schemer. Mirkele had never had a captive's proper shame, not when she was a plump young woman proud of her dark hair and dark eyes, and not now either. She had grown old and thin as a wolf in winter, but still proud, now of this granddaughter.

The women would have hated Elske if they could, but not being able to do that, they hated Mirkele the more.

The vengeance on grey-haired Mirkele was good, better even than when the last of her sons was slain in far-off battle. But an unaccustomed lightness would be taken from the Volkaric when Elske entered into the Death House so that she might follow the Volkking into Death's great halls and serve him there until the sun burned out. For Elske had been fed of the honey which Mirkele received from the Volkking whenever a boychild was born, and the sweetness of honey cake was on Elske's breath and her skin was the color of pale new honey, and her greeting glance sweetened the day around her as honey sweetens water. Elske was different from the Volkaric, as small and dark and different as her grandmother, but no schemer, no deceiver, and even the jealous women named neither of them coward. Elske was like the flowers that suddenly swept across the meadows in the spring, appearing without warning, gone almost before they could be seen, delicious in color and scent, a brief gladness. But unlike the flowers, smoke-eyed, bright-hearted Elske had lingered among the Volkaric season after season, until now, when Death would lead her away from them all and the women would have their revenge.

At last, with the harvest sun high in the sky over him, the Volkking rose up before his throne, and would not move or speak or hear, all the long afternoon. The Volkking stood stiff before his throne, a dead man, yet living, and his silent people watched. Seated on the hard ground around him, as numerous as the grasses in the lands he ruled over, they waited with the Volkking until—long into the star-pricked night—Death felled him.

Then the captains dug out the shallow lake for his Death House, and covered its dirt floor with straw, and wove together dried reeds for its walls, and made its low roof out of straw and branches. That done, they carried the Volkking within, and set the torch into its stand by his head, that he might have a light beside his eyes. All around his bed they spread full half of his treasure. At last they came out again, to drink the King's mead and eat the festal meat.

Then the women sent for the Death Maiden. Small in the silver wolf cloak, she walked through the moving shadows of the fires, her bright face hidden in the darkness of her hair. She turned neither to right nor to left as her bare feet took her up to the doorway of the Death House.

The people of the Volkaric watched, silent, as she approached her fate. At the low entrance, she halted—her back to her watchers—and dropped the cloak around her feet, for the Death Maiden must enter to the Volkking clothed only in her nakedness. The people saw a glimpse of white skin, and the tumbling fall of long dark hair, and she was gone.

Now the greatest among the Volkking's captains emptied their drinking horns, set aside their robes and weapons and followed the Death Maiden, themselves naked. The people of the Volkaric, listening, heard what they could not see. They heard the Maiden's cries as the Volkking's captains held her down and raped her—as cruelly as they could, in a fury of grief and mead. Listening, the Volkaric beat on their thighs with their hands, to carry her shrieks of fear and pain into the Halls of Death to honor the Volkking. The Volkaric drank deep of the honey mead, beat their thighs, listened to the terror from within and sometimes themselves howled like wolves, the war cry of the Volkaric. When the captains were done, they would leave Maiden and Volkking together, and the last captain would turn at the doorway to lay the torch on the straw floor. Then the Death House and all within it would burn to dust.

But on this night, for this Volkking's death, when the Death Maiden no longer cried out, and the beating hands had tired, and throats were too raw to howl again, and silence flowed like night out of the low doorway of the Death House, flames erupted—

The captains had not emerged.

Great flames roared forth, driving the people of the Volkaric back with their heat. The flames seized the Death House in their red-fingered grasp and tossed it up into the empty sky as King and Maiden and treasure, and captains, too, in a burial fit for the greatest of Volkkings, all were at once devoured.

Chapter 2

ELSKE WAS AWAY to the east when the sky behind her began to glow on the horizon, as if a small sun—perhaps a child sun taking his first clumsy, confused steps—had lost his way and was trying to rise in the west, at night. Elske had often looked behind her, anxious to see that light. Only then could she know that Mirkele had finished the death meant for Elske. When Elske at last saw the western sky stained with fire, she turned back onto her own way with a lighter step.

There was no path, but Mirkele had instructed Elske carefully: Go to the east, up into the hills. Elske moved quickly over the rough land. Having seen the fire behind her, she had no further need to look back. The wolf cloak she wore was too warm for the mild night, and the sack she carried on her back was heavy with baked wheat breads and smoked meat strips, and her winter boots, too; so Elske was bathed in a cool, cleansing sweat. Her grandmother said she must travel to the east and the north, away from the gentle southern lands where the Volkaric war bands marauded. If the men of the Volkaric ever found Elske—

Mirkele had told her: She must go to the eastern hills and not stop to rest until she was the night and a day distant from the Volkking's stronghold.

Darkness wrapped itself around Elske like friendly arms, concealing her soft footsteps in its own noises. Elske slid through the night like a boat through water.

She had never seen a boat, of course. But her grandmother—

Elske could feel the emptiness beside her, where Mirkele had once stood. All the twelve winters of her life had been lived in Mirkele's company, in the Birth House where the Volkking had placed the little, dark southern captive. In the Birth House, Mirkele lived apart from the others, whose houses crowded together against the King's walls. Mirkele was midwife, and she also kept those unwanted female children who survived their births, until the spring when she must take those unnecessary babes out into the northern wildness, and leave them there to feed the wolves. That had become Mirkele's work, after she had been captured and set aside for the Volkking, that he might admire her dark southern beauty and be the first to rape her.

But her grandmother—

Elske now told herself the story she had often been told, but told it silently, her voice kept inside of her head, as she traveled east. Her grandmother had been no maiden. Mirkele had deceived the Volkaric war party with her slight girl's body, and her silence. Mirkele was clever, and she had kept silent until she could understand the language of her captors, and learn what they had planned for her. She kept silent, and never said that she had

7

been a wife and borne children, until she spoke it into the Volkking's ear.

The Volkking's wrath at learning this had fallen not on Mirkele, who deserved it, but on his own men, whom he shamed with beating, and shamed by keeping their sons for his own, and shamed by mocking their ignorance of women. Mirkele he set apart, to midwife the women of the Volkaric and to bear whatever children were got upon her; for the Volkking wished her to live and not—as the women hoped—die.

The streams Elske splashed through now were cold on her bare feet and ankles, and that refreshed her, helping her along her way, just as the sharp stones and bristling undergrowth pricked, to speed her on. All of that night's journey Elske remembered her grandmother, filling the empty place beside her with memories.

She remembered Mirkele when her grandmother's hair was dark and her voice sweet as she sang the babes to sleep; she remembered how Mirkele would look up from where a root stew bubbled, or glance over at Elske as she showed the steps of a dance; and she remembered Mirkele's gladness, as if her life among the Volkaric were no more trouble than a moth, fluttering at her face. But when the Volkking chose Elske Death Maiden, something changed in Mirkele, as if this last was the smithy's anvil blow that hardened her to steel; and Mirkele's hair began to turn grey.

Elske remembered Mirkele in their own language, the language of the southern cities. This was one of their secrets, that Elske could speak Souther. Another was that Mirkele had taught Elske to read

8

letters, and to scratch words into the dirt, as she herself had been taught, when she was a girl, in her father's many-roomed house. In their secret language, Elske gave her grandmother her true name, Tamara, and she called the Volkaric as Tamara had, Wolfers.

"Wolfers know only fear and greed," Tamara said. "They cannot taste the sweetness of honey."

Tamara had instructed Elske: She must travel to the east until she came to a path made by merchants carrying goods northwards from the wealthy cities of the south. Years ago, Tamara had been seized from her home and husband, and then falsely bartered for gold by the Wolfer captain to merchants who spoke of that path, leading eventually to a great city in the north. The foolish merchants were stripped of life and goods by that same captain before the day's end, and Tamara was taken to her life among the Volkaric. "Well," Tamara always ended the story, "and so I have you, my Elskeling."

Two times earlier in her life, Tamara had escaped the Wolfers, but not the third. She instructed Elske: "Travel northwards. Listen to me, and haven't you always had goodness happen for you? Maybe you will reach some place to winter over, but if winter does come down before you reach safety, that will be a gentle death."

Elske knew that Tamara's end in the Death House had not been gentle. She also knew, however, that in her death Tamara had taken revenge on those who had seized her from husband and children, from her birthright, too, and she had taken revenge for the two young men who once gave their lives for hers, in the first Wolfer raid she survived. So Tamara had a good death.

Night's darkness cloaked Elske, covering her as the winter snows cover mountains, from peak to foot. Elske moved with the weight of darkness on her shoulders, on her head; and she tasted it in her mouth like the flavorless rills that ran so fast in spring melts. Now there were trees around her, tall, thick, dark shapes, rooted, and the spaces between them—into which she moved—blocked sight with their dense blackness. She heard the rustling of leaves at her feet, and a sighing wind, and occasionally the owl's questioning cry. It was the harvest season. Wolves would not yet be on the hunt and bears would be fatted for winter, slow and sleepy. The darkness smelled empty, clean, safe. Elske felt herself part of the darkness, moving steadily through it, as invisible as the night air.

Because she could not tire, Elske did not tire. It would be a day, or maybe two, before any of the women went out to Mirkele's hut, so much did the Volkaric fear her. The women would draw close to the hut, and hear nothing. They would enter to find—if animals hadn't carried them all away—the bodies of the babes in Mirkele's care. "I *am* caring for them," Tamara always said before she and Elske snapped the necks of those girl babies, giving the wolves bodies as flesh to be eaten, not living babes as prey. In this, too, Tamara defied the Volkking; had it been known that the babes had been killed before being fed to the wolves, it would have meant Tamara's death, and Elske's, too. But she always said, "I set these children free from life before they know any greater harm than hunger." On that final night she sent Elske away before the slaughter. "You go off now, Elskeling, Elskele. I do not fear my death when it makes your life." And Elske obeyed.

So the women, when they dared to approach the Birth House, would find the babes dead, the larder empty and the fire cold. They would think they saw Mirkele's revenge for the loss of her granddaughter.

In part, they would have seen truly. Tamara's hope, and Elske's, too, was that they would not see completely. Tamara's hope, and Elske's, too, was that the women of the Volkaric would think that such a girl as Elske would go gladly into the Death House. So foolish and fearless a girl would want no more for herself than to satisfy those around her. Tamara's hope, and Elske's, too, was that the two sharpened knives the old woman had strapped to her own feet, invisible in the night, would lie undisturbed in the ashes of the Death House, as unrecognizable as the grey hair Tamara had stained dark with the blood of the slain babes.

As to the captains, their hope lay in the nature of drunken men—drunk on their desires for the Kingship to come, drunk on the heavy mead and the pride of their importance to the King, drunk with rape. Even if they are warriors tried and trained, drunken men cannot defend themselves against a sharp knife, and well-honed hatred.

Tamara's and Elske's best hope was that the Wolfers would believe that these captains had chosen to follow the Volkking into deathlong service. "After that," Tamara said, "the new Volkking will be busy enough, finding some harvest in his fields, sending out swift raiding parties to fill his storerooms and build his treasure troves, filling women's bellies with his sons. Why would he chase down an old woman, crazed with age and grief? With his people to keep under his hand and winter to survive." And so they hoped Elske would be spared her life.

Day came greyling first, and then golden shafts of light greeted Elske from among trees, and she walked towards them. She stumbled, with the weight of sack and memories, and with the uneven ground underfoot where undergrowth tangled around her legs. But the warmth of sunlight tasted sweet on her tongue, and brought her fresh sweat.

Deep in forest now, she let the eastern hills pull her to them. She could see but a little distance ahead, into thickly grown trunks and fading leaves on low branches. She could hear birds, and a chuckling of water.

Elske followed that watery sound to a brook that tumbled across her way. Without dropping the sack, she knelt to drink. She had carried in her hand the small loaf that would make her day's dinner, and when her thirst was refreshed with icy water, she walked on—pulling off little bites of tough, nutty, dry bread, chewing them slowly. With food, more of her strength returned.

The sun moved across its arched sky path, as slowly as Elske moved up steep hillsides. When at last the sun lowered at her back, Elske halted at a stream. She dropped the sack from her back and put her face into the water. She finished her small loaf and took out a piece of meat to chew.

There need be no fire that night. The air was warm enough and she could do without the light. When darkness closed around her, she wrapped herself in the wolf cloak, even knowing that this sleep made the last ending of Tamara. For Elske, now, everything must be unknown and companionless.

Chapter 3

WAKING, ELSKE SATISFIED her thirst and set off into the rising light. Damp air rode a lively breeze and she lifted her face to it, in welcome. All across the grey morning, Elske kept her own silence in order to hear the day's voices, the whispering wind, the hum of insects and, starting at midday, rain thrumming through the trees with a noise like the beating of tiny drums. No sunset troubled the end of the watery day. No stars troubled the sky as Elske lay down to sleep in the company of trees and stones, inhaling the dark, rich smell of wet earth.

During the night the sky emptied itself of rain and the sun rose up into a blue field across which clouds ran like wolves, hunting, or like a herd of deer, fleeing the wolf pack. By full sunlight, the earth and stones were warm against the soles of Elske's feet. This untraveled wildness was crowded with undergrowth and thick with trunks of trees, a place where boulders hunched up out of the ground. After that day's rough travel, Elske lay down under her cloak and her tiredness opened its arms in welcome as if sleep was a lost child come safely home at last.

The fourth morning's air hung quiet and moist

over steep hills. There were pine trees here and their fallen needles made a soft carpet under Elske's feet. Instead of growing warmer as the day wore on, the air grew cooler. It was the afternoon of this day's travel when Elske came at last to the merchant's path of which her grandmother had spoken.

The path was broad enough for two men to walk abreast; it was worn down to dirt and scarred with the tracks of boots and what Elske guessed might be hooves. Tamara had told her about horses, four-legged and tireless, large enough to carry a grown man on their backs, strong enough to bear a bar-rowload of goods. Under Elske's eager questioning, as they sat alone with the babies in the Birth House, Tamara told her about the sea and the boats that rode on it, and about cities, cones of salt, beds that were feather mattresses set on boxes to raise them above the floor, pearls, like river-polished pebbles but white, and round, hung in strings around a woman's bare neck, and dolls, miniature lifeless people for little girls to play with. The more Tamara told, the more Elske asked, until Tamara's tales made that other world so real Elske could recognize the tracks the round hooves of horses made in the dirt path. Elske placed her feet carefully on the dirt and turned to the north, as Tamara had instructed.

That night Elske built a fire and sat by its warmth, chewing on bread and dried meat strips, feeling how the empty spaces around her guarded her solitude. She slept deep and awoke at first light.

The merchant's path made easy walking. Elske moved on into winter and the north, through air the sun could not warm. She walked, and listened, and when she heard thudding sounds behind her, she knew she was being overtaken.

But no human foot stepped so.

Then, straining to hear, she heard voices, so it was human; and more than one.

They were men's deep voices, and one lighter that might be a boy's or a woman's, and although many of the particular words were strange to Elske, it was the familiar language of the Volkaric they spoke. The voices drove away the forest silence as they argued about the speed of their travel and the sharpness of their hungers. The thudding steps accompanied the voices and Elske hoped that she might soon see a horse, and touch its long velvety nose with her own hand. She was listening so hard behind her that she stumbled.

Stumbling upright, she heard the voices see her.

First, the footsteps ceased, human and animal, then "Hunh?" she heard, and "Father?" and "Look!" "Who's—"

A conversation was held in lowered voices.

Elske did not turn around; she started walking again.

"Hoy!" a man's voice called. "Hoy, you! Stranger!"

Elske stopped. The forest kept close around her, trees hovering nearby.

"Friend?" the voice asked. "Or foe?"

Elske waited four heartbeats before she turned to begin what would be next in her life.

"It's a girl," the lighter voice said. "What's she doing alone? What's she wearing?"

There were three of them, one a boy, and behind the three, two beasts which she guessed to be horses. The horses' gentle-eyed heads were level with the men's broad, bearded faces.

The men of the Volkaric had their women pluck out the hairs on their cheeks, to leave long, thin beards growing from their chins, but these men had such thick beards that only their mouths showed, as if they went bearded for warmth, as an animal wears its fur. All three wore short cloaks over trousers stained with travel. The two younger had yellow hair but the older had hair the color of dried grass, and grey streaked both his head and beard. Two sons with their father, Elske guessed. Merchants, from the packs on their own and their horses' backs.

"Friend or foe?" the father asked again.

How could Elske know? She only knew the word *foe*.

"Maybe she doesn't speak Norther," the older son suggested.

"She's small and dark-haired, so she could be from the south," the younger agreed.

Elske guessed now at the meaning of the father's question, but before she could speak her answer, he asked, with his finger pointing at her, "You good me?" in Souther so awkward that it took Elske a moment to understand that this was the same question.

Before she could answer him, he stepped closer. Behind him, the horses stamped. He pointed to his own chest with a finger. "Tavyan," he said. He pointed at the young man. "Taddus," he said, and then named the boy, "Nido."

The boy pointed to the older man's chest and said, "Father." Then he bowed at Elske, grinning widely. "May we be well met," he added in Norther.

"My name," Elske said then in the Norther they had first used to her, "is Elske." She might have added, like the boy, *May we be well met*, but she didn't know what this would mean.

"You speak our language?" Taddus asked, surprised.

Elske answered him carefully. "There are—different words." Then she addressed herself to the man, the father. "I can hear you, almost, what you say. Not every word."

The path on which they stood threaded through this deep forest like a well-hidden secret, so there were both time and safety for all the questions the men had.

By careful attention Elske understood that Tavyan, the father, wondered where she was going, and she answered that she was traveling to the north. He asked about her parents and she could say she had none, only a grandmother newly dead.

Tavyan asked her what country she came from, and that meaning she couldn't guess. He asked her again, and again she couldn't answer, until Nido interrupted impatiently to say, "What land, what people?" and Elske could tell the father, "The people of the Volkaric."

They looked to one another, wary, and said nothing, all three ranged against Elske.

"The Volkaric are yellow-haired," Tavyan said to her, "blue-eyed. Like us."

"My grandmother was taken captive from the south. They say I am like her."

"But why have you left your people?" Tavyan asked.

Elske told him nothing false. "My grandmother sent me away."

"Well," Tavyan said. "Well, then. How far—?"

"Father." This time it was Taddus interrupting impatiently and Tavyan gave way, making his decision, asking her, "Shall we four travel on together? We also go to the north." He explained, "The city, Trastad, is our home."

"Trastad." This could be the northern city Tamara's merchants had hoped to reach, as if Elske might complete the journey Tamara had begun, as if their lives were still connected. She answered Tavyan with a smile, "Where else should I go, and who else travel with?"

So they set off, with Elske in the lead. She had answered their questions and any she had for them could wait until they halted at nightfall. Tamara had always told Elske stories, tales of foreign people and their foreign ways, tales of watery oceans stretching out as far as the eye could see, tales of a Kingdom hidden away safe from the rest of the world, where the King looked on his subjects as a gardener looks on the plants whose well-being makes his own. In her stories, Tamara had spoken of men like these three, whose work was carrying goods from one place to another, for buying and selling. Merchants traded goods for gold, as if each merchant were a Volkking, to have his own treasure-house.

Elske listened carefully to her traveling companions. In their talk, his father and brother scolded Nido for speaking foolishly, and teased him for his laziness, and for wandering off the path. Nido pestered them to tell him how many more days it would be before they were home at last, until they told him sharply not to be so impatient. They talked about men they had done business with in the southern cities, and whether the cloth Taddus had insisted they purchase would please the women of Trastad or if, as Tavyan predicted, it would prove profitless.

Elske liked the sound of that word, *profitless*; it was narrow and tidy, like the Birth House in Tamara's care.

The men spoke quickly and with much argument, although they often laughed. Elske wished she could walk backwards, to see their faces. The Volkaric laughed at another's pain, or shame; their laughter was as sharp as their swords; like swords, laughter was used to wound. The Volkaric argued over things that could be taken, a bowl of stew, a pelt, a woman, and they talked only to give orders. These three used talk differently.

Nido talked the most. He thought they had been ten days and nights on the path, for he had been counting carefully. He thought the mother would be watching for them over the sea, and asked could he be the one to go up behind her and put his hands over her eyes to surprise her, and her new baby, too. For weren't babies born in summer?

Taddus scolded his brother for talking as if they had arrived safely home already, tempting fortune to do ill by them, and said something about Elske that she didn't understand.

"She wouldn't harm us," Nido argued.

"Don't go ——ing her," Taddus warned. "She's Volkaric."

Elske turned the sound into letters in her head, as Tamara had taught her. T-r-u-s-t-ing.

"She's trusting us enough to travel with us," Nido argued. "That's evens up."

They spoke in Norther, but with a difference.

Elske's accustomed language was like the broth made from gnawed bones, but this language of theirs had meat in it, too, and onions, and other unknown foods, even pinches of salt.

"How do we know she's not leading us into an ambush?" Taddus asked his father.

"How does she know we won't rape her or sell her as a slave?" Tavyan answered. "I've decided that she'll travel with us, and that settles that."

Taddus ignored his father's last words. "You know what they call them, in the south. Wolfers. You know that, and do you know why?"

"She's not like a wolf," Nido said. "Anybody can see that."

"Wolves," Taddus continued, "will smell out a pregnant doe, and they'll trail after her until she gives birth. Then the wolves take the helpless newborn, and the mother too weak to escape. That's what Wolfers are. They know nothing of mercy or law, government or trade."

Elske said nothing, and asked nothing, not when they spoke of things she knew, not when she wondered at the meaning of their words. She walked and listened.

When they halted at sunset, with four it took almost no time to gather wood and start a fire. Elske had her own loaf and scraps of dried flesh, which she offered around to the others. They turned away from her food. In turn, they offered her a round, speckled-red object. "Apple," they called it.

Elske took it into her hand. The apple was hard, not as heavy as a rock, palm-sized. A short twig rose out of its top, like the cut cord on a newborn. She looked across the fire to Nido's face, shadowy in the firelight, then to Taddus, and Tavyan.

Tavyan held one of these apples in his own hand and said, "Eat." He bit into it.

Elske tried to tell them. "My grandmother spoke of apples, and trees with white blossoms in the spring." Tamara had also told of little cakes, like bread only so light and so sweet with honey and something called raisins that, speaking of them, Tamara smiled to remember what it was to have such a cake in her mouth, and taste it. Elske held out her hand, the apple in her palm. "I never thought I would eat an apple."

"— it," Nido urged. "There's nothing to be afraid of."

T-r-y. Elske put the new word away in her head and promised him, "I'm not afraid." She opened her mouth and bit into the apple. Her teeth cut through its tight skin and she heard a sound—like frosty grasses underfoot just before the snows begin—as her teeth closed around the flesh and a bite fell off it, into her mouth. She chewed it. The taste was like—clear as water, and sweet, like Tamara's winter medicine of water with three drops of honey stirred into it. But this apple was dense as a turnip, this apple was food. Elske opened her eyes to smile. Two of the watching faces smiled back at her, but Taddus asked his father, "Do they know the value of the skins they wear? Do you think she knows how much her cloak is worth?"

"You don't think to take it from her, do you?" His father laughed.

Then Taddus, too, smiled at Elske. "We won't harm you."

"Why should you harm me?" Elske asked, and

took another bite of the apple. When these Trastaders smiled, their teeth gleamed white, especially when the smiling man was bearded; these Trastaders smiled freely.

"And you won't harm us," Nido announced.

"Why should I harm you?" she asked, her smile broadening.

Nido added, "You couldn't, anyway, you're only a girl," at which both Taddus and Tavyan laughed, and warned Nido that he was too young to understand what harm girls could do to a man. Then Nido became angry, and asked why, if Taddus felt that way, he was in such a hurry to get home and get married?

Like Nido, when Elske finished the apple she tossed the core into the fire, where it sizzled and steamed and sweetened the rising smoke. A white crescent of new moon hung in a black, star-speckled sky above them, the fire had burned down to bright warm coals, and they were all tired; so they lay down and slept.

In the morning Tavyan showed Elske what their journey would be. "The mountains lie between us and Trastad," he said. "We are heading for the pass," he said, and took a stick to draw in the dirt. Elske crouched beside him. "This line is our path, running north." Then he drew uneven lines, approaching the path and forcing it to turn west, "Mountains," showing how the path turned back towards the north and east, between the jagged lines. After the mountains, the path he drew became a river, he said, as he ended it with the letter T.

"Trastad?" Elske guessed, and he said, "Beyond Trastad is only the open sea. At this time of year, most of our merchants return to Trastad by sea."

Elske was studying the lines in the dirt.

"You can drown in the sea," Nido told her, but she couldn't understand what was so important in that. "Men do, sailors, all the time."

"That's nothing to do with us," Taddus pointed out to his brother, and Tavyan, too, ignored his younger son, saying to Elske, "It's only a roughly drawn map."

"Map," Elske said, shaping the word in her mind. Now that she had seen a map, she could travel on her own—if she wished—to Trastad. Now that she had seen a map, she couldn't lose her way. Without thinking, she wrote the word with her finger in the dirt. Then she stood, and picked up her sack.

The others were staring at her. At last, "You know letters," Nido said.

Elske sensed some danger. "My grandmother taught me."

"Do all the Volkaric know letters?" Taddus asked.

To think of that made Elske laugh, and when she laughed the danger was gone. "The Volkaric didn't care to know, and what need did they have? They had no parchment, or"—she remembered the odd little word, a Souther word—"ink."

"Father," Taddus said again, reminding them that the morning was going rapidly by.

"My brother's bride awaits him," Nido explained to Elske.

"And we all have winter moving towards us," Taddus said.

"Two good reasons for haste," Tavyan said, and they set off.

For that day and the next the path took them

west, until on the third morning they came to a broad, shallow stream, its stones gleaming in the water. This stream led them back to the north and east. Then, every day the mountains came closer, taking up more of the sky with their white peaks, and the stream the travelers climbed beside ran away behind them, down rocky hillsides. Rain fell, so cold that Elske wore her wolfskin boots, which kept her legs and feet as warm as summer.

Taddus wished he could have such boots. "Not for myself, for Idelle. My wife, as she soon will be, when we return. At the Longest Night, Idelle and I will become a husband and his wife," Taddus told Elske, proud to say it, and eager.

By the full moon they had entered a high valley, its narrow meadows and steep hillsides dusted with frosts. There another stream tumbled down into the valley bottom and this new stream followed the valley to the east, curling and coiling between mountain steeps.

These mountains were so high that the travelers fell asleep before they could see the moon risen into the night sky, and awoke after she had once again slipped behind the mountains. They were accustomed to traveling together, now, and Elske knew much that she had not known before. She knew that a wife was the woman a man of Trastad had chosen to be his lifelong companion, promising never to move another woman into his house; marrying his wife, a man became a husband. She knew that Nido had three sisters waiting at home, two of them older than he but the last younger, and his mother expected another child, which Nido eagerly hoped would be a boy. The reason for this was the

Trastader customs of inheritance, and Elske needed many questions to understand these. By Trastader custom, when he married, Taddus would live with his wife's family, where he would become the inheritor of her father's wealth, all other children of the father having died. But Tavyan, too, must have an heir, which Nido would be, as a son. But if the expected baby was a boy, then there would be another heir for Tavyan's property, to feed the family and give dowries to the daughters. So Nido would be able to apprentice himself to a ship's carpenter, which was his desire. And if the boy did not live? But Nido would be already apprenticed, contracts signed, fees paid; so then one of his sisters' husbands must inherit the business. It was all arranged by law.

"Law?" Elske asked.

Elske learned that Tavyan was bringing back from the south not only rich fabrics and colorful threads to stitch them, but also two barrels of a drink called wine, for which the richest merchants of Trastad would pay many coins. "Wine is cheap in the south, where grapes are plentiful," Tavyan explained to Elske, "but comes very dear in Trastad." The horses also carried many cones of the finest salt. Because this would be a Courting Winter, Tavyan told Elske, there would be much call for salt.

Elske asked what a Courting Winter was. They told her that every second year great and rich families from many distant lands sent their sons and daughters to Trastad, where they were welcomed, for a price, into the best houses of the city. These Adeliers, as the foreigners were called, were offered various entertainments, dances, feasts and Assemblies, during the course of which many of the sons chose wives, many of the daughters husbands. Whatever the Adeliers made of the opportunities Trastad offered, Tavyan said, the Trastaders made profits.

Before they left the shelter of the high valley, snow had caught them twice. Then the stream they followed led them out of the mountains and through steep hills, growing deeper, its banks becoming steeper as other streams ran down from the north and west to join it. By the time the land became rolling hills, their stream had become a river, and they were drawing close to Trastad. "How will you live," the three asked her now, "in Trastad, in the winter?" Elske had no answer; how could she know how to get food and shelter in Trastad? "We'll help you," they promised her. "Don't worry."

Elske had never thought to worry.

The river looped through gentle country, close to the city; here the land was cleared and farmed. On the last night they slept in the stable yards of an inn. Just as Tamara had told, the inn bustled with activity of hosts and guests and animals; it offered foods richer than Elske had even imagined, and rooms with beds. But Tavyan preferred to dine on bread and onions, and to sleep the four together, close to their horses and goods, discouraging thieves.

When they asked her what the Volkaric did with someone who stole, Elske couldn't make them understand that only the Volkking owned treasure, so that a man could steal only from the Volkking, which was treason. For treason, a man's feet were cut off and they drove him away, crawling, to feed the wolves. "I never saw this, but my grandmother remembered," Elske told them. "We had no thieves," she told them, and she thought that the Trastaders must honor this in the Volkaric.

But "Brutish," Tavyan said, and "Cruel," Nido said, shaking their heads. Taddus said nothing, but only because they were so close to Trastad that he could think only of his Idelle.

They met no other travelers. "At this time of year, merchants choose to travel by sea," Tavyan told Elske. "So would we have, except there was a storm from the northeast and I have no wish to die by drowning. We found horses to carry our goods, and set off, leaving the sea captains in the port awaiting fair weather. Also, one of us was impatient to be home."

"We risked the Wolfers," Nido interrupted, proudly.

"We'll be home before we are expected," Taddus said.

"They'll be expecting us to come by sea," Tavyan said.

"I think Mother must have had a boy. There have already been three girls and only two boys," Nido said. "It wouldn't be fair if it wasn't a boy."

"You must wait and see," his father reminded him. "Like Elske," Tavyan said, "you must wait and see what chance will be offered you."

Chapter 4

TAVYAN HAD DRAWN another of his rough maps, showing Trastad. Although it was a single city, Trastad included three islands, lying in the sheltering arms of land where the broad river spread out into the sea, and hamlets and farmlands on the mainland. The island at the river's mouth, the largest, was Old Trastad, "where the first traders settled. Old Trastad is where the most important business of the city is conducted, by merchant houses and merchant banks, in the great marketplace. Also there are taverns and inns, as well as the Council meeting hall and of course the docks, warehouses and shipyards."

"Council?" Elske asked.

"The men who rule Trastad."

"The Council is your Volkking," Elske said.

"We want no King when we have our Council," Tavyan said, and Elske asked, "Where is your own house?"

On the middle island, Tavyan explained, called Harboring, where most of the lesser merchants lived, behind and above their shops, and the craftspeople, too, and manufacturers. Harboring had its own taverns and livery stables, although not so large or many as were to be found in Old Trastad. The last island, most inland and thus most protected from the sea, had used to be farmland but now the wealthiest merchants—the great Vars—built their magnificent villas there. Logisle, this innermost island was named, for the lumber it had supplied to build the great docks of the city, and the bridges that joined the three islands to one another, and to both banks of the river, also.

The Trastaders were famous builders of bridges, Tavyan told her proudly, drawing quick lines in the dirt to join the three islands to each other and to the mainland.

"Then will I be close to the saltwater sea?" Elske asked.

"Close enough to touch, if you wish. Ours is a seafaring city. Can't you smell it?"

"But you don't see the ocean from Harboring," Nido said. This last path on this last day of journey was a roadway broad enough for six men to walk abreast. On this road they saw some other men, fishers and farmers Elske was told; some of the men were accompanied by women whose hair was wrapped around with colored cloths. These men and women stared at Elske, in her fur boots and wolfskin cloak, but when she stared back at them they looked away.

The bridge, when they came to it, stood as tall as a house above the river's watery surface. Elske crossed over to the island on planks of wood, with the water visible between them, looking down on the river as a bird might, from above. On the island the dirt road had been covered by stones, some small and sharp, some as large as a fist—to make walking less dusty in dry weather and less muddy in wet, they explained to her. Just beyond the bridge, a man hailed them from his small, steep-roofed house.

The man spoke to Tavyan. After some talk, Tavyan took out a purse of coins and gave some to the man. When he rejoined his three companions, Tavyan said, "The taxer reports a storm, not four nights past, lasting from afternoon on through the night, and all the next day and night as well. There was tidal flooding on Trastad, but no loss of merchandise. Some boats may well have been lost to the storm, those carrying Adeliers, but most merchants have returned."

"No other urgent news in the city?" Taddus asked.

This new street was crowded with people moving in both directions. Between tall, close-built buildings the stony road climbed and dipped, and they followed it.

"No news," Tavyan said. "So, no fires, no fever epidemics over the summer. No sudden deaths. We may well find all as we left it."

"Except there will be the baby. You hope for a boy, don't you?" Nido demanded.

"I have only a small store of hope," Tavyan answered his son with a smile. "So when I expend any of it, I think not of more sons but of lower taxes. Tell me, Elske, must the Volkaric pay tax moneys to their King?"

Elske told him, "The Volkaric have no money."

"They are a fortunate people," Tavyan laughed.

Nido asked, "Then who pays to keep the streets cleaned of garbage and offal? Who hires justices to say when a law has been broken, and name the punishment, and who sets guards over the cells? Who gathers together the tribute money for the Emperor?"

"The Volkking pays tribute to no one," Elske said. "And if his people please him, then he will give them all they need."

"What if they displease him?" Taddus asked.

"None wish to."

"Are his people slaves?" Nido asked, but Elske didn't know that word.

"What do you think of Harboring?" Tavyan asked Elske. His hand waved about him, indicating people and doorways, houses crowded together until their roofs made a single line, and he told her, "All the storehouses will be filled by now, and wood chopped and stacked, with winter coming down on us. Attic spaces will be piled high with round cheeses, and barrels of salted fish, and boxes of smoked fish. The cellars will be crowded with sacks of ground wheat and stacked onions, turnips—"

"Ugh, turnips," Nido said.

"Come spring, you're glad enough of anything not salted, even turnips," Taddus reminded his brother.

"You're just acting—" Nido started to answer, but his father cut him off, explaining to Elske, "Trastaders lay in great stores, before winter comes. Our lives depend on being ready for the worst. Should things fall out other than we expect, well, then, we will feast in spring, but we are like bears, fattened for winter."

"Especially the Courting Winters," Taddus said, "when there is so much profit to be made from the Adeliers. This winter, Father's house should make—"

"Let's add up our profits in the spring, when they

fill our pockets not our dreams," Tavyan warned his son. "What *is* it, Nido? Have you fleas in your trousers?"

"May I go ahead, Father? May I surprise them? They'll expect us by sea, and I can surprise them. Elske can lead my horse. She's strong enough and she's not afraid of horses. Are you, Elske?"

Elske took the rein without a thought, and Nido dashed off. Her eyes were full of the faces and dress of the people around her. Smells crowded the air as closely as houses crowded the sides of the streets. Was the entire island of Harboring filled with houses, tumbled upon one another like onions in a basket?

They came at last to an open gate beside a narrow timber house in a row of narrow timber houses, where Nido stood watching for them. "It *is* a boy!" he called. A plump woman watched with him, and two younger women stepped out of the doorway. All three wore dark dresses, protected by aprons; all three had their heads wrapped around with colored scarves. A little girl, her hair also covered, hid behind the opened door. The older woman—the mother, Elske guessed—greeted Tavyan with pink-faced surprise. "I thought, if you lived, you'd be another sennight at least," she said. "I am glad to greet you safely home, my husband."

"You have another son to learn your trade, Father!" Nido cried, and his mother asked him to hush, now, if he'd be so good.

Tavyan moved all of them through the gate and into a small open yard beside the house, with two out-buildings against its far wall. He and Taddus took apart the packs the horses carried, and instructed the others where to carry each item. The mother bustled about, promising a hot meaty stew for everyone, repeating again and again how Nido surprised her, knocking on the shop door as if he were a customer, and how she was wiping her hands dry on her apron when she saw who it was. "Didn't I scream?" she asked her older daughters, who agreed that their mother had frightened them out of two years' growth with her screams.

Nobody remarked Elske, who stood silent and aside, although the two older sisters looked as if they might have, if their father hadn't had them hurrying about so.

Finally, Nido and Taddus were sent off to take the horses to the livery, and then run back so that their mother could serve up the meal, if they wanted food in their bellies this day; because Tavyan had much to do arranging his goods, and taking his inventory after the summer shopkeeping. And this was a baking day, especially now that there were so many to feed. Now that they were safely returned, more bread would be needed. And who was this person?

"This person is Elske," Tavyan said, waving her forward. "Bertilde, I present Elske, who joined us on our journey. Daughters? Dagma, Karleen, Sussi, I present Elske to you. Don't be shy, my little Sussi, she's very friendly. We'll be glad of another hand, with so many in the house, and Elske is both strong and willing."

"I never asked for a servant," Bertilde humphed. "Nor a pretty one, neither. And what is she wearing under that barbaric cloak? It looks like animal. What kind of creature have you brought to my house, Husband? Look at her hair!"

Elske did not know *servant* or *pretty*, but she had

heard Tamara spoken of in just that way, all her life. The girls—as thick-bodied, short, round-faced and blue-eyed as their brothers and parents—ignored their mother and urged Elske inside, and so she did not know how Tavyan answered his wife. The girls were proud of their cook room, warmed by a fire in the hearth, over which a cauldron bubbled, proud of the long table at its center now displaying a line of shallow wooden troughs in which bread dough was rising, proud of what they called glass in the window. They knocked on it with their hands, and suggested Elske do the same, but she did not wish to. She watched through it, to the yard, where Tavyan had an arm around his wife's waist as he spoke to her, and two cats strolled out of the shed, one with a bellyful of kittens.

The sisters called her into the shop at the front of the house, to admire its windows and its empty shelves. At the back of this room, a narrow staircase climbed up.

Elske had heard from Tamara that there were such dwelling places, one level resting on top of the other; so she was not surprised. Each of the three rooms above held a bed, with a mattress as deep and puffy as a summer cloud, and each had a small window under the low roof. Elske could not take it all in at first sight, the wooden floorboards, the whited walls; and the sisters enjoyed her amazement.

Back in the cook room, she stood to the side while the mother ladled out wooden bowls of stew and Dagma set them around the table, and Karleen sliced off chunks of pale bread and set out metal spoons. By the stone hearth, Tavyan crouched low and looked into a little box where a baby slept. A cradle, they called it, used only for a baby to sleep in.

They ate seated on benches facing one another across the wooden tabletop. Elske ignored the talk and ate until she could eat no more, however much her mouth still longed to taste the tastes of meat and broth and onion, carrot, turnip and other flavors she had no names for. "Ouff," she said, at the fullness of her belly, and looked up when the others laughed.

She had forgotten they were present. Her bowl was empty and theirs were still almost full. "Oh," she said, and put down a half-eaten chunk of bread.

Bertilde now seemed pleased with her. "We Trastaders have forgotten the taste of hunger. I think we do not enjoy our food as much as Elske does."

"I do," Nido asserted, and dipped bread into his bowl, and they all laughed again.

The baby fussed then and Elske went to quiet it. This was an easy task, with only one baby, and he well-fed and warm, his swaddlings dry, and with a lap to himself. Tavyan, his wife and children talked among themselves and she could listen unobserved as she gently rocked the baby back to sleep. "I've not coins to spare for a servant," Bertilde said, so now Elske knew that a servant belonged to a wife. "And it will be many years before we have no daughter's hands to work beside mine," she said, so Elske knew what work a servant would do. "We'll give her one of Sussi's worn dresses. She looks little more than Sussi in age, just a child, but she can't stay. However good-tempered she might be. However skilled a nursemaid, if you look at her now."

"Where would we keep her, besides?" Dagma asked. "On the floor in here?"

Elske felt as fat and contented as the baby on her lap, and thought the cook room floor would make a fine bed.

Nido couldn't be long distracted from his own interests, and announced, "Tomorrow, at first light, I will apprentice myself to the ship carpenter. You'll give me the coins, Father? Elske," he called to her, "I am going to become a builder of ships. And now, when my father and my new brother, Keir, who will inherit my father's trade, wish to have ships of their own, I will be a partner in their growing riches. Until we will be so wealthy, father and brothers, such great Vars of Trastad, that Taddus will be chosen one of the Councillors—won't you, Taddus?"

"It's not impossible," Taddus said, "when I represent two such merchant families."

"When do you go to Idelle, Taddus?" Dagma asked. "She has been waiting all these long days, sending her aunt to ask at the docks what ships have come to port, carrying what traders safely home."

"I'll see a barber first—"

"Yes, or your beard will frighten her off forever, and you'll never get sons to inherit the property she brings you," Karleen said.

"You go with him, Husband," Bertilde said. "You also need barbering, and you can bring back news about the losses from the storm. I've heard two ships were seen to go down."

"Drowned men sink under the waves. It's from filling their bellies with water, when they try to breathe water," Nido told Elske, with the same plea-

36

sure the war bands took in telling of their battles. He told her, "When they rise up again they are black and swollen with death, and the soft parts of their faces and flesh are eaten—"

"We don't need to be reminded," his mother said.

Tavyan said, "There is nothing anyone can do now, to make or mar those fortunes. So let us consider a fortune we have at our disposal. What shall we do with Elske?"

Elske hoped they would let her sit by the fire with the sleeping baby on her lap, and feed her again when she was next hungry.

Bertilde asked, "Can't she hire herself out elsewhere as a servant?" and Elske understood that in other houses a servant might be wanted.

"I could marry her," Nido said.

"You're still a boy," Karleen said, then asked, "How old are you, Elske?"

The warmth of the stones against her back had made Elske drowsy, so it took her a moment to answer. "This will be my thirteenth winter."

"You look younger, but that's still too young to marry," Dagma decided.

"What do we know about her?" Bertilde asked.

"She's strong," Taddus said. "She's clever."

"She knows letters," Tavyan said. "Reading and writing."

"She kept us from fighting," Nido said, but "How would a girl do that?" his father demanded, and Nido answered, "Well, we didn't, did we? Also, Elske never once complained."

"She seems to know about babies," Bertilde said. "If she kept her cleverness to herself—for who wants a servant who can read?—she might find a place in one of the great houses, in a Courting Winter."

That night, Elske slept beside the warmth of coals, and woke early. She had the fire built up before anybody else stirred in the house; although, having done that, she could only sit beside it and wait for what the morning would bring.

After their morning meal, the two men left the house for Old Trastad, leaving the women in charge of the shop and the home. Bertilde kept Nido back, to accompany her to the marketplace on Old Trastad, where she hoped to find a good fowl for the pot, and cabbage, and a fat, sweet onion, too. Elske, clothed now in a dress that rested light as a summer wind on her flesh, despite its long arms and tangling skirts, asked if she might go with the mother, but Bertilde told her that Nido couldn't be expected to be protection for two women. So Elske stayed with the baby in the cook room, and when Karleen came running in with the troublesome news of eight kittens born, with none needed or wanted, Elske snapped their delicate damp necks while the sisters watched horrified through the window. She placed the bodies in a sack, which she left beside the shed.

"She could have spared one!" Karleen cried, when her mother returned.

"Taddus will remove the remains," Bertilde answered. "None of us enjoy getting rid of kittens, so stop your sniveling, Karleen, and you, Dagma, spare us your outrage. You're not children. You should be glad Elske was here, or you might have had to drown them yourselves."

"But why drown them when by snapping their necks they die quickly?" Elske asked.

No one had an answer for her, and when Karleen

reported Elske's heartlessness to her father, at their meal, Tavyan told his family, "We've determined today what to do about Elske, at least until the Longest Night. Elske? Tomorrow, Taddus and Nido will take you to the house of Var Kenric, who is Idelle's father. You will serve Idelle, until she marries."

Nido was holding his hands in front of him and twisting them, saying, "Snap! Snap!" until Sussi wept again and Dagma said, "That's not funny, Nido," and his father told him to behave himself, when he was at table.

Elske asked, "And after she marries?"

Taddus explained it. "I will be the husband. You can't be my servant when we have traveled as equals."

Elske didn't argue although she didn't understand. After all, the Trastaders had their own ways as much as the Volkaric, and like the Volkaric, the Trastaders preferred their own ways. Who a servant was, for what work and uses, that she could guess at; and it was no more than who and what every woman of the Volkaric was.

"By Longest Night we'll have found you another place, for many houses take on extra servants in a Courting Winter. That's my decision," Tavyan told her, as if Elske had argued. But Elske had no such wish.

Then the men told the gossip and news they had brought home from the city. Two ships had come into harbor, both with sails ripped out and one half-masted, reporting what they knew about the wrecks of the storm. It had not been as bad as it might have been, and none of the Adeliers had been lost. "Which is a piece of luck," Taddus said, "although—" and then his shorn face lit up with laughter.

There was one Princess, he reported, laughing with Tavyan at the story, one Adelinne who had refused to be sent below decks with the rest of her kind during the storm. The waves were tossing the ship about, as if it were no more than a leaf falling, and all the other Adeliers on board were weeping and vomiting below, making a great moan. This was trouble enough for the captain, who cared only about keeping his ship afloat, but here was this girl—no more than a girl, young for an Adelinne—stamping her foot at him, while the gale grabbed at her cloak. No, she would not go below, she told him. She didn't have to obey him, or anyone, because she was a Queen and obeyed none but herself.

Tavyan took up the tale. She was a brat, the captain had told her bluntly, a misbehaved and misguided brat, and if she was his own daughter she'd have the flat of his hand across her backside. But if she wouldn't be sent below, he couldn't waste the time worrying about the waves washing her overboard, so he turned his back on her.

When the captain next thought of her, Taddus continued, there she was hauling down a sail, a sailor at work on either side of her, her hair hanging down wet, and her cloak soaked and dragging. She wasn't afraid, not of waves, wind, water or drowning. She'd been as good as a sailor in the storm, the captain admitted, even though he'd have liked to throw her overboard with a stone tied to her ankles, for the trouble she'd have caused him had harm come to her.

"Well, it's a good profit we make from the

Adeliers, so let them be a trouble," Bertilde said, but nobody answered her because Dagma was exclaiming, "Who would want to marry such a girl?" and Nido said he wouldn't, and Tavyan said he hoped this Princess had a rich dowry, because she would need it to overcome the reputation this story would earn her, growing fatter as it was told throughout the city until they would say she was sailing the boat alone, the captain clouted across the ears and sent about his business. Taddus wondered how she could have not been afraid, for the one storm he'd been caught in had been enough to overfill his stomach for sailing adventures.

Elske asked, "A Queen? What is it, if she is a Queen?"

"The Queen is the wife of a King," Dagma told her.

"As a Varinne is the wife of a Var," Taddus explained. "Idelle's father is Var Kenric and her mother thus becomes Varinne Kenric."

"But this girl—this Adelinne who claims to be a Queen—isn't married, so no King has given her the title. So she's a liar, as well," Dagma laughed. "I pity the family that has her for guest, this winter."

"They'll be given recompense," Bertilde said. "I wouldn't mind giving up a bedroom to have some Adelier filling my purse with coins."

"Just wait until I'm a shipbuilder, trained and proven," Nido told her. "After Taddus and his sons have multiplied Var Kenric's fortune, we'll build you a villa on Logisle, and you can fill it to the roof beams with Adeliers."

"By that time, I'll be too old for such things," Bertilde said.

"She must be swollen with pride," Dagma said, "this Adelinne. And ignorant, to think she can fool us as to her station."

"She can't be too proud," her mother answered, "if she is sent to Trastad to catch herself a husband. Don't waste jealousy on her, Dagma."

"I have no jealousy," Dagma answered, but Karleen said to Elske, "My sister wishes her Henders were not a farmer. She will miss the easy life of the city."

"I am perfectly content with my choice of husband," Dagma said.

"As you should be," her father told her. "You'll be wife of a goodly house, and the flocks that feed around it."

"You're the one jealous, for any husband," Dagma said sharply to Karleen, who answered, "I need no lout of a husband, thank you, Sister," and Elske wondered why, with stores against winter, warm fires and soft dresses, these girls should still speak as bitterly as the women of the Volkaric, who were the first to go hungry, and kept farthest from the fire. Her own belly was too full for bitterness.

Chapter 5

TADDUS AND NIDO delivered Elske the next day to Var Kenric's house and service. As they crossed the center market of Harboring, Nido pointed down an alley. "See that sign? With a ship's wheel painted on it? My master's workshop is there." In only seven years, Nido told her, he would be a journeyman carpenter, sailing on merchant vessels as a skilled craftsman.

The street they walked along branched down towards the riverside now, and there were no more taverns or market squares; the houses rose three stories tall and their shops were kept in separate buildings, beside. Taddus knocked on one of the wooden doors, then told Elske, "The Varinne hasn't left her bed since winter. They say she is ill with the death of her sons."

Before he could tell her more, a grey-haired woman, pale as a parsnip, her grey dress covered by an apron, opened the door and asked them to step inside. "Idelle sits with the Varinne at this hour," the woman said to Taddus, who answered that he only wished to introduce Elske. "Elske, this is Ula, Idelle's aunt. I will return this evening," he said to

43

the woman, who answered, "I should hope so, young master. May we be well met," the woman said to Elske, who responded in echo, "May we be well met," and the woman said, "Aunt, not servant. My husband was Var Kenric's brother. When his ship went down, so many summers ago that I can no longer remember his face, I came here to live, to be of what use I can. So you are to be our young lady's maidservant. It's true enough that the Var is a busy man," Ula told Elske, "and with no one to share his burdens—until our young mistress weds this handsome fellow, of course. But you go off now, young men. I have affairs to manage."

Tavyan's sons left Elske to make her own way among these strangers and Ula hurried her upstairs to show her the chamber where she would sleep on the floor beside Idelle's bed. "You'll be comfortable," Ula told her. "Now we'll fit you out with a dress proper for Var Kenric's servant, and shifts as well, I expect. I'll teach you how to scarf your hair, first thing; you'll not want it hanging loose. And stockings, I wager you have no stockings. Luckily I've stockings to spare, for you can't go about bare-legged and be dead by midwinter. So we've undertaken to clothe you as well as house you, and feed you, and I hope you prove worth the trouble you're causing. Put your cloak in here," Ula told Elske, opening a chest at the foot of the bed. "I hope you're strong," Ula said, lowering the top of the chest. "I've been needing a kitchen girl for years, and it's worse now with the Varinne useless. There's only the two of us to get everything ready for the marriage day and the marriage feasts, since the Varinne has taken to her bed with grief and is determined to die there."

44

Elske followed Ula back down the stairs, and drew the high stockings she was given up over her knees, put on the light shift and the grey long-sleeved dress Ula found for her, and protected her skirts with an apron. Ula wrapped her head around with a soft white scarf, to cover all of her hair. She was told to knead bread dough while Ula watched, "for cooking's a burden I'll gladly share, now there's a servant for the house. The sons died of fever, one after the other; it was the spotted fever and it broke their mother's heart. Aye and mine, too, truth be told. They were lovely boys, a great loss to their father," Ula said. "The sooner Idelle gives us her own sons, the better off we'll all be."

Elske looked around her. This cook room was furnished like Tavyan's, but it was larger, with more cupboards, more plates and mugs on shelves, and a bigger hob. A fish lay waiting on the table, and when Ula had shaped four round loaves, and covered them with a cloth, she turned a knife to it. As she slit open the fish's belly, a young woman came into the room. She was thick of body, like her aunt, and had a broad, Trastader face, with freckles spread across it as plentifully as stars across a night sky. Her eyes were pale blue, her dress a dark blue, and her head scarf a duplicate of Elske's. She was taller than Elske, and older; when she spoke her voice was soft. "Is this the girl, Aunt?"

"This is Elske," Ula said. "I've shown her her place in your chamber."

"And Taddus?" the young woman asked eagerly.

"He's a man, with a man's day's work to get done. He'll come calling tonight, he said."

There was a disappointed pause, then Idelle

greeted Elske. "May we be well met. Taddus said you've no experience serving in one of the better homes, but can you cook? Launder? Sew?"

Elske shook her head, three times.

"I've never trained a servant," Idelle said, worried, and "I can learn," Elske offered.

"You can hem the bed linens, which is an easy, if time-consuming, task. That will help."

Ula reminded her niece, "Don't forget the work of the marriage feast. Even an inexperienced pair of hands can clean pots, scrub floors—"

"When I've no need for her," Idelle reminded her aunt. "She is first for me. There are not many weeks left before I marry."

Elske thought that she was learning if not what a servant was, at least what a servant did. As she came to know, a servant did what she was told, from first light to late into the night. The preparations for a wedding and the celebration feast—the cleaning and polishing, the ordering of game and fish from butcher and fishmonger, of sweet rolls from the baker and barrels of ale from the brewer, so that all might be ready on the day—those preparations, added to helping Idelle at her dress and wrapping her hair with scarves, accompanying her to the market, hemming the bridal bed linens—all of this kept Elske fully occupied.

Most evenings saw Taddus come to the house, to dine with Idelle and her father. Elske did not serve them, not being skilled in waiting on table, but when the plates and pots were put away, when the floor was scoured clean and Ula was satisfied that all was ready for the morrow, Elske was sent to sit by the fire in the front room, with its table and candlesticks and whitewashed walls, to join the three who had pulled their chairs up close to the fire, on these cold nights. When Var Kenric had talked with Taddus about stores and sales, profits and investments, he went up to make his nightly visit to his wife and Elske remained, turning the hem on the bridal bed linens. It was necessary for a servant to attend a courting couple. This made no sense to her, but a servant asked no questions, as Elske learned.

One of the first nights by the fire, while Elske sewed, Taddus and Idelle sat at the table to compose the announcement which made public offer of Elske's services as maidservant.

When Idelle saw what Taddus wrote, "You can read? And write?" she asked in surprise. "But our merchants and bankers wouldn't want maidservants who know such things. It's not as if you were a manservant," Idelle said to Elske, and Elske agreed that she was not a man.

"Still, it might prove desirable," Taddus disagreed, and wrote, adding, *She is experienced with babies.* "Is there any other use you have, Elske?"

Elske, a stranger in Trastad, could not tell him.

"She can sew a good hem," Idelle said, and her cheeks turned pink, as if that were a blushing matter. "She is always willing, and she doesn't tire."

"Father said that the men who seek to hire you should come first to our house, Elske," Taddus told her, as he wrote down Tavyan's name at the bottom of the paper. "He wishes to see you well-protected."

"Thank you," Elske said. "My thanks to Tavyan, as well." Her stomach was full with the fish soup she had helped to prepare, served with slices of thick bread; her stockinged legs were warmed by the fire while thick snow fell silently outside; a winter night covered the city but she would sleep on soft furs beside Idelle's high bed. What more could she ask for?

She had never had anyone near her own age to talk with before, not any sister or even a brother, only Tamara, who was a grandmother and wise. Idelle was four winters older than Elske and soon to be a married woman, but the two lived companionably, walking out to the marketplace together, talking about the gown Idelle would be married in and the nightdress in which she would present herself to her new husband. "I had no fortune when he chose me, so he chose me, not my fortune," Idelle announced, so vehemently that Elske knew she doubted it.

Elske could tell her young mistress, "He was impatient to be back in Trastad."

Idelle blushed. "Young men are always eager when a marriage bed awaits them. Should my nightgown have lace at the neck?" she asked Elske. "Would a man desire such finery?"

Elske could not say. It seemed to her that, except to marry, the women of Trastad feared men, except for their fathers, and brothers; and the fathers, brothers and husbands mistrusted all other men. The women of Trastad could not go out of doors alone, lest they be set on, and ruined. Ruined, Elske deduced, meant raped, although Idelle seemed to anticipate having Taddus in her bed. "So it is good to be raped by a husband?" Elske inquired, and Idelle covered her face with her hands before she said, "When it's your husband it isn't rape. Rape is when the woman is unwilling. When the man forces her."

Among the Volkaric, the women were neither willing nor unwilling. They had no will in the matter, just as they had no marriages.

Seeing that Elske did not understand, Idelle explained, "If a woman is ruined, no man will have her to wed."

"What if," Elske asked, "a woman is willing?"

"A woman *must* be willing for her husband, or how will she get her children?"

"What if," Elske asked, "a woman is willing for a man not her husband?" If a woman bore the Volkking a son she got honor and importance, and other men then wished to rape her, this woman who had produced a son for the Volkking.

"No woman would wish such a thing," Idelle told her. "Or else why would any man look for a wife?"

Elske did not know and could not have said. All she could do was accompany Idelle to the great marketplace, and to the shops that crowded around the Council Hall, whenever the needs of house or wedding sent the young woman out of doors. In Trastad, if a female servant was the only companion a woman's house could afford her, then the female servant made her company, to keep her safe. A Trastader woman did need her safety guarded, Elske learned. The young men of Trastad made a game of teasing women, especially young women. Elske walked at Idelle's shoulder through crowds, and when someone approached her mistress too close, or too roughly, or with words that were too bold, Elske stepped forward. Seeing Elske there, "We only jest," they might say, turning to find another woman to trail, adding as a parting unpleasantness to Idelle, "If you were prettier, Varele, I'd take more trouble over you."

The days went slowly by. When Taddus came in the evenings, he sometimes brought men of the city whose houses needed a maidservant. Often, the man would be pleased with Elske and then Taddus would come the next afternoon to take Elske to meet the mistress of the house. But always the Varinne would say, "She will not do." Even though Elske looked like any other Trastader serving woman, with her hair scarfed, under a man's protection, still "She will not do," the Varinne would report to her Var. Elske was found too young, too inexperienced, too old to train, too ignorant of the ways of Trastad or too clever.

The Longest Night drew closer and still Elske had been offered no place. Var Kenric's house was hung with greens, to celebrate the season and the marriage. The bed linens were hemmed and folded up into the chest at the foot of Idelle's bed, ready for the wedding night. Snow piled high in the courtyard behind the house, where evergreens showed black against the whiteness of the snow. It was full winter, almost the Longest Night. "A place will be found for you, Elske," Idelle assured her, uneasily. "Somewhere. Soon. Maybe tomorrow."

They were returning through the empty streets of Old Trastad from the bakeshop where Idelle's marriage cake would be made. There would be bad fortune on the marriage if the guests were offered no marriage cake of dense, heavy sweetness, rich in honey and nuts and ale-soaked raisins, so they had stayed on, discussing ingredients with the baker. They walked back in the long darkness that devoured winter's brief day. At one corner they almost ran into a group of young men, Adeliers accompanied by two servants. The Princes held their heavy cloaks close around them, and were wrapped also in the perfume of ale. They leaned into one another, joking and cursing in Souther. The servants followed behind, carrying jugs of drink.

Elske knew, immediately and without question, that Idelle was in danger. She smelled danger as strongly as might one of the wolves whose skins made the cloak she wore.

The darkening air was thick around them. The snow-covered street was empty of people, the shop-fronts shuttered at day's end. Sounds were muffled in these twisting streets.

The young men stumbled by, laughing. Then Elske heard them halt, turn and come to walk only a few paces behind Idelle, boasting to one another about their knowledge of women, speaking about Idelle in her heavy woollen cloak, "one of these precious virgins of Trastad. Plump as a honey cake, isn't she? Would she be sweet in the taking?" they asked, and answered themselves, "Who's to stop us finding out?"

Although she didn't know Souther, Idelle seemed to understand her danger. She began to walk more quickly, concentrating on the snowy ground ahead of her feet.

"And a maidservant, too. Two's double one, and always will be," one voice said and another answered, "She's a child, too young to be worth the trouble," but he was hooted down. "Where are your eyes, fool?"

Elske pretended to trip in her haste to get away, and she fell forward. She used her hands to break her fall, and heard laughter from the young men behind. The snow stung her skin as she reached beneath it; and when she scrambled back to her feet, she held one fist-sized rock in each hand.

Now the Adeliers made their move, and rushed ahead to face the two women. Idelle started to cry out, a thin wailing cry, pleading for kindness.

Elske kept her hands under her cloak. She considered the seven laughing young men.

Two were so ale-sodden that they were obviously no danger. One, with full lips and a jewel in his ear, she counted their captain. All had eyes bright with eager cruelty, like a war band going together into battle. Two of the Adels held back the menservants, who now called out warnings in Norther. "Run, Varele. They'll ruin—"

Elske stepped between Idelle and the young captain. "Quietly now," she advised her trembling mistress. "Your fear will make them the more cruel."

Idelle raised her hands to her face, and whimpered into her fingers.

Two young men grabbed her from behind, and she screamed out.

Elske screamed, too. But when Elske screamed, it was the war cry of the Volkaric that came out of her mouth, a howling like the voice of a wolf. The cry wound around the narrow streets as if they were in the wild and merciless northlands. She howled again and the Adels loosened their hold on Idelle. They turned to their captain.

This young man paused where he stood, his jewel glinting in the lantern light. Elske saw in his eyes a tingle of fear and his own pleasure at the fear. Quick, she swung her fist at him, and hit him on the side of the head.

He fell sideways onto his knees in the snow.

The other Adeliers stood wordless. And watched. Idelle, too, had fallen silent.

Elske howled once more as she bent over the young man and lifted his head by the thick, dark hair. She smiled down at this drunken Adel Prince with the rich jewel in his ear, knowing what revenge she would take on him.

Holding the second stone like a fist, Elske raised her arm and smashed it into his lip and nose. Then she let his head fall back.

Now it was the captain who whimpered, and his hands covered his face, and he curled up on the ground. "Help me!" he cried.

The snow beside his hidden face stained out a bright red.

The servants, now free, called to Idelle and Elske. "Run! Run! We have no weapons! We can't help you! Run!"

Idelle sobbed, asking Elske, "What have you done? What have you done?" But Elske turned to the Adeliers, three now lifting their fallen captain, and spoke to them in Souther. "If you had succeeded, you would all have been dead men."

They stared at her.

"*Fruhckmen*," she named them, the Volkaric word. They didn't know the language but they understood her meaning.

Now Idelle was running awkwardly home, her feet tripping on her own cloak in her haste and fear, but Elske knew they had no more to fear from these Adeliers, these cowards. And their captain would be marked for life for what he was. She'd seen his bloody teeth in the snow. She'd split his lip like a nutshell.

● ● ●

When Idelle told her story to Ula, and then again to her father after he had returned in the evening, there was a great commotion. Var Kenric pressed Elske over and over, "And she was never touched? Never harmed?" When Taddus came to call, Var Kenric pulled him aside and spoke to him in a low voice, in the corner of the front room.

Idelle sat wrapped in a blanket in her chair by the fire, sometimes weeping in remembered fear. They gave her wine to soothe and strengthen her. "If it hadn't been for Elske," she kept saying, and Ula stroked her hair and spoke to her as softly as if she were a little child.

After a time, Var Kenric said quietly, "I thank you, Elske." He had started to add, in warning, "But you—" when he was interrupted by a pounding on his door.

He opened it to four men accompanied by servants carrying lanterns. The men stamped their feet in the snow and asked to enter the house.

"Certainly," Var Kenric said. "May we be well met, gentlemen." He offered to take their cloaks and he offered tankards of ale. They shook their heads, declining to give up their cloaks, declining refreshment, and to persuade them he said, "It's a cold night."

"Colder for some than others. You must know, we've a gravely wounded princeling on our hands."

At that, Var Kenric called for Elske to join them around the table, leaving Ula, Idelle and Taddus near the fire.

The four visitors were thickset Trastaders and one stood taller than the others, a bear-like man with heavy-lidded eyes and a thin mouth. Elske didn't know how they would deal with her. Among the Volkaric, reward for courage was given as swiftly as death for cowardice—but she was among Trastaders.

One of the shorter men spoke. "You have attacked and injured an Adel."

"Yes," Elske agreed.

"Why would you do such a thing?"

Elske found herself talking to the bearlike man even though he was not one of her questioners. "That one was the captain, and the others only followed him. They hoped to ruin Idelle," she said. Then, seeing by their faces that she had not answered them, she explained, "If a wolf pack is after you and you can chase off the leader, the others will not stay to fight."

She thought it was the tall man's judgement that would rule the others.

"They meant rape," Var Kenric said. "I don't understand why you are here, Vars, and under the darkness of night as if in secrecy," he said, although Elske guessed he well knew. Idelle's father was trying to help her, she could see. And thus she saw that she needed help.

The big man answered Var Kenric. "They say they were only teasing, only flirting, they had drunk too much and were stupid with ale. They say, these guests of Trastad, these Adels who have come here for the Courting Winter which puts them under the Council's protection, they say that the attack was unprovoked."

"But that is not so," Elske said.

"We wonder, how you could know they intended

harm to your mistress, when they speak Souther," he answered, and watched her face carefully.

"Ask the two servants," Elske suggested.

"The servants have been sent out of the city, and so cannot be questioned. The young men deny everything. They demand that we punish you." He kept his eyes on her face.

Her death, then. Elske didn't know what else there was for her to say, so she said nothing. These men had come to take her to her death and only waited for the tall man to speak the order. She would give Idelle her wolfskin boots, for the young woman had admired them.

"Are you not afraid?" the tall man asked her.

Elske shook her head.

"And were you not afraid when there were seven of these Adeliers ready to attack and rape you both?" he asked.

She corrected his mistake. "There were only three, for two held the two servants back, and two more were soft-legged with drink, not dangerous. There was only the one who was truly a danger to Idelle."

"No reason for fear, then," he said, with what might have been a smile. "And if the princeling dies?"

"Why should he die?" Elske asked. "I gave him a scarring blow, not a killing."

"But how could you be so certain they planned ill?" one of the others asked. "I want to be merciful, but I don't see how you could be so certain they planned ill."

Elske tried to explain. "When men take too much mead, and they are together, and each wants the others to know his manhood—such men are as dangerous as a pack of wolves at the hungry end of winter. They smelled dangerous, and they said Idelle was a precious virgin of Trastad, and they asked one another, 'Who's to stop us?'"

"But how do we know—?" one of the shorter ones started to ask, before another cried him down, demanding, "Do you care more for the profits of these Courting Winters than for the safety of our women?" but "Will you have it known abroad that such an attack went unpunished?" the first countered.

The tall man gave his orders. "Speak no more of it. Let the servants carry tales, as they will, being servants, and all the Adeliers will hear soon enough from their own servants, and from Prince Garolo's face when he reappears in their midst. The story will be told, and it will grow, and if we neither punish nor praise this girl—if we say nothing, as I advise—then the story will act as a deterrent for years to come. It will be known that the Adeliers may not with impunity act like beasts in Trastad," he concluded, with another small smile that was not a smile.

"But I think the girl had better come with me. I am in need of a nursemaid for my three daughters. I would like my daughters," he said, unsmiling now, "to be in the care of someone who can defend them."

"What will your wife say, Var Jerrol, to such a choice?"

"My wife will say what I say," the man answered. "Come now, what is your name?"

"Elske," she told him as Var Kenric called across the room, "Daughter? Make your farewells to Elske."

"But who will be my servant?" Idelle asked. "Elske was to stay with me until I marry."

"You'll be safer apart, now," Var Kenric told his daughter. "I'm sorry you leave us, Elske, but this is the better way. When my daughter has no maidservant, then she could not have been the Trastader maiden who was attacked in the street. When you have been hidden away in Var Jerrol's house, nursemaid to his daughters, you could not have been that half-wild servant from off island, for if you were, who could trust you with his own helpless children?"

Elske knew Var Kenric meant to remind her of how great her strangeness was, how perilous her position in Trastad, as a warning not to protest. She needed neither reminder nor warning. And she would move warily in her new position, for this big Trastader was as dangerous as any man of the Volkaric. She bade farewell to Taddus, and to Var Kenric and Ula, and sorrowfully to Idelle, whom she wished joy on her wedding day. Then she followed the four men back out into a night filled with dark falling snow.

Chapter 6

THE PARTY MOVED silent as a Volkaric war band through the night. Snow muffled the sounds of their footsteps and the only light came from the lanterns carried by the servants.

Elske moved in their midst like some captive of great worth being taken to the Volkking.

After they had crossed the snow-covered bridge to the old city of Trastad, the party divided. Elske was to go on with the tall man, Var Jerrol, and his two servants. Parting, Var Jerrol said to his companions, "One of you will take the notice down from the door of the Council Hall," and "We'll see to that," they promised him. "Good sleep, Var," they bid farewell to one another, adding that this was a good night's work. "These foreign Adels need to be ridden with a short rein," they said. "Good sleep, Var."

The icy air was thick with falling snow. The four made their way, turning now left, now right, past ship chandleries and livery stables, warehouses and taverns. Then they were walking between the flat faces of tall houses, their ground-floor windows shuttered but the upper ones showing cracks of light that lit the snow as it fell.

At one of these tall houses the party halted. The door opened as if they had been watched for, and they entered into a small room. The tall Var told Elske, "The wolf cloak must be burned," taking it from her. And those were all the words he spoke.

A maidservant gave Elske a candle, and led her up three flights of stairs. She opened a door into a dark, cold chamber that contained a bed, a chest and a short-legged box made out of flat tiles. As Elske watched, the servant struck a tinderbox to light a fire in the box, blew on it until the flames burned eagerly, then took three pieces of wood from a basket and fed them to the fire. She half-closed a metal door at the front of the box. "Once your room warms, you should close and latch the door of the stove," she told Elske, and left the room.

Stove, Elske thought; and she thought she understood; she had already learned *latch*. It was wonderful, Elske thought, to keep fire tamed in a box that took its smoke away with pipes and chimneys. Winter in the one-roomed houses of the Volkaric was a choking season, unless you opened the shutters and let clean icy air blow through.

Elske looked about her to see what the candlelight revealed. The bed had fat covers lying on it, and pillows, too. Two small windows were tucked under the low ceiling, and they showed a black curtain of night, with little white flakes blowing up against the outside of the glass. She set the candleholder down on the wooden chest, hung her dress on a peg beside the door and latched the door of the stove, closing in its fire. Then she climbed up on the bed. She slipped down under the coverlet, as if all her life she had been used to such a bed. But she did not sleep. She remembered.

She remembered the orderly quiet of Var Kenric's house, and the days as Idelle's maidservant, days as like one another as one onion to the next; and she remembered the young men's threats in the lonely street. She remembered the strength of her arm against their captain; remembering, she noticed what she had not seen at the time, which was how easily cowed they all were—Idelle, the Adels, the servants.

What she would be now, Elske did not know. Nursemaid, if she could believe Var Jerrol, and she had no reason to disbelieve him. Had he not taken her under his protection? But Elske knew enough about Trastaders to know he would have his own uses for her, for his own profit.

Remembering, Elske noticed again Var Jerrol's eyes, how they had measured her, and then she noticed how he had—having taken her measure— given orders to arrange the outcome to his will. Among the Trastaders she had met, only Var Jerrol might be dangerous, Elske thought.

And then she noticed that she had taken her own measure of him.

Her legs and shoulders were already sleeping, but a newly born person behind her eyes struggled to stay awake, just a little longer, to ask if Elske had also noticed this: that she could change things. For had she not changed everything?

Almost, she reminded herself, changed everything to her death. And now Elske noticed that while, like any Volkaric man or woman, she did not fear death, she would, like any Trastader, prefer to live. Her further safety was up to her, Elske thought, as sleep finally overmastered her.

Wakened by the door—opening—and somebody entering the room, Elske sat up in a room filled with sunlight. She had slept well into the morning.

A red-faced Trastader girl, wearing an apron over her dark dress and a white kerchief around her hair, stood at the foot of the bed, her arms full of cloth. Elske waited for her to speak. The girl stared.

This went on until Elske moved to get out of bed, setting her feet on the floor.

"Odile says you're to dress and come down. Into the cook room." Her message delivered, the girl left the room.

Elske bent down to see out the windows.

Black bare-armed trees grew up out of the snow, and grey stones made a low wall at the end, and beyond that stretched a river so shoreless it had to be the sea, Tamara's sea.

"Oh," Elske said, aloud alone, and "Oh," again.

That morning the sky shone so clear and so blue that the sea sparkled deep and bright, blue as the tiny bellflowers that appeared in the brief Volkaric spring, and bluer. Blue as only itself, the sea shone back at the shining sky, outside her window.

Elske laughed out loud. But she could not linger. She dressed and followed the stairways down to the entrance hall and then followed her nose.

The large cook room was filled with the odor of bread and porridge. A thin woman stood at the long wooden table, her knife raised. The carcass of a rabbit lay before her, skinned, its guts removed, the head and paws chopped off. The woman had blood on her hands.

"You'll be the girl," she greeted Elske. She didn't wait for any response. "I'm to feed you and then take you to the master. That's Var Jerrol, in case nobody told you, and I'm Odile, housekeeper for the Var. His wife is so worn out by childbirth that she is dying of the coughing sickness, so there are the little girls to look after. Do you know anything of children?"

Elske said, "I only know about babies."

"What, how to get one?" Odile laughed, loud and short, like a dog's bark, and drove her knife into the shoulder of the rabbit. "How old are you? Are you bleeding yet?"

"This is my thirteenth winter and no, I am not."

"It'll be any day, from the look of you, and what's your name? Sit, I've porridge."

Elske sat on the bench and the woman dipped a bowl into a cauldron set on the hob, then set it steaming down on the table. Elske took the spoon the woman gave her, and ate.

After a bite, "Good," she said, and it was. Porridge was food to fill a belly, and keep it full. "Elske," she said, between mouthfuls. "That's my name."

Odile cut the rabbit into pieces which she dropped into a second, smaller cauldron, then swung it on a metal hook back over the open fire. "That's done," she said. "And you're fed. Now you go to Var Jerrol. I'll warn you, you'd better tell him whatever's true. He'll find you out easy as breathing if you lie to him, and that'll be the end of you."

So openness would be her safety, here in Var Jerrol's house, as much as it had been what kept her safe among the Volkaric. Elske followed Odile to a chamber off of the entrance hall. When she entered that room, she saw the Var sitting straight-backed in a chair, and he was busy with the many papers opened out in front of him. Shelves on the wall held leather boxes, and squares were on the walls, most colored, one blank. The man was writing.

Elske went up to one of the colored squares, to look at it more closely. This was not cloth, although when she touched it, it was as smooth as her skirt. This square showed a man's head, smaller than a real man's head. Although it was as flat as glass, it didn't look flat. The man stared off, as if he saw something over Elske's shoulder. But when she turned there was nothing to be seen.

Var Jerrol paid no attention to her.

Elske went to the blank square. Now a face filled it, dark-eyed, a girl's face, with dark thick eyebrows over eyes of so dark a grey they reminded her of rainclouds, and wolf pelts. The girl had a short nose and her hair was worn Trastader fashion, under a scarf. Except for the color of her eyes, the girl looked a great deal like Tamara when she was thinking out the day's work. The girl looked so much like her grandmother that Elske smiled.

The face smiled back at her, as if it were alive, and happy to see her.

She stepped back, and the girl stepped back. She reached a hand out, to touch the face, but the girl's hand reached towards hers, until their fingertips touched. But all Elske felt was flat and cold.

"Elske," the man spoke from behind her, and she whirled around. "It's all right, it's a beryl glass. Don't be afraid."

"I'm not afraid," Elske told him, and now Var Jerrol

smiled at her, to say, "Of course. I'd forgotten."

"But who is she? And where?" Elske asked, turning back to the beryl glass.

"She's you. That's you." He rose to stand beside her, and she saw him appear also beside the girl. The girl's face, her own, was not a broad Trastader face, although neither was it narrow, like the Volkaric. "The back of the glass is painted silver, and that causes it to reflect what is before it, as the harbor on a windless day reflects the sky and masts, or the river water its banks. But come over to the window," Var Jerrol said. "Let me see you by daylight. You don't look strong enough to have smashed the Adel's mouth."

"And nose," Elske told him.

"And nose." He smiled again.

She explained it to him. "I had a stone. Actually," she added, for perfect openness, "I had two stones, from the street, because I smelled danger when they turned to follow us and I could hear what they said to one another. I needed to keep them from ruining Idelle."

"So you do speak Souther. Yet you are Volkaric."

What did he know of her, Elske wondered, and why would he know anything about her? But she had decided to keep no secrets and by the time he finished asking her, he knew about her warrior father, dead in some distant battle, her Volkaric mother and Tamara, who let her live, and raised her. What he did not ask, he did not know. "Why did you leave?" he asked and "My grandmother sent me away," she told him. He desired to know no more, but said then, "I am the eyes and ears of the Council. Do you know what that means?"

"You tell the Council the secrets you learn," she guessed.

"In part," he said. "Also, I hear their worries and their schemes, and I set my spies to gather information the Council needs, to settle their worries, to enact their schemes. I do not tell everything, Elske, just what they need to know. You will be safe in my house. If you are nursemaid to my daughters, and unseen, the misadventure will be forgotten." Then, in a different voice, he asked, "You can read? As the posted notice claims?"

"I know letters," Elske answered.

The Var rose and took down one of the leather boxes from his shelves. This turned out to be sheets of paper, sewn within a stiff leather cover— not a box at all. The cover was made so that it could be opened to display the pages one after another. She could see words on the open page and reached out a hand to touch them. The page was smooth, flat, and the letters lay smooth and flat upon it. "What do you call this?" she asked and "A book," he answered. "Can you read it?"

Elske studied the letters, making the sounds in her head, until she remembered them well enough to read him the tale of the eagle who was shot with an arrow fletched with his own feathers, a story Tamara, too, had known. When she was done, he returned the book to the shelf and said, "I've kept visitors waiting. Odile will take you to my daughters." He went to the door and opened it, that she might leave him. Following her out of the room, he reached out his hand to greet a cloaked man, who was just then crossing the hall in loud boots. "May we be well met," Var Jerrol said to this guest, and to the manservant he said, "Bring us hot drinks," and Elske was forgotten.

She went back into the cook room where Odile asked what she was to be paid for her labors and when Elske said she did not know, promised to settle it with the Var. "It's hard to put a price on the kind of work you'll be doing for him," she said. "And he'll work you without recompense if you let him." Then, "I don't know where you come from, to know so little of the world," Odile added, and laughed. She led Elske up two sets of stairs, to knock on a wooden door and open it without waiting for an answer.

This was a large room, where the serving girl who had awakened Elske sat sewing and two little girls, of one and two winters, whispered together on a bed. There was a cradle set near the warmth of a tile stove. Windows let in sunlight, and there were two beds with small chests at their feet, as well as a round table at the center of the room with four chairs around it. When Odile led Elske in, the sleeping baby was the only one who didn't stare solemnly.

"Here's the new nursemaid," Odile announced. "Elske. And that means you"—she jabbed the girl with a finger—"will be back in the cook room—where I have need of you, what with the Courting Winter, and the master's meals, and the Varinne's dainty stomach. Your soft days are finished and I don't want to hear any snuffling on that account." The girl rose from her seat.

Odile spoke to the little girls with more courtesy, and in a gentler voice. "Our oldest—she's two. Can you give a curtsey, Mariel?" The child shook her head no, and sucked on a finger. "And this is

Miguette," Odile said, as the younger, just steady on her own legs, took her sister's hand and bobbed downwards. "The baby is Magan. The sewing is an old cloak of Mariel's we're taking up. You can sew, can't you?"

"Mine," Miguette said, pointing to the cloak.

"Little girls can't get sick," Mariel said. "Poor Maman is sick," she told Elske.

Odile and the serving girl left Elske with the two little girls and the sleeping baby. Without a word, Elske sat on the low seat beside the cradle, took up the cloak and continued the hem where it had been left off. She knew the sisters were watching her from the bed where they sat, each with a doll in her hands. When the baby woke, Elske could ask Mariel where the clean cloths were, and where the baby's soiled cloths were kept, and so they would grow comfortable with one another.

By the time bowls of fish soup were brought up for them, and chunks of bread with honey to pour on them, the little girls had grown comfortable with this stranger. Elske noticed this, and noticed, too, that her spirits rose to have little children in her care, and for companions.

The Longest Night arrived and passed by without Elske having time to do more than silently wish Idelle well. Not only were Var Jerrol's daughters in her care, but also Elske could be summoned to the cook room to assist Odile; for the cook was kept busy, as the Councillors met with Var Jerrol to plan and manage the Courting Winter. The men needed to govern the high spirits of the Adels, so these young men were taught sword-fighting by two masters of that art, and when the snow was packed solid in the streets they had permission to race their horses, and when weather kept them inside they were taught dances and songs. The city feasted its guests frequently, and regular Assemblies, with hired entertainers, were held in the Council Hall. Still, the Adels had too much time for drinking and quarreling and making mischief, and that interfered with the Council's intention of bringing them to marriage by the end of winter. Luckily, the Adelinnes understood their purpose in Trastad and caused no trouble.

One day, as Odile unrolled a pastry crust over the top of the fish pie she was preparing for a tableful of Councillors, in satisfaction at her work she announced, "I may have been a bad woman, but none can say I'm a bad cook."

"Was it difficult to become bad?" Elske asked, hoping to cause Odile to laugh.

Odile obliged her, turning the bowl in her hands as she pinched the crust down into place. "The opposite of difficult, Miss Curiosity. It's a short and easy road, but not—as some say—scattered over with flowers and pieces of gold. The law of the city had me bound for the cells, but Var Jerrol took me instead. All the servants of his house he's rescued from the cells, and that keeps us loyal. You, for example. If the Var hadn't fetched you home with him that night, where do you think you'd have lodged the next, and all the rest of your life? And that wouldn't have been long, down in the cells. You'd have not wished it to be long, either."

"But if the Adels threatened to rape Idelle, why is it I who would go to the cells?" Elske asked.

Odile shrugged. "The law places Adeliers under the Council's protection, so when you harm an Adel you have transgressed against the law. Justice does not always harness well with profit, as any of our merchants will tell you. So Var Jerrol brought you here, to keep you from the cells; and let the world think you in the cells—for there is no doubt the world has thought of you, and spoken of you. Let them think you if not dead in the cells, then dying there." Odile laughed again. "You're fat for a corpse," and Elske laughed with her. She placed the fish pie into the baking oven and asked Odile, "Why were you a bad woman?"

"Oh, well, I was young. I had a husband but his boat went down in a storm, driven onto sharp rocks, and I left childless and penniless. A widow without property has nothing to attract a husband. So I stole what I could, usually from visitors to the city, and they found me out and set me before the Council. 'Why did you not go whoring, woman?' they asked me. With the cells awaiting me, I wished I had. But Var Jerrol claimed me for his cook. The Council didn't like to say him nay. None of them naysays any other, if they can help it, and no one wants to cross Var Jerrol. He's given orders to have you trained at waiting table."

"I think I will obey," Elske said, and earned another bark of laughter.

"The Council knows that without Var Jerrol, whose ships carry his spies as well as his goods, whose whores pick the heads but not the pockets of our visiting merchants and traders, their own profits might fall off. He keeps Trastaders, too, under his eye, for men who look to profit will often be tempted to take profit where the law forbids it. The city is full of thieves, Elske, and not all of them sleep rough in streets and stables." But Odile could not be long diverted from her instructions. "He has said you are to wait at table under Red Piet. When you do that, Saffie will watch over the little girls."

Elske, wondering if her safe place in the house would be at risk with this more public task, asked, "What if I prefer not?"

"I'd prefer so, if I were you, my missy, unless you prefer the cells. They might send you there to serve this Fiendly Princess."

"An Adelinne has been sent to the cells?" Elske asked, then answered herself, "No, they would never; but she must trouble them severely. Is she the Adelinne who wouldn't go into safety in the storm?"

"The very same and a very devil, they say. Uncooperative, disobedient, proud, uncivil, she refuses to go to the Assemblies. She demands to be taught swordplay. She tries to take part in the street races—she doesn't know her purpose here, and doesn't wish to. No maidservant will stay long with her for her temper and tongue, each as bad as the other, both sharp as a sword, hot as a firebrand. And she offers her servants no coins. Now, you do this second pie, fold the pastry over the top, as I did—yes, over, and pick it up from the two ends—yes, and lay it down. Pinch it tight, lest the good juices be lost. *And* she has run away so often they keep her in a locked room, they send her under guard, this Fiendly Princess, when she must be out in the city. But you'll make a good cook, Elske. You're a clever one, aren't you?"

Elske was more interested in the Adelinne. "She must have courage."

71

"And if she does, what good will that do her," Odile decided. "Obedience and beauty get more marriage proposals than courage, and wealth gets the most, and you are needed upstairs in the nursery now, unless my ears deceive me."

As the dark winter days went by, Elske was kept busy, with all she had to learn and all she had to do. Var Jerrol gave her a book of animal tales to read to his daughters, to begin the widening of their world. "With wealth, and knowledge gained from books, my daughters will make wives worthy of any man," he told Elske. "And why should my daughters not marry as well as any Adelinne?" He also had Elske taught to serve at table, having her practice by serving him whenever he dined alone on the golden plates he brought out only for those occasions. All that long winter, Elske stayed within Var Jerrol's property, but she was not restless. The little girls gave Elske wild nursery games and wild nursery laughter, and that lightened the long darkness. Var Jerrol explained his importance to the Council, how his ships brought not only information and goods, but also rarities from foreign lands to introduce the Trastaders to the newest luxuries, embroidered silks, silver filigree, peppercorns. Odile gave her the gossip of the house and the city—how the Varinne had brought a good fortune to her husband but failed to give him a son, how his own housekeeper had named High Councillor Vladislav, the wealthiest Var in Trastad, father of her child, how a clever thief had emptied a merchant's strongbox in broad daylight.

Elske only saw the Varinne when she took the daughters to her. The Varinne didn't have the strength to have the girls linger, but she was always glad to see them. Once or twice, when Elske had wrapped the two older girls up warm and taken them outside to fall down in the snow and make snowballs to throw at her, she saw the pale face at the window, looking down at her lively, healthy daughters.

Eventually, winter loosened its grip on the land. Then it rained as often as it snowed, but when the sun shone out of a clear sky, the sea shone back blue. Some few boats ventured out, fishermen hungry to end the winter shortages and eager for profits. As soon as it was safe to travel, the Adeliers returned to their homelands and whatever futures they had made or found during the Courting Winter.

When she no longer risked recognition, Elske could carry the basket for Odile, with Red Piet and Piet the Brown accompanying them to the shops and markets. She grew accustomed to the city, the many faces and crowded streets, and to its smells—a combination of offal and salt air and bakehouses, with their roasting meats and yeasty breads and honey-nut cakes. The sea was now a familiar sight, jigging at the edges of the land.

Elske was growing out of her girlhood, and she started her woman's bleeding that winter; the little girls were growing, too, and so were the days which stretched now into one another, with only a shadowy darkness to act as night. Elske could bake a meat pie, now, or a fish pie, or an apple pastry, and the daily porridge and loaves of bread. She could prepare a meal, if Odile was taken with her women's pains, and she could stand beside Red Piet to wait at table when the Var entertained guests.

The serving at table, she discovered, was one of Var Jerrol's uses for her; for some of his guests were merchants from the south, come to Trastad to buy lumber, furs and ores. These merchants were cautious when Var Jerrol sat with them, but if he was called away they would speak unguardedly in Souther. Afterwards, the Var called Elske into his chamber and asked her to recite what the merchants had said when they were alone and, as they thought, unheard. She reported to him their disgust at the delicate whitefish the Trastaders ate pickled in vinegar and onions, their hopes that the Council would approve their offering price for a hundred-weight of ore and their calculations of how much their profits would increase at that price. She reported when they schemed to mix fine ground grain in with a shipment of spices, assuring themselves that the simple Trastaders would not know the difference between the pure and the diluted.

The merchants also spoke among themselves about wars and Wolfers, about the ambitious Counts who ruled over the cities of the south, about diseases and their cures, and about magic weaponry; there was always information they wished to keep to themselves, lest the Trastaders know and take advantage.

"I don't blame them," Var Jerrol remarked to Elske. "I am the eyes and ears of Trastad and much of my wealth comes from information which—when I know it—also protects the city and its people."

Elske never made the mistake of keeping anything back from Var Jerrol. She knew that Var Jerrol trusted her reports and noticed that he smiled, with a private pleasure, whenever he saw her. But she believed that information was her true work for his house, for some of the merchants were more than merely greedy. Some had secrets.

Once she reported to Var Jerrol what three merchants of Celindon had said to one another when he left them alone with glasses of wine, and Elske there to keep them filled. The merchants had spoken in lowered voices of something called black powder. When Elske repeated that name to the Var, he looked at her long and silent, dangerously, before asking, "What did they say about the black powder?"

"They said that you were ignorant," at which news Var Jerrol smiled, and she added, "Thus, they said, their supplies of lumber were assured."

"Did they say what lumber had to do with the black powder?" Var Jerrol asked, his eyes intent upon her face, as if he could read there more than the words she spoke, as if although she might not know more, still he would find more there, in her face, in her eyes, and seize it to himself.

"No. They spoke as of something they all already knew. Although they did observe," Elske reported, remembering carefully, "that your stables were lined with saltpeter, and that in Trastad the waste from the copper smelters is dumped into the rivers."

Var Jerrol lowered his eyelids, to think about this. After a long time he looked at her again. "If you're as clever as I think, Elske, you are also a danger to me. Are you so clever?"

"Yes," she said.

"Well," he said; then, "Was there anything more these merchants said?"

"That was when you returned."

"Go back to my daughters now. But Elske," he ordered her, "this is no matter you need to remember. Unless, of course, you hear anyone else speak of black powder, and that you must report immediately."

Elske almost laughed to hear him instruct her thus; and he almost smiled as he watched her face.

Var Jerrol smiled seldom now, for when the Varinne coughed, she coughed blood. The apothecary said she wouldn't live to see another spring, and so he allowed her to open her windows on fine days to taste the warm salty air, and hear the voices of her daughters while they played in the gardens.

On days when Elske accompanied Odile to the markets she saw more and more swollen bellies among the young wives of Trastad. Each market day she looked for Idelle. But when she found her—a manservant three paces behind—Idelle's belly was as flat and empty as Elske's. Idelle was glad at first to meet with Elske, but that gladness soon washed away and she said, "As you see, I will have no baby to welcome Taddus home."

"As I see," Elske answered.

Idelle sighed. "But it could happen that our second winter bears more fruit than our first. It often happens so, I've heard that. You've always been luck to me, Elske," Idelle said. "Maybe meeting you will bring good fortune."

Odile called Elske away then, for the Emperor's messengers had arrived to collect the tribute money and Odile was poaching a redfish whole, to be the centerpiece of their dinner. Var Jerrol would feast the messengers and then give to them the chest of tribute coins. It was to meet this expense that the grandfathers of the present Trastaders had first opened their houses and their city to those Adeliers; the profit from the Courting Winters made up most of the tribute. The tribute bought peace, safety in which they might continue their trading.

The long, sun-filled summer days ran on. Sometimes the sky was clear and the sea blue. Sometimes storms whipped up white-headed waves that roared against the stone seawall. Sometimes the water ran grey between the mainland and Trastad, and all of the sea beyond was grey, too. The summer air blew warm over three-islanded Trastad, and the Trastaders kept out in the air as much as they could, because summer's stay among them was only brief. As long as it wasn't raining, the little girls in their light summer dresses stayed outside in the warmth and light, until they were sent inside to sleep.

There came a day in full summer—but it was really a night; that was part of the wonder of this time, sunlight at night. In this golden evening the Var's older daughters ran about barefooted, laughing, singing, dancing, delighted with themselves, delighted to be themselves with the light washing around them like water, and the baby sat upright in the grass, clapping her fat hands in admiration of her sisters.

Elske and Odile sat beside the Var's two young apple trees, watching. The air hung so sweet neither of them wanted to gather the little girls together and end the day. Mariel's high laughter rolled along the grass behind the wooden ball she was chasing. Then Odile murmured something in her low woman's voice. Magan fell sideways, fussing now. And Elske had a sudden sharp memory of Tamara, standing in the doorway of the Birth House, speaking in just such a low, rough voice, with just such sounds of laughter and misery coming from the room behind her. The memory sliced into Elske.

"Whatever is it? Whyever are you weeping?"

Elske shook her head, and wiped her eyes on her apron, and wept more tears, and didn't answer. The babies and toddlers she and Tamara had left out for the wolves, after winter had drawn back, were just such children as these three. Those Volkaric girls would have grown fatter and more clever, just as Magan had over the spring and summer, and grown into small ladies like Mariel who danced like a flower in the wind. Miguette, not yet two winters, was already secretive and solemn like her father. To think what might happen to these three little girls in their helplessness, and to remember all those for whom the Volkaric had no use, and so she and Tamara had wheeled them by the cartload out to a stony place, and been able only to end their short lives quickly— Elske's heart felt as if it were being ripped apart by wolves.

She had not even noticed that great change in herself, to have a heart where before she had had none.

Chapter 7

NOT THAT ELSKE deceived herself into thinking she was a Trastader. She only knew what she no longer was.

Fall was a short, fat season in Trastad, busy with preparing vats of salted and smoked fish, pots of fruit and jars of honey; busy with filling the pantries of Var Jerrol's house for the long winter. Only those fish caught by ice fishermen, who spent winter mornings dangling baited hooks through holes they sawed in the ice, would be fresh food for Trastad in the winter; and it was the high price those fish brought that made the discomfort and danger a risk worth taking for the fishermen.

The fall was busy and brief in Var Jerrol's house, but it was not sweet, for the Varinne was dying. The household fell quiet around her as she made her way into death. The air in every chamber was thick with sorrow, and the food they ate tasted bitter with loss, so that when the Varinne had at last breathed out the end of her life, even though it was the deep dark of winter something light came back into Var Jerrol's house.

Since it was not a Courting Winter, the Trastaders

could go quietly about their own business. Elske went once to visit Idelle in Var Kenric's house, accompanied by Red Piet. On this occasion, she had a mission for Var Jerrol, but she hoped to hear also that Idelle was with child. This hope was disappointed and Idelle could speak only of the sadness that stained her life. So now Elske saw two grieving women, Var Kenric's wife and daughter, each inconsolable, gazing out from behind his windows. One wept for the past, one for the future, and when Elske found Taddus in the counting room she could see that he was eager for spring, to give him the reason to leave the gloom of his home.

Elske's mission for Var Jerrol was to ask Taddus about a rumor that had reached Trastad. In his travels of the summer, had Taddus heard of an exploding ship? Yes, he had, but he didn't credit the rumor. Could a ship, and its crew of eleven men, with its two tall masts and its long keel, simply fly apart up into the air? Taddus had heard tales but none of the tellers had been eyewitness to the event and when he asked in which city's harbor the event had happened, none of the tellers agreed. Each had heard it from a friend; each friend had heard it from the sole survivor of the catastrophe.

The tales told of the sky filled with charred pieces of wood, and parts of bodies, and the water of the harbor clotted with debris. The tales had a ship riding peacefully at anchor and then—without warning, with no sound as of galloping hooves to herald danger—a roar filled the air. Everyone agreed about the sound; it was thunder trebled. But nobody could agree about what they had seen—an explosion of fire, a sun burning in the harbor, the air darkened with evil-smelling smoke. Taddus shrugged, telling Elske this. "So the rumors go. And the rumors go farther, too, with talk of demon warriors risen in the south, come to lay everything waste and barren. The Wolfers are their slaves, and run before them, rumors say. But we are distant enough, here in islanded Trastad, Elske. You needn't fear."

"I'm not afraid," Elske answered him. "I was sent to ask."

"If I had married you, we'd have a child by now— do you think?" Taddus asked her suddenly. "But I will be named Var this spring, or the next, and that will give Idelle a new place among the ladies of the city. Maybe that will console her."

Elske joined in that hope, and left him there with his coins and his dreams and his books of cost and profit. She bid farewell to Idelle and called Red Piet from Ula's kitchen to escort her back to Var Jerrol's home.

"I suspect this is no demon army, but some new weapon of war," Var Jerrol said, "and I would not wish Trastad to be surprised by such a weapon. Such weapons give too much power to those who wield them, and cause dangerous fears in those who know of them. You are a girl and you may wrap your ignorance around you, but I am the eyes and ears of the Council."

"You think this is the black powder," Elske decided.

He wore the mourning band for his wife across his chest, but now he smiled at Elske. "Perhaps I should marry you. Other men have clever wives to work beside them."

"Why should everyone suddenly think of marrying me?" Elske demanded, and he smiled more broadly but did not tell her, so she could only laugh. Then he dismissed her, to return to the little girls. "And why *should* I marry again?" he asked as she turned to leave him.

"You wish for a son," Elske told him.

"Go now," Var Jerrol ordered, "before I change my mind."

Var Jerrol sent a party into the south, men willing to risk the hazards of winter travel for the sums Var Jerrol offered. When the survivors of the party returned, marked by blackened, frostbitten toes, fingers and ears, they brought with them a captive, a nervous, quick-eyed man, who asked question after question. Elske translated between the man and Var Jerrol. "What is he going to do with me? Why was I taken?" the man asked. "I'm not a wealthy man. How can they hope for ransom from a simple apothecary? Have you no pity for me? Can you not pity my wife, who must wonder what has befallen me? I'll reward you, I promise, Elske, whatever you ask. A rich husband? If you'd just tell me what he wants. Jewels? In my own city, I have the ear of the Count. The Count will give you whatever I tell him, if you help me get away."

The apothecary grew bolder with food and drink and warmth and rest. Var Jerrol shared meals with his captive, but kept Elske always in the room, to translate. As the man looked around him more, he no longer asked Elske to help him escape. At last, one day, he inquired of Var Jerrol directly, "What do you desire of me?"

Var Jerrol, who like all of the merchants spoke

some Souther, answered this question himself. "The formula for black powder."

The apothecary laughed, then. "I thought it was something like that. Well, it's simple enough—for a man who knows its secret." He watched Elske, as she translated. "But I need some incentive to persuade my secret from me. For I'll have broken faith with the Count, and his writ will be out on my life."

"I could make you glad to tell me anything I asked of you," Var Jerrol said, but the man only laughed again, and suggested, "You prefer to have me tell you willingly, and truthfully."

Var Jerrol didn't argue.

"If I'm to lose everything, I'd be a fool to ask nothing in return. I'd need a new home, and large wealth," the apothecary said. Var Jerrol nodded, eyelids lowered; he accepted the bargain. "I might want a new wife. Young, and unknown to any man, to get my sons upon. I might want Elske," the apothecary said.

"Elske doesn't wish to marry you," Var Jerrol said.

"What do her wishes matter?"

"In Trastad, no woman weds against her will," Var Jerrol said. "Not even a servant. Besides, she is Wolfer bred and raised. And who would take such a woman into his bed, where he must sometimes lie helpless in sleep, when he has taken her against her will? You're safer with the wife I find for you," Var Jerrol said. "Now, tell me what you know."

The apothecary sighed, and then announced cheerfully, "I know everything." As he spoke, Elske repeated the information to Var Jerrol.

Mixed in proper proportions, the ingredients for

black powder responded to flame by bursting apart. Like a pig's bladder, when children fill it with air and then knot its neck; if the children drop it into a fire, it blows itself apart. Black powder explodes, the captive said.

The evil smell that accompanied the explosion was burned sulfur, familiar to those who lived near where iron and copper were extracted from their ores. It was charcoal, ground fine, that gave the powder its black color. Charcoal was in short supply in the south, where the forests had been cleared to farmlands to feed the growing citizenry, and there was little wood to burn down to charcoal. Thus, unless the apothecary was mistaken, Trastad would find more and more ships come into its harbor, to be filled with lumber, for use by the southern manufacturies of black powder.

Yes, a city could easily be taken with the black powder, its walls breached by the explosion. There was even talk that some of the Emperor's armies had long tubes, out of the ends of which the black powder propelled sharp pellets, to kill a man before he could come close to you with his drawn sword. This was killing your enemy as soon as you could see him, and he could have no protection against you. But the apothecary doubted these stories, for why didn't the long stick blow up in a man's hands when the fire flashed through the black powder?

Oh, yes, there was a third ingredient, to be ground in with the others, and the joke was it could be found in any cellar, on the wet walls, and it could be found growing atop any manure heap of every farm. This third ingredient was the pale saltpeter that, added in proper proportion—things must always be in the right proportions or the powder wouldn't work, it was knowledge of proportion that made the apothecary's information so valuable—made the black powder. Now, if the distinguished gentleman would give his word to the bargain—?

Var Jerrol would, and offered his hand to seal it.

Then the apothecary could easily write the formula down, if Elske would bring him paper and pen.

She set them down before him, and watched as he wrote, and saw how simple it was.

At this point, Var Jerrol sent Elske from the room, and she never saw the apothecary again. She never asked about him, either, for she had seen Var Jerrol's eyes.

Winter's end finally came near, the ice melting out into the sea, first, and then separating into chunks on the rivers. When the grass grew green and the apple trees threw lacy shawls of blossoms over their shoulders, Var Jerrol began talking to Elske about the proper education of his daughters, that they might attract husbands worthy of their father's position. He wished them to learn not only letters and numbers, but also how to mount and ride a horse, and even sword skills, that they might defend themselves, and even to have some knowledge of trade, and banking.

The long, honey-colored summer days flowed over Trastad. Piet of the brown hair asked for Elske's hand in marriage and she declined him. Var Jerrol warned her that when he himself wed—for he had chosen his new wife—Elske must leave his house if she would not take Brown Piet. He warned her that she was approaching her fifteenth winter, entering her marrying years, so she should look about her for a man who pleased her most. He would give her a dowry, Var Jerrol said. But Elske had no desire to marry.

She had chosen her future, he said. The city would give her as maidservant to an Adelinne, to serve the young woman during the Courting Winter, to companion her to the Assemblies and other entertainments and probably, since most of the Adeliers spoke that language, to speak her familiar Souther. Elske would be sent to Var Vladislav, High Councillor of Trastad, the wealthiest of its citizens, master of many vessels and a large banking house, possessor of vast forest estates on the mainland, and farms and copper mines as well. She would be just one among many maidservants in his great villa on Logisle. This must be her future if she would not marry, Var Jerrol told her and waited again for her answer.

Risking his displeasure—for she found herself unwilling to bend to his will—Elske again declined to take a husband. She had no desire for any man to husband her, she said, and while there would be an emptiness in her heart where the little girls had lived, still, her choice was to be sent away from them.

"Do you think to overmaster me so easily?" he asked, and she laughed, partly for the pleasure of seizing her will from him.

"I don't think to overmaster you at all," she said. "I'm not such a fool."

She accepted the purse of coins he gave her, and wished him well with his new wife, wished the daughters well with their new mother, and when the cool, brief days of autumn spilled over the three islands, Elske said her farewells to Var Jerrol's household, made her curtsey to the new Varinne—as round and rosy as the first had been slim and pale—and followed Red Piet for the last time through the stony streets of Trastad. They walked past docks and warehouses busy at the concluding days of the trading season, and over the bridge to Harboring where—as she knew—Idelle awaited Taddus's return with the sorrow of an empty cradle, and then across another bridge to Logisle. There, the stone villa of High Councillor Vladislav opened its heavy doors to Red Piet's pounding.

The manservant told Elske she must go around the side of the palace, as he called it, and reminded Red Piet, before he closed the door upon them, that he should know better than to come pounding at the *front* door of the High Councillor's palace.

"You could marry me and come back to Var Jerrol's," Red Piet said to Elske, then.

"Why does everyone wish to wed me?" Elske asked him and he told her, "To keep you safe among us, and have you in my bed. But you won't marry me?"

"I'm to serve the Adelinne."

"And after that?" he asked her.

"How can we know what comes after?" she asked him, bidding him farewell.

Alone now, she followed the sandy path around the villa, passing tall empty windows, passing through gardens where the last of the summer roses faded on their thorny branches, passing into the kitchen gardens—herbs, and the tall stalks of onions trampled down onto the dirt, the green fronds of carrots, waiting in the earth and apple trees behind all—passing on to a plain wooden doorway. The villa was like a bird, with its two wings spread out. The central section rose up four stories, its windows growing smaller with each ascent; it needed four great chimneys. Elske faced one of the wings, only two stories. She could look into the windows and see dried herbs hanging in bunches down from the rafters.

Then the door opened to her knock, and the same stern manservant urged her inside. "You've come from Var Jerrol. You're to be maidservant to our Adelinne. You're called Elske," he told her. "I am steward to the house of Var Vladislav, who is the High Councillor of Trastad." As he named his master, and gave him his title, the steward became even stiffer than before, and more dignified.

Elske said nothing, and this pleased him.

He led her down a narrow dark hallway, past a large cook room—where three open fires burned, and several young women were at work at a table, and cauldrons steamed on the great hob—into a moist, windowless washroom. There two vats of water boiled over open fires, and two women stirred them with thick poles while a third watched them at their work. The third woman introduced herself.

"I'm housekeeper to the High Councillor. Var Jerrol has sent you to us, and Var Vladislav takes his spy's word for you, so who am I to question? We are to have the Fiendly Princess for our Adelinne. For they've sent her back, to angle again for a husband, and you are to be her maidservant. Carry on here, girls," she said, and "Yes, Missus," they answered her.

They were stirring around among white cloths,

sweat running down their red faces and chests heaving with the effort. The housekeeper took Elske by the arm and led her out of the washroom, then down a long hallway, lit by dim daylight.

There was first a room where servants dined but Elske would not, and then storerooms holding food and linens, pots, brooms, stacks of wood for the stoves, as well as eight large copper tubs for bathing. At the end, a door opened onto the entrance hall of the villa. There, the housekeeper allowed Elske to look into the two reception rooms, one for the Varinne when she had callers, the other for the Var to conduct his business. She pointed out the room in which the Var and his family dined, and the large dining room where the Var entertained. There was also a ballroom, the walls hung with beryl glass, which in daylight made it as bright as outdoors. At the foot of the broad staircase that rose up from the back of the great hall, the housekeeper told Elske, "Under no circumstances will you ever go up into the family's private apartments."

"Yes, Missus," Elske said, having no desire to ascend. The housekeeper, satisfied, opened a door beside the staircase, to allow Elske a brief glance into a room smaller than any of the others she had been shown. This room had windows that opened onto the front gardens of the villa. There were maps spread out on a table at the center and books standing in rows on the shelves. "Sometimes the Adelinnes like to read," the housekeeper said, "although what care *she* might take of the Master's books, I don't like to think. That will be your responsibility, Elske. Also, her mischiefs and even crimes will be on your head." Then, giving Elske no chance to protest, she opened a door into the wing opposite the kitchen wing. "These are your apartments."

Here the hallway had broad wooden floors and polished wooden walls; it was lit by candles in wall sconces. One doorway, of dark carved wood, opened off to the left, and that was a small anteroom with the bedchamber beyond. The bedchamber had a waist-high row of windows, the sills deep enough to sit on, a stove with its bucket of wood beside it, a table, a cupboard fitted into the wall, a chest, a chair with arms and a small stool, as well as a high bed, the four posts of which were draped around with a heavy cloth. A beryl glass hung in a thick gold frame, and a bowl of flowers was set out on the table. All was in readiness.

The anteroom was where Elske would sleep, the housekeeper explained, on a pallet that was now rolled up, and Elske could just set her pack down here.

Across the hallway was a privy room, and at its end a reception room furnished for dining. "She, of course, does not bring her own servant, so you must also wait on her at table. The meals will be brought to you, and if she requests any particular delicacy, you may send word to me. Also, the Adelinne may take exercise on the villa grounds. Can you remember all that?"

"Yes, Missus," Elske said, keeping all expression from her voice and face. If she could not remember such simple instructions, she would be a sorry creature.

"The Adeliers will start arriving any day now, but until then—what use are you?" the housekeeper demanded and said, without waiting for Elske's answer, "The washroom always needs an extra hand. You can work there until your Fiendly Princess arrives. Well, she was little more than a child the last time they sent her here to find a husband, perhaps the years have improved her, although they say she was the demon imp himself."

"Yes, Missus." Almost, Elske was eager to meet this troublesome Adelinne.

Elske's two companions in the washroom were farmers' daughters, come to the city to try their chance at marriage and pleased to be servants in the High Councillor's villa, where any man who wished to court them would know their superior status. At first they mistrusted Elske. "You've the look of a house servant. Soft."

"But I'm not," Elske protested, and later they admitted, "You're stronger than you look." They became more at ease with her, and told her what they knew about service to the Adeliers. "You'll take meals with your Adelinne, unless you're accompanying her to an Assembly, or to a ball. Or a feast, sometimes there are feasts," they reminded each other, and advised Elske, "You'd better make good use of the winter because afterwards—everyone says, everybody knows—the girls who are maidservants for Adelinnes have been ruined."

"Raped?" Elske asked, and they covered their mouths, muffling their laughter.

"What do you think of Trastad, if you think that? Where did you come from to think such a thing? No, those who serve the Adelinnes are spoiled for other employments, because they have developed a taste for rich food and wines, and entertainments, for the company of people of higher station. No house will hire them, afterwards. They go to the inns and taverns, to work there, and that's the end of their hopes."

"Hopes for what?"

"For a husband, and children of their own. What else should a girl hope for? Although, I've heard of maidservants going off with their mistresses, but I wouldn't want to do that. Who is anything other than a Trastader, I pity that man or woman."

"But even if he's a Trastader," the other said, "I'd never marry a herder, however great his flock."

"No, nor any man who goes off to work in the mines, and not a fisherman, neither—for those too often never come home again."

"And when they do, they smell of—"

"Oh, agreed, agreed. I'd never wish—"

"A clean, well-mannered house servant would do me very well."

"Nor a sailor, neither. Unless he already owned a house of his own where I might live should his ship be lost."

"A house servant looks to his wife's comforts."

Elske took her meals alone in the apartment her Fiendly Princess would occupy, and slept on her pallet in the ante-chamber. Often, she stood at the bedchamber window, leaning her elbows on the deep sill, looking out to where the river ran, silvery in a dawning light, black under the stars. As best she could, in her secluded position, she was considering how she might secure further choices, and what they might be—once this, her first free choice, had played itself out.

And then, one morning, she was summoned from

the washrooms and presented by the housekeeper with two new dresses, and new stockings also, and a pair of soft leather boots. "The ship's in port, and she's on it, and all the others are arriving, too. Well, if she wants a more richly dressed maidservant, she'll have to see to you herself. Don't fail us, Elske."

Elske spent that afternoon awaiting her mistress's arrival, but no one came. The next morning a small sea chest arrived, and a heavy trunk. Elske shook out the Adelinne's dresses, and hung them in the dry, clean air of the washroom to freshen them. She placed on the cupboard shelves the shifts and stockings, underskirts and the cloths for the Adelinne's monthly bleedings. This Princess had clothing that was no more plentiful than Var Jerrol's daughters, and no finer, either. This Princess also had hidden among her shifts a sharp dagger, its blade as long as Elske's hand and its hilt iron, worked into the forms of a bird and a bear—the bear on its hind legs, the bird with its wings outstretched—one on each side, and each rounded to make a firm grip easy. It was not a rich weapon, but it was well-made, and well-honed. Elske hid it away again, back among the folded shifts.

Elske waited alone in the apartments all that second day, too, and still no one came. Most of the time she watched out of the window. Only sheep moved about on the wide lawns. Little boats, some small enough to require only a pair of oars to move them, some with a single red sail raised on the short mast, moved along the river. She began to think that perhaps the Adelinne would never arrive, but deep in the second night there came a pounding at the chamber door. Elske leapt up out of her sleep.

The door opened and the housekeeper stood there, a candle in her hand, a scarf around her shoulders, her grey hair loose. "Well, they've found her," she said to Elske. "She thought she'd be able to have her own way loose in the city, but Trastaders have good noses to smell out foreigners." Then turning from Elske she said, "Come here, my fine Lady. Step forward. You'll have to sleep in your filth, for I'm not asking any of my girls to heat bathwater at this hour. Get"—with a shove against the back of the tall young woman—"in now. There. This is your maidservant."

The young woman walked into the room without a glance at Elske, as slow and unconcerned as if she was not the object of the housekeeper's scorn and irritation.

One of the servants gave his candle to Elske, who took it without a word. The door was shut, again.

Elske turned to greet her mistress.

Behind her, a key turned in the lock.

Chapter 8

THE YOUNG WOMAN glared at the thick wooden door, as if she were devising suitable punishment for its misconduct. Her long, hooded cloak had a thick band of mud at its hem, and the boots that showed under the cloak were equally travel worn. She was tall, and seemed taller when she drew herself up and let the hood fall back. Her long brown hair hung tangled. She had a pale, oval face, with a long straight nose and wide mouth; her forehead wrinkled as she drew her dark eyebrows together in vexation. She was two or three winters the older, or so it seemed to Elske.

The Adelinne stood with her shoulders high, as if she faced an enemy, not a locked door. She unfastened the clasps at the neck of her cloak and let it fall to the floor behind her as she turned to move through the narrow doorway from Elske's anteroom into her own unlit bedchamber.

Elske had seen Volkaric women in a fury of vengeance; she had seen furies of fear and sorrow in the women of Trastad; but this Adelinne was not furious as a woman is. Hers was an imperious anger, firm, steady; you could warm your hands at it. Elske picked up the cloak and hung it on a peg—first it must dry out, and then she would brush it clean. The heavy woven wool, dyed dark blue, the smooth blue lining—these were rich cloths, although this was not a cloak made for harsh winter.

Elske heard the chest being opened, then its lid dropped down, impatiently. She heard the cupboard doors creak apart, and a rustle of fabric, and more rustling. Then the Adelinne spoke, her voice curling out of the doorway. "Enter to me," the voice said, in clumsy Norther.

Elske obeyed.

The Adelinne had lit the oil lamps and now she stood at the window, looking out at the darkness. She had changed into one of the heavy nightdresses Elske had folded away and she spoke without turning to look at her servant. "My travel dress—those—you must wash."

Elske gathered the dress, the underskirts and the shifts up in her arms. "Yes, Missus," she said.

At that, the Adelinne spun around, and Elske saw that her eyes were blue, the color of the sea under a clear sky, a deep, bright blue.

"Say me 'my Lady,'" the Adelinne said, pointing at her own chest whenever she said "my Lady." "Yes, my Lady. This you say to me. What I speak, do you hear it?" she asked.

"Yes, my Lady," Elske answered.

"There is—to eat?" She gestured at her mouth with her fingers.

"No, my Lady," Elske said.

"They"—her hand reached out and rotated—"keyed me."

This wasn't a question, and Elske didn't know if

she was supposed to answer or not.

"These dolts and dimwits. She doesn't wonder why we should be prisoners," the Adelinne muttered to herself in Souther, her voice quick in her own tongue, as quick as song. Then in Norther she said, "I am sleeping hungry. You not rest here." She pointed to the floor. "Not to sleep next me." She added in Souther, "So your spying will have to be confined to the daylight hours."

"I am not a spy," Elske answered in that same tongue.

The Adelinne stood absolutely still, her hands quiet in front of her. The blue eyes were fixed on Elske. "And a liar, too."

Elske's spirit rose to meet that scornful glance. If the Adelinne thought that Elske could be bullied by a false accusation then she had a surprise waiting for her, like those foolish Adels and their pretty-faced captain. Elske's eyes rose to meet the Adelinne's and she saw, with an unspoken breath of her own surprise—"Oh!"—that the young woman would welcome a battle. She explained, "If I were here for that use, my old master, Var Jerrol, would have told me what to listen for, and how I would report my information to him. Var Jerrol is the eyes and ears of the Council," she explained. "My Lady."

"Why should they have given you to me, when you know my language, unless to know my thoughts? But what should they hope a spy to tell them of me? They starve me into confusion," the Adelinne said, and ordered, "Take those dirty clothes out of this chamber, then return to me. I don't understand, and you will not sleep until I do."

Elske obeyed. She was not at all sleepy, and she

was curious, too, to know how the Adelinne would seek out understanding. When she returned her mistress seated herself in the chair and challenged Elske to show her skills as a hairdresser by combing out the knots and tangles in her hair. "It's been more than a day since I've put food into my mouth," the Adelinne told her. "I've drunk from public fountains, but that's not like good bread and meat in the belly. Nor strong wine, either."

"No, my Lady," Elske agreed.

"You'll be useful to me, to teach me Norther," the Adelinne said, and admitted, "I think you know why they have locked me in." And Elske answered, "You are that same Adelinne who stayed out on the ship's deck during the great storm two years back. Disobedient, they said. They complained that you ran away. You are the Fiendly Princess."

The Adelinne answered her quickly. "Not a Princess, a Queen. I am the Queen that will be. Or ought to be, if I can keep them from exiling me, which is their plan. Marrying me off to some poltroon pip-squeak princeling from some distant land—that's their hope. They wish to be rid of me and they think that if I am out of the Kingdom they can crown my brother. And Guerric thinks he can rule. . . . So, I am called the Fiendly Princess?" the Adelinne asked, not displeased. "And what do they call you?"

"Elske."

"Elske. And you were a servant of this Var Jerrol? This eyes and ears of the Council, you were his spy?"

"Since I speak Souther," Elske explained. "I could tell him how the merchants hoped to cheat him in trade, or what they said about the black powder. I knew what they spoke of when they thought they couldn't be understood, when I served his guests at table."

The Adelinne turned her head at this, to look up over her shoulder at her servant. "What do you know of this black powder?" but this question Elske chose not to answer. She met the blue eyes with her own grey glance.

The Adelinne looked long at her, then said, "I will ask again later. When you know me. When you know it is safe to answer me truthfully," she said.

Elske didn't doubt that time to come. There was in this Fiendly Princess something to which Elske's spirit answered.

The Adelinne went on. "The Kingdom lies so far from the world, news comes to us so slowly, we could be lost and taken before we even know that there are the weapons to destroy us." She turned around again and Elske went back to working the comb through the tangles. "I think any man might have this weapon in his hand, and why should not I, too, possess it? I don't wish to be ignorant on the subject of black powder. What were you in Var Jerrol's house, besides his spy?"

"I was nursery maid to his three daughters. After the Var remarried, it was better that I leave his house. Once the Var had a bride, his house had no need of me."

The Adelinne turned again to look at Elske full. "You shared his bed?"

"Why would I do that? The Trastaders protect women from ruin. Women are dear to the Trastaders."

"Not dear enough to be masters of merchant

houses, Elske, not even the widows. Nor of inns, nor of ships, not even in the market stalls, and never dear enough to sit on the Council," the Adelinne answered. "And that's too dear a dear for my purse. You were not the Var's bedmate, then. Nor any other man's?"

"No, my Lady." Elske patiently worked the comb through and through the tangles, until her mistress's nut brown hair hung smooth down her back.

"A pity, that. But it can't be helped. What skills do you have? Besides a gentle hand on the comb."

Elske could only answer everything she knew, since she didn't know why the Council had placed her with this Adelinne. "I speak both Souther and Norther. I read and write in both tongues. I can figure with numbers. I know how to care for babies, and children, and something about cooking. I can snare small animals and skin prey of any size, dig over soil, plant it and harvest a crop. I can serve at table," she said. She thought of her most recent experiences. "I can launder clothing. I can mend with a needle and thread."

"And do you know the streets of the city?"

"Of the two other islands, yes, Old Trastad and Harboring. Logisle is not familiar, but I think I might be lost anywhere on three-islanded Trastad and find my way."

"I *will* know their use for you," her mistress warned her, but promised, "And so will you. Braid my hair. Maybe you will do well for me, as my maidservant. But tell your masters, I will look through you like glass and see their plans, let them imprison and starve me as much as they will. You will be a window for me to see through to their intentions."

"I am not glass," Elske said, "and I don't know how to be such, not even for you, my Lady. If that is what you require in your maidservant, perhaps you should ask for another. I can help you in other things, as in teaching you their language, or perhaps finding food, but—at most I can be your beryl glass, and that cannot be seen through."

Something in Elske's words caused the girl to smile, some secret mischief amused her, and she rose to look at herself in the room's beryl glass, as if that would hide her from Elske. Seeing herself, her mouth set firm. "I'll not be forced to any husband," she said, whether to herself or to Elske, Elske didn't know, although she spoke as if Elske had thought to contradict her. "Who thinks he can force me will pay with his own blood for that. Sooner or later, he'll pay. I can be patient," she said, thoughtfully. Then she demanded, "You said food? You've food hidden here? You have a friend to let us out?"

"If I go out the window—I was only outside the once, the day I was brought here, but I saw kitchen gardens, or I think they might have been."

"I want bread and meat, and wine."

"I saw trees, so perhaps there might be apples."

"Only apples? But I need sustenance," the Adelinne protested. Then she surrendered. "Bring me my cloak. I'm going with you."

"I think, better not, my Lady."

The Adelinne drew herself up, her shoulders high and proud. "You say no to me?"

Elske explained it. "If I can't climb back in, and they find me outside in the morning, then that is one kind of disobedience, which they may punish. But if you're out—and it's you they've locked into her room, for they never locked me in while I have been alone here—then they may take stronger measures against you. If you've already once been lost to them—"

At this, the Adelinne smiled again. "As I have." Then she frowned again. "You will do this," she determined. "You will go out the window and immediately climb back in. If you can do it then so can I. My cloak is clothing enough for night. Do it," the Adelinne ordered.

Elske obeyed, fetching in both cloaks, pulling on her fur boots.

The bedchamber's narrow windows opened outwards. Standing sideways, Elske could easily slip through. She opened a window and climbed up onto the deep sill, and looked out.

It was a lightless night, with the moon at half and behind clouds, the stars hidden, too. The dark air breathed a great silence, over all the grounds of the villa. Elske stood on the windowsill, listening to the darkness. On this windless night, the river greeted the land with little watery sounds.

"Go. Now, Elske."

Elske sat down on the broad stone sill. Her feet did not touch ground. She couldn't remember how high these windows were, so rather than jump, she rolled over onto her stomach and slowly lowered herself. Almost immediately she felt solid land underfoot. Her shoulders and head reached above the open window.

"Well? Can you get back in?"

Elske reached her arms up and over the sill, and pulled her weight up. Her boots scratched at the wall for purchase and she found she could thus push her body up, to scramble back onto the sill, so she dropped back onto the ground.

With a grunt the Adelinne dropped down beside her, then said, "Wait for my eyes."

Elske waited. The air had an edge to it, a knife blade edge of cold.

"What's that?" the Adelinne demanded at her ear.

"What, my Lady?"

"That sound, like—is there a river here? Is it the sea?"

"The river. The High Councillor lives on Logisle, the inmost island, and his villa lies on the riverside. By daylight—"

"Are there boats? Does he keep boats here?"

"Yes, little—"

"Then I could go home," she said, her voice in the darkness filled with longing. "Oh, Elske—" the Adelinne said, and then her voice changed and she said, "A small boat would never survive the open waters, I know that as well as any other fool. When you report to them what I say, tell them I know that I can't run away by sea."

"Why would I tell them anything you say?" Elske asked.

"Why indeed?"

"And why would the Council want to know what you say?"

"As to that, they're employed to keep me here by those who wish to keep my throne from me, and so they are my enemies."

"The Council employs me but they don't own my choices," Elske said, understanding now. "Might not they be so employed by your enemies?"

"I cannot think," the Adelinne said. "I must get

food. Hunger and judgement don't harness well together."

"This way, my Lady," Elske said and moved off, but "Am I to follow you?" the Adelinne demanded. "When I know the way," Elske said, and the Adelinne announced, "I know my own way." But she let Elske lead.

The blank, dark face of the house showed no light other than their own windows. Elske moved swiftly back around to where she remembered the kitchen gardens. In the dark, the villa seemed longer, taller than she remembered, the kitchen wing farther from her own than she would have guessed. Beyond the kitchen entrance she came upon the low stone wall that edged the gardens. The Adelinne started to enter the garden but Elske held her back.

She pulled herself loose.

"Farthest in that direction," Elske pointed, "are trees. I think they may have apples on them. What lies in here, and where, I don't know." She kept her voice low, as muffled as the night sky.

The Adelinne answered at the same pitch, but angry. "Do you think I complain of hunger because I am soft with having been waited upon?"

"No, my Lady," Elske answered. "I don't think you are soft. Nor do I think you have been much waited upon." She waited for an angry expostulation, but it did not come.

"Well?" the Adelinne asked.

"I will go down for apples if you gather what you can find here."

This they did. Elske went on to blindly reach fruit down from low branches, then she returned to where they had separated, to wait until the

Adelinne found her. Night lay over them as undisturbed as a heavy robe as they crept back along the side of the villa until the light guided them back to the opened window. Her mistress stepped up on Elske's cupped hands to make an easy ascent back into the chamber. Elske clambered after her.

Her mistress had tied her cloak up around its burden of plump onions. She bent to untie it while Elske pulled the window closed.

"Were there apples?" The Adelinne held a hand out, and when Elske gave her one, she bit into it. With the apple held in her teeth, she shrugged off her cloak and went to the cupboard, from which she took the dagger Elske had hidden there. "I'll have two of the onions," she said. "And you? What do you want?"

Elske added one onion for herself, out of curiosity. With the onions, her mistress threaded two of the apples onto her dagger, which she held into the flames of the open stove. As they heated, their skin blistered and blackened, and then it split. A liquid, clear and sweet-smelling, like the blood of the apple, oozed through the split skins. The onions, too, bled so. The chamber air was perfumed with the smells of cooking onions and apples.

They ate gingerly, so as not to burn their fingers, and without speaking. The stove consumed whatever they did not—the thick papery outer layers of onions, the cores of the apples. "Better," the Adelinne said, and said no more. She merely went across to the privy and returned, to climb up onto her bed.

Elske picked up the cloak from the floor and placed the uneaten apples and onions into the cupboard. She had never expected to be locked in, and she couldn't guess how long it would be before they were released. Furthermore, she had never seen Var Vladislav, or spoken with him, so she had no idea how he planned to deal with this willful Adelinne. They two might well spend the whole Courting Winter locked into these rooms together.

Elske thought she could be in worse company for a winter's imprisonment. She blew out the flames of the oil lamps.

The Adelinne's voice spoke out of darkness. "I sleep behind closed doors."

Elske pulled the door closed behind her and returned to her own pallet for what was left of the night.

There were no windows in Elske's antechamber, and so she did not know what hour of the night, or morning, it was when she was wakened by the sound of a key turning in the lock. No other sound followed, so she returned to her slumbers. How long after that it was that the door was opened and one of the kitchen maids set a tray on the floor, Elske couldn't say.

The tray was covered with a white cloth. Under the cloth were two bowls of porridge, with spoons, a platter of bread and cheese, and two cups of ale. Honey made a sweet pool at the center of each of the bowls of porridge.

Elske pulled on her dress and then looked out into the hall, where the light showed her that morning was well begun. When she returned from the privy, she saw that a jug of water and a bowl had been set down beside the tray. The water was warmed, for washing. There had been no summons nor sound from beyond the bedchamber door, but the wooden door was so heavy and the villa walls so thick that Elske was not sure she would have heard any sound her mistress might have made.

She pushed open the door. A still mound lay on the bed. The fire in the stove had burned out and an early morning chill lingered in the room. Elske slipped into the chamber and took chunks of wood from the basket, opened the door and laid them on the glowing ashes. She blew into the heart of the fire until smoke rose in thin wisps. She closed the stove again.

Turning, she saw that the still figure had not moved.

Outside, beyond the windows, beyond the grass on which sheep grazed, the river was flowing, and beyond that she saw the mainland shore, where forests stretched back endlessly.

"Leave me," ordered a voice behind her.

Before drawing the door closed behind her, Elske said, "There is a tray here, with food, when you wish it, my Lady."

It wasn't long before the door opened and the Adelinne stood in it, her wrapper tied at the waist, in stocking feet, her face expressionless. "The chamber pot is ready. You may bring in the tray," she said, and withdrew to sit at her table beneath the windows. Elske brought in the tray, and uncovered it. She removed the chamber pot and emptied it into the privy, then returned for whatever service might next be required.

Her mistress ate hungrily, spoonfuls of porridge. She drank at the cup of ale, took a chunk of bread and finally asked impatiently, "Do you expect to be asked to sit down with me?" She thrust the second bowl of porridge into Elske's hands. "Do you need to be *told* to eat? What do you expect?"

"I don't know what to expect, my Lady."

The dark blue eyes studied her suspiciously. "I can tell you to expect no coins of me. My purse is empty. Have you never served an Adelier before?"

"No, my Lady."

"Eat then, Elske, and trust me to instruct you how to serve me to my satisfaction. And I don't mind admitting that you have thus far proved satisfactory."

Elske smiled to hear that, for if she had a choice of masters this Adelinne would be the one she chose.

"Of course," her mistress went on, "good beginnings can lead to bad ends. But today, I will walk out and you will accompany me. While Adelinnes are usually taken out only for display, to flirt and attract, we *are* permitted exercise in good weather. When there are entertainments, Assemblies, and dances, you must accompany me." She watched Elske's face, as if it were a page of words she was puzzling out. "As my maidservant, you eat what I eat, and when we dine, we dine alone. At feasts, you serve me and do not eat. You may have the bathwater when I am done. Now, you may sit on the stool, and eat your porridge," her mistress told her, and Elske obeyed.

Her mistress remained lost in thought for some time.

Then, "When you return this tray to the kitchen, tell them I will bathe this evening. Also tell them I require wine with my midday meal, and tell them also that I have no coins in my purse."

"Why should they know anything of your purse?" Elske wondered.

"Because those who serve the Adeliers expect coins for every service. But my gold is already spent, and much besides, too."

Elske protested. "I don't wish to tell them that, my Lady, for your sake. These are proud servants, for this is the house of the High Councillor—"

"Servants too proud to take coins?" Her mistress was doubtful.

"Too proud to ask for coins," Elske said, "and also ashamed not to be given them. It is better to tell them nothing of your purse; they will assume that your purse is fat and it will be only a matter of time before you fill theirs, when we come to the end of the Courting Winter."

"You presume to advise me?"

"Why should you wish the house servants to neglect you?"

"You presume to know better than I how to deal with servants?"

"Yes, my Lady, since I know them a little and you know them not at all."

The Adelinne stood up then. "I think I know now why they chose you for me. They think your disobedience will be their revenge on me. But understand this, Elske: I will be obeyed. I will not keep my pennilessness a secret, as if I were ashamed. Any person who serves me, and any man who courts me—which is unlikely, since they send me dowerless to Trastad—will take me for myself alone. I offer nothing more."

"Yes, my Lady," Elske said. The Volkaric would not wear their pride on that shoulder, but that didn't mean they went naked of pride. She picked up the tray.

"All the same," her mistress said, now, "I will ask you *not* to tell them in the kitchen that my purse is empty."

In the cook room, Elske delivered her Lady's instructions.

"She wants wine, is it? And a bath? She's realized how soft a bed she's sleeping in, and quickly, too, hasn't she? It didn't take long for her to show us her true colors, this Fiendly Princess. You'll soon be wishing yourself back in the peace and quiet of the laundry room, Elske."

Elske did not think so, but said nothing. "Will more Adelinnes come to this house?" she asked, and they told her that for the High Councillor to take in even one was unusual. So Elske asked when the Assemblies would begin, and was told, "All in good time, tell her. Tell Lady Impatience that."

"She will walk outside today."

"You must be with her at all times, especially such a one as she. If we were to send her back ruined to her home, other fathers might keep their daughters from us, and there would be no Courting Winters in Trastad, and then where would we find the gold to pay the Emperor's tribute? She is in your keeping, Elske, and if harm comes to her, you are for the cells."

"Why should harm come to her?" Elske asked, and the other servants exchanged knowing looks.

"She is the kind of Adelinne who puts herself in harm's way. She does not behave as a Princess ought."

"Because she is a Queen," Elske explained.

"And I am the Emperor's daughter," they laughed.

Elske returned to her mistress's bedchamber, where she was told, "Fetch my cloak. I am restless."

The proper way to the outside was through the dining chamber, a door that opened onto the lawns they saw from the windows. Outside, a wind blew, but not ungently, and her mistress instructed, "You will follow me."

"Yes, my Lady," Elske answered and fell into step behind her mistress, but the Adelinne said, "You must keep close enough that we can speak," and Elske stepped obediently up to her mistress's shoulder, remaining just a little behind.

They walked towards the river, where on this morning two boats were tied up at the dock. The Adelinne asked, "Where are you from, Elske? What people? What land? You must be a foreigner, because the Trastaders do not speak Souther."

"I am of the people of the Volkaric," Elske answered, but seeing that the Norther word meant nothing to her mistress, she risked saying, "I am Wolfer."

That halted the Adelinne. She turned to face Elske, placing them face-to-face where they stood between the villa and the river, and no one to overhear their words. The girl looked directly into Elske's face and her eyes shone with the blue of the sea.

"You're the one who split his face open, aren't you? Don't deny it. Not if it's the truth. It was you, wasn't it? They hid him away, they told tales, but we all knew— and he deserved it, and he was not the only one who needed his vile heart showing on his handsome face. I was but a child two years ago, but if I'd had the chance—and my weapon— Is it true, what he boasted? That he'd had many virgins of Trastad?"

Elske could not answer what the Adel had done except for the time of their meeting, when he had done nothing, she having forestalled him.

"*Was* it you?" her mistress demanded. "Rumor said, it was a man disguised as a maidservant, a Trastader trick to protect their women from the Adels. Rumor said, a girl's brothers had ambushed the Prince, to revenge her ruin, and there was a great skirmish that left many Trastaders wounded. Rumor said, the girl was a Wolfer and she ripped his face in half with her teeth."

Elske could not still the laughter in her throat. "It was only a stone. He was only a coward."

"It *was* you."

"Yes, my Lady." Elske didn't think this Adelinne, this Fiendly Princess, would fear her, or condemn her; and she was right, for at the acknowledgement the Adelinne smiled, a smile like the warmth of a fire on an icy winter's night, as heady as the wine-rich autumn air they breathed. "It was *you*. I never thought I'd meet you, and now I have. You gave me courage, two years ago, Elske, and since then, too. I wished to be you, when I didn't even know your name."

The Adelinne reached her hands out from under the cloak she wore, and removed the gloves she wore. She held her right hand out to Elske, as if they were two merchants closing on a sale, and she bowed her head to Elske, as if they were two swords-men ending a match, and she looked Elske in the eye, as if they were Wolfer captains, about to risk their lives in battle. The girl took Elske's naked hand in hers and said, "I give you greeting, Elske. I am Beriel, who will be Queen in the Kingdom."

Chapter 9

THE TWO WALKED on, down to the river's edge, Elske once again at her mistress's shoulder, close enough for speech. In appearances, nothing had changed; but the Adelinne had given Elske her name, and so everything had changed.

"Beriel," Elske said, "the Queen that will be." There was no question about that. Every word the Lady Beriel uttered, and the manner of her speaking, every gesture of her hands and turning of her body, were those of a Queen. Elske knew this, although the Volkking like the rest of his people having no wife, the Volkaric had no Queen. In the Lady Beriel's high-shouldered way of standing and her refusal to give way, Elske could see what a Queen must be.

At the river's edge the soil was moist and the grass grew thick. A salty wind blew against their faces, from the south and the sea. These drew Beriel's thoughts in their direction, for next she said, "I *could* take one of these little boats, if I never ventured far from shore. Perhaps. If there were no storm. I'd know Pericol from the water and if I had coins in my purse, I could pay my way through

Pericol. Although, it's never sure what gold will do, when you offer bribes to thieves and pirates," she said.

"I have coins," Elske offered, for she did. Var Kenric had given her some, in gratitude, and Var Jerrol had paid her a servant's wages; she kept them hidden in her Wolfer boots. "You might take them."

"I will not give over my land," Beriel said, not hearing Elske's words. "In the north of my Kingdom, the forests stretch up the mountainsides, like dark waves running up snowy sands. That country yields up not only timber but also iron, and there is silver, too, buried deep in the mountains. There are lakes in my northern lands, as full of fish as the sea. A great river runs through the Kingdom, with water as good as wine to drink, and to lie in that river, to swim through it, is as if sleeping through a dreamless night. Can you swim, Elske?"

"Swim?"

"I will show you. The fishermen taught me when I was a girl, before my nurse discovered us, and you also must know it. In the south, the soil is black and rich. In the south, all autumn long, apples sweeten on the trees—"

"I never had an apple until I left the Volkaric."

"I am afraid I will never see my land again, Elske."

"Why should you not? If you wed no Adel, and you are the Queen that will be?"

"You know nothing," Beriel said then, swinging around to face Elske in a Queen's quick fury. "But I promise you this, I would fight to the death to keep my throne."

Elske wondered, "Why should you not become Queen, if it is your throne?"

"Because they will bring me down, if they can. If they have not already. Speak no more of it," Beriel commanded.

Now they walked along the river's edge, far from the broad front of the villa. Beriel seemed lost in thought from which she would sometimes emerge to ask a question. She asked about the wealth of Trastad and Elske told what she knew. Beriel asked about the tribute paid by Trastad to the Emperor, but Elske knew little of this. "Who is this Emperor?" she asked in return, so Beriel told her, "He rules the east. They say he is as tall as three men, and he never sleeps. They say he makes caskets of the bones of those his armies have slain, to hold his riches. The story goes that he traded his daughter to an alchemist in exchange for the formula for black powder. But nobody has seen this Emperor, and his lands lie so far away even the great ships of Trastad have never crossed the distance, so I don't lose sleep over him," Beriel said.

"Could a man be as tall as three men together?" Elske asked, for if this were false, then all the rest was doubtful.

"Are you a simple after all?" Beriel asked, but gave no time for an answer.

This young mistress was like none of the women of Trastad, nor of the Volkaric, either, for all that she was as protected as the one and as fierce as the other. Elske thought, walking at Beriel's shoulder, that if she were a man, and there were battle, she would rather ride to her death for this Lady than for the Volkking, whose terrible revenges earned him obedience. She would rather face danger for Beriel than for Trastader coins.

Elske also thought it strange that Beriel could be forced to the Courting Winter, and a second time, too; and she wondered by what means her mistress had been made obedient.

That question was answered in the quiet evening, when the maidservants had brought in the copper tub for a bath, and given Elske the jug of scented oil to sweeten the hot water they carried in, one following the other, steam rising out of the top of their buckets. When Beriel—her brown hair loose for washing—stepped out of her shift and lifted a foot to step up onto the footstool, Elske saw that the Adelinne was belly-swollen with child.

Beriel, naked and proud, glared at Elske.

As she soaped the long, thick hair, and poured jugs of rinsing water through it, Elske understood that Beriel must find a husband to marry, and before the Longest Night, too, for she must be near four moons from her time; if this was the first child she carried, when a woman showed latest and least, she might be nearer. So perhaps she was three moons from the birth?

Beriel leaned forward and Elske poured rinsing water, which fell over her head and down her slim shoulders.

But Elske had never heard of marriages performed among the Adeliers while they were still in Trastad.

"I will wash myself," Beriel said.

When Beriel sat in her chair by a stove so warm that the occasional drops of water sizzled on its tiles, she told Elske to bathe before calling the maidservants to empty and carry away the tub. Elske obeyed, slipping out of her dress and stockings and shift to climb into the tub, and sit there in its failing warmth before taking up the cloth and soap.

Beriel watched this, whether Elske permitted it or not.

"Is it a crime among the Wolfers when a girl has a child before she has a husband, then?" Beriel demanded. "Are such women punished?"

"No, for women—"

"Do they exile them? Execute them? In the Kingdom, a royal Princess is so punished. The people do not have so strict a law over them as do the Lords, and the Lords run with a lighter rein than do the members of the royal family. What are you going to do now, Elske?"

"Soap my hair, my Lady."

"No, about me. What will you do about me? My shame is yours, when you serve me and I carry shame with the child, for all that the real shame is someone else's."

When Elske had finished, she climbed out and dried herself on her underskirts. Beriel by then had covered herself with her night shift. "Then there must be no child," Elske said. It seemed simple enough.

"You know how to rid me of it?" Beriel's face was transformed by relief. "Have I wasted all of my coins, and two gold chains and a silver bracelet, too, and the medallion of my mother's house, given to me by my grandfather—? Have I gone skulking around this islanded city, looking to rid myself of this burden in my belly, have I slept cold and hungry and unguarded—? And all the time you were waiting here for me? What do I do? Drink something? Is it a potion? Is there danger it will kill me? Don't worry, I'll drink it, but I'd rather know those dangers

I face. Or do you reach inside me, to—?"

Elske understood. "Ah, no, my Lady—"

"I should have guessed that the Wolfers—"

"My Lady, I mean when you have birthed it."

Beriel withdrew back into a cold pride. "You said, 'There must be no child.' And I believed you, and now I am betrayed."

"My Lady, I don't betray you. A woman can give birth and still have no child on her breast."

"Ah." Beriel nodded her head several times. "I see. But how will you do this, Elske?"

Elske had no answer ready. "Give me time to consider," she asked.

"Take all the time you like," Beriel granted it, almost gaily, "so long as you are ready when I need you." But then she covered her face with her hands, as if to hide from her own thoughts. "But if I must birth it, where will I go to hide until it comes? I think I *am* lost."

Elske asked, "Why should you hide yourself away? It is winter and your gowns are heavy. When I have altered the waists, the child will be hidden under the high, full skirts."

Beriel uncovered her face, to consider this. She looked down at her belly under the heavy nightgown, and nodded. "Perhaps. Perhaps I may go undiscovered. If I do, and if I live, I'll have revenge," she said then. "My brother, who led them to me, my cousins, who raped me, again and again, until they had filled my belly—"

"Why should they wish to ruin you?" Elske wondered.

If the sea could hold flame, that would have been the color of Beriel's eyes. "Because I am the Queen

118

that will be. And my brother—he is the King that wishes to be, although I am the firstborn, and thus named royal heir, by law. But I am also the first female to claim my inheritance through this law. Years before, with my mother's birth, came a new law that a female might inherit her father's domain if she were firstborn. But my mother gave up her own claim to her Earldom to marry my father, the King. Neither she nor my father now wish me crowned—despite the law, despite the word of the Priests and the will of my people, despite my own worth and my brother Guerric's base nature. If they have their way, I will be wed into another country; and now if I do not cooperate in that, then I will be driven from my rightful place by the shame my brother has placed on me. If I live, whatever else, I will return to take these cousins, and this brother, too, if I can lay hands on him, and I will feed them black powder until their bellies are swollen with it, and I will put their heads into the fire so they breathe in flame."

She stared at the dark window.

"I'll have them screaming, swearing they never meant me ill, begging for mercy. As I never did, when they came at me."

Beriel caught her breath and looked back at Elske, as much like a wolf as a woman. "If I do not die in childbirth." As she said that, Beriel's voice sank.

"Why should you die in childbirth?" Elske asked.

"That is the fortune of women," Beriel announced.

Elske was puzzled. "I have been at many births and but few deaths."

"You know midwifery?" Beriel stared at her, wordless, shook her head as if amazed, and then laughed, as if she were a girl again and not a ruined woman, her belly filled with the child her rapists left in her. Laughter flowed out of her, until she could ask, "Who are you, Elske? What were you, among the Wolfers?"

"I was the Death Maiden," Elske said.

"Which is?" Beriel asked, her voice now quiet, dangerous.

Elske explained how the Volkking journeyed into the land of the dead with his treasures around him and the Death Maiden to answer his needs. "That is a terrible custom," Beriel said, but Elske answered that it was the feeding of infant girls to the wolves that she had learned to think terrible. "The Death Maiden was given food when others went hungry. I was kept clothed and sheltered, for I was good fortune to the Volkking."

"You are ignorant," Beriel told her angrily. "These Wolfers are brutes—albeit straightforward brutes, unlike more civilized men. Oh, but Elske," Beriel said. "Where would I be if Tamara had not saved you?"

Rain fell hard the next morning so they remained in Beriel's apartments, and Beriel called for needles and threads; for her gowns, she told the housekeeper, had been ill prepared. Elske worked at altering her mistress's clothing and this occupied them until the midday meal. After that, because the rains had stopped, they walked again, following the tall stone wall that hid the High Councillor's villa from the road. Eventually, this wall ran in among a woods and became no higher than Elske's knees. That was what Beriel had been looking for. "That is our way out," she said quietly. "A way out and back in, if we wish it. So we have the road, now, as well as the river, and the window always ready to be opened. Let them think they have me prisoner, when I am not."

That evening, Beriel turned to the matter of Elske's dress. "You must alter, I think, two of my gowns to fit yourself. I'm taller than you are, and you're rounder—except now, of course."

"But I have my own dresses and the Var supplies aprons."

"You don't understand," Beriel told her. "Don't be stupid, Elske, not now. The menservants and maid-servants display the wealth of their Adeliers, so a poorly dressed servant bespeaks a poorly filled purse. If I wish to answer any doubts, then my servant must be richly outfitted."

So Elske and Beriel took out her several gowns, one after the other, and selected two for Elske to wear when she waited upon her mistress at the feasts and Assemblies. One of the dresses given to Elske was as red as groundberries, the other as green as the leaves of crawling ivy; the fabric cut off from the hems, to shorten them, would make scarves to wrap her hair. The gowns Beriel kept were blue and golden and wine red; some of them were sewn over with golden threads, so that they glittered in the lamplight. "You'll set me off well," Beriel told Elske, pleased. "My last maidservant was chap-faced and clumsy and I wished to murder her, at least once each day."

Elske was cutting out the stitches that held a skirt to a bodice.

"I have no use for a stupid servant," Beriel said. "Although if I had been more clever myself, I might not be in this predicament. Elske, you must not tell anyone about the child," Beriel said, then. "Whatever I choose to do you must not speak of it. Although I can't even think about what to do. Other than find some boy stupid enough to take me for bride, and take him for my husband. And that will make him King, to gainsay my will, to share my high position, to keep me tamed. What other ways have you thought of, Elske? Have you thought of another way than marriage? Another way than death?"

"I can see two or three," Elske answered.

"You can see," Beriel echoed her. "You are one of those who can always see another way, aren't you? And that's a gift, Elske. Do you know what a great gift it is to see a way through, or past? Although, when it's not your belly or your crown, vision comes easier. But if I am ignorant, must I not also be innocent? Yes, I think I must, and if innocent then guiltless. So can I give the matter over into your hands, Elske?" Beriel asked.

"Yes, my Lady. Of course." Let Beriel choose which way and Elske would then work out a plan of events. "The ways are—"

"Tell me nothing. I wish to know nothing of it," Beriel said. "You must never tell me what you do, Elske. Give me your word on that."

"I give you my word," Elske said, surprised. She had never been asked for her word before. Before, she had not had a word of her own to give.

"No, Elske, this is not so light a thing, your word," Beriel said and stood before Elske, where she sat on the low stool, sewing. Beriel crouched down until their heads were level and reached to put her hand on Elske's shoulder.

"*Swear* to me that, no matter what, you never will reveal to me what has happened to this baby. Swear it," Beriel insisted.

"I swear," said Elske, who had sworn to nothing before in her life.

"Give me your hand on it," Beriel insisted as she stood up again and held out her right hand. Elske reached up to put her own hand into her mistress's. "For I know myself," Beriel said. "Whatever I feel now, I know that I will ask you. I will try to persuade you, order you to obey, force you. You must give me your word, for I trust you more than myself in this."

"I promise, my Lady," Elske said, the words rolling up from her heart and out of her throat as heavy as stones.

"That last Courting Winter, you would have been no older than I am now," Elske said, on one long evening. She was still at the work of sewing her mistress's gowns. "This is my fifteenth winter, and I am still young for marriage."

Beriel stood by the window, staring out into the darkness, and answered, "It has been days since I've seen boats on the river, and it feels cold enough for ice to form."

"But you had no choice but to return to Trastad, did you?" Elske asked.

"What else could I do? At least, I am far from where I am known, and watched, and hated, and now betrayed by a brother. He has no thought for the people, their labors and well-being. He cares nothing for law, or honor. How can I give my land and people to such a King?"

Elske could not answer this.

"My grandparents wished me Queen," Beriel said. "The Earl and his Lady, those two, and the people, my people: They have backed my claim. I know this, even though I was young when my grandmother died. That is when my grandfather gave me her golden medallion—"

She stopped speaking and turned back to the night.

Elske watched how the white needle slid into the heavy fabric, and came out again, joining skirt to bodice.

"When we are in the city," Beriel said, "as we go about in this Courting Winter, I promise you I'll be watching for a woman. I will know her when I see her, for she took the medallion from me, and promised me help, and although I waited where she told me—waited through the whole night and the next day—she never came back. If I see her, I'll have my medallion back—or she'll wish she'd never gulled me."

Elske stitched.

"The coins and the gold chains were nothing to lose," Beriel said. "But the medallion was put into my hands that I might remember, always, that I am the Queen. And I gave all to that woman. I've been a fool, Elske," Beriel said, turning around and in a fury.

Elske said nothing until she thought to offer again, "I have coins, my Lady, which are yours if you want them."

"You are a fool, too."

"Why should you not take them?" Elske asked.

"You are poor and a servant. It isn't fitting that I should take your coins."

"How can I be poor, when I have coins and no need of them?"

"It's of no matter, anyway," Beriel said. "No man will ask for me, and I wouldn't have any of them anyway. We are all of us here in Trastad because no one in our own lands will have us. So we hope to find marriages where we are not known, except for our faces and our purses." Beriel returned to the window, and said, "I have no purse and my face does not please." She stared back out into darkness.

Elske sewed, and thought about this baby Beriel would have, how it might be gotten rid of without discovery. Death was easiest, as is often the case, but with the river frozen over the body presented difficulties. The land, too, would be frozen hard, and what did a people do with the bodies of its unwanted babies when there was no wolf pack to feed them to? A babe could be easily killed, by smothering, by a knife thrust, by drowning, strangling, exposure in a winter night, or its neck snapped like a kitten. If the baby must die, to save Beriel, the killing wasn't the problem; but the body presented difficulties.

Then Elske thought of the holes in the ice through which the fishermen pulled their catch, and her eyes filled with tears as she thought of thrusting a small body down into the icy black river.

Elske could begin to understand why the Trastaders cared so much about a woman's ruin; it had to do with these babies. For the Trastaders valued children. It was a deep grief when a child died, and a lasting sorrow when a woman proved barren, as Idelle feared.

Elske sewed on, blindly. In one house a child was desired, in another unwanted; the world worked backwards. But if that was the way of it—and that *was* the way of it—why not move the child from the one place to the other?

"When will your babe be born?" she asked Beriel.

"I don't wish to think of that," Beriel answered.

"Nay, but you must, my Lady. And you must think of bearing the pains silently. The women of the Volkaric give birth with no crying out," Elske told her mistress.

"What any woman can do, I can do," Beriel declared. "Don't doubt my courage. When the time comes—"

"When will that be?" Elske persisted.

"How should I know? I've never had a child before, and my mother would have no reason to tell me. I've heard the servants counting backwards say it takes ten moons to make a baby."

Elske sewed, the needle leading its trail of thread in and out, and the fabric lay heavy and warm as a cloak over her legs.

"It has been eight moons since I had my woman's bleeding," Beriel told her reluctantly. "Or perhaps it's only seven. How could I find time to count the moons, when— I will have those cousins under my heel," she promised Elske, with another swift change in spirits. "I will take my brother by the hair and cut his throat open. My cousins I will drop into the lake, with stones tied to their feet, let them stand beside one another there, and have the skin eaten off of their hands and faces, the eyes eaten out of their skulls. Let them stand together as they stood by my bed." Beriel overmastered her anger then, and rested in the law. "They plotted to bring me down, and that is treason."

Elske sewed, and made her own choice under her own law: The child who would be born she would choose not to kill unless she must.

Chapter 10

ON THE DAY of the first Assembly a fine, misty snow fell through grey air. Snow dusted the road, and the cloaked shoulders of the young men on horseback. The Adels rode to the Assembly, displaying their horsemanship and their fine trappings, as well as their high-stepping mounts. The Adelinnes rode in covered chairs, each chair carried by a pair of menservants, while the attendant maidservants walked alongside.

Elske wore her wolfskin boots for the long walk from Logisle to the Council Hall; once there she would change them for soft indoor slippers. She wore her second-finest dress, the red one, and a head scarf made from the cloth cut off to raise the hem. At this first Assembly, and throughout the Courting Winter, Elske would take her place among the other servants at the back of the hall, to watch over her mistress while Beriel took her pleasure.

"Although what pleasure anyone could take in these . . . Assemblies," Beriel said, spitting the last word out of her mouth as if she had bitten into a wormy apple. "We parade around the great hall say-ing nothing, although many words are spoken and there is much laughter. Everyone looks everyone else over—it's a horse market, a pig fair, no different. And the Vars watch us, drinking their wine, their greedy eyes counting up all the profit we bring them."

Elske admitted, "I'm curious, to see everything."

"I've already seen everything and everybody—or no one and nothing very different—two years ago," Beriel grumbled. Then she had a cheering thought. "Later, when they think they've got our measure, we'll be allowed to visit the markets, and the shops—to look at furs and feathers, sweet cakes, anything that amuses us, anything they hope to sell to us. We'll be allowed to wander," Beriel remembered. "We'll make our freedom out of that, shall we?"

"If you wish it," Elske agreed. She took a careful look at Beriel. The babe did not reveal its presence, beneath the high waist and full, heavy skirt. Beriel looked in fine health, fat and ripe. Elske had noticed this among the women of the Volkaric, too, towards the end of their child-carrying months; they would bloom out, not like flowers but like ripening foods, plump onions, swollen grains of wheat, and—now that Elske had seen them—round and reddened apples.

Elske entered the hall four paces behind her mistress, who looked neither to left nor to right, but stepped into the midst of those Adeliers who had already gathered. Elske joined the servants.

The wide hall was as tall as ten men standing on one another's shoulders, and there was a railed balcony to which Adeliers hoping for privacy in conversation could retire. This balcony rested on spiraled wooden pillars, and it was in the cloistered area behind these pillars that the servants gathered. Fir garlands hung around the windows and long tables covered by bright woven cloths were set out with platters of dainties, both sweet and meaty, as well as jugs of mulled apple cider, which mingled its spicy smell with the sharp odor of the greens.

The finely dressed Adeliers, smiling, looking about, talking, moved around the room in a promenade. From the balcony came the music of six lutes played by six men wearing the Council's livery. The Adeliers paraded, and watched themselves parade. The leading merchants of the city took part in this opening promenade, black-garbed figures with the bright ribbons of office across their chests.

A manservant standing close to Elske pointed out the wealthiest Adels and named the Trastader dignitaries; he instructed his fellow servants in their behavior. Servants kept to the background, but as long as they remained back they could move around freely, conversing with whomever they wished, and even—he said, and winked at Elske—make their own matches. He himself, he admitted with a smile for a yellow-haired maidservant standing at his elbow, had been married after the last Courting Winter.

In the hall, Adels and Adelinnes kept arriving and arriving, Princes and Princesses, Counts and Barons, the heirs and heiresses of large fortunes, the distant cousins of great men, until the room grew crowded with the sounds of their voices, and the colors of their clothing.

Elske saw that Beriel kept herself aloof. Sometimes, as they passed, an Adelier might speak to Beriel. She would answer, hold out a hand whether it was a young man or young woman who claimed her attention, then walk on. They would follow her with their eyes.

Beriel walked by putting one foot in front of the other, her hands at her sides. She drank by raising a goblet to her lips, and ate by taking bites. She did nothing extraordinary. Other Adelinnes were more richly clothed, their hair more beautifully dressed, their faces more lovely. Even the Adels wore more jewelry than Beriel, and many of them moved with a more graceful step. And yet, watching, Elske could see how unlike her mistress was to the other Adeliers.

When he spoke from behind her, Var Jerrol used a low voice to tell her, "Don't be alarmed." Then he drew her aside, so that it would be difficult for any of the other servants to hear what they said to one another.

"May we be well met," Var Jerrol said to her. Laughter lay behind his eyes, although his face expressed boredom. "So the Fiendly Princess doesn't wear you down with her demands?"

Elske waited silently to hear his purpose. Var Jerrol was not a man to spend his attentions without making a profit from them.

"What does she tell you about her homeland?" he asked her. "Could you travel to it, and know how to make your way around in it? What are its riches, has she told you? Its weaknesses?"

Elske chose her answer carefully, to tell nothing false, and answered him, "I know only that her homeland is beautiful to her, and precious."

"She will be Queen there?"

"I think her parents wish her brother to be King," Elske reported, "and so they hope to marry my mistress into a foreign country, whence she can't claim the crown away from him."

"So her claim is good, and thus they fear her," Var Jerrol said. "As I think they might well, now I've seen her for myself. Tell me, Elske, if you know, what she names this land."

"The Kingdom," Elske said.

"And can you also tell me, in the Kingdom, if they have black powder for their wars?"

"She has told me of no wars," Elske answered.

Var Jerrol moved away then, motioning her to follow. He led her among servants and then among the overseeing Vars, keeping her beside him as if she were not a servant. "We'll take cider, shall we? You haven't answered me about the black powder."

They approached one of the food tables and Var Jerrol poured the drink from a jug into a silver goblet, which he gave to Elske, then took another goblet for himself. Elske again made her choice for plain truth. "She has heard talk of the black powder, rumors. She has no more experience of it than I do," she said, and filled her mouth with the flavor of liquid apples.

Var Jerrol's hooded eyes studied Elske. "Do you enjoy life in the High Councillor's villa?"

"How could I not?" Elske asked, wondering what he wished to learn now.

"The food, as I hear, is of rare delicacy."

This was nothing. "My mistress is locked into her chamber at night," Elske said. "There is no need," she said.

"No need," he agreed. "In exchange—for I think

132

your Fiendly Princess will have seen us speaking. She doesn't miss much, I think," Var Jerrol said, as if he had not paraded Elske out for all to see. "If she asks, can you tell her we didn't speak of her?"

"Why should I lie to her?" Elske asked. She had Var Jerrol and he knew it. He opened his mouth as if to answer, then shut it. He looked out over the crowd of Adeliers in their brightly colored gowns and coats, their glittering rings and necklaces, the white arms and necks of the young women, the broad shoulders of the young men.

Elske, easily locating her mistress, saw an Adel approach Beriel to offer her a goblet and gesture with his hand towards a table spread with food. Her mistress took the drink with a sternness of expression that the young man—himself in a fine brocaded jacket, his chest crowded with heavy gold chains—smiled his way through. Seeing the Lady halted, two more young men approached, and she gave them no warmer welcome.

"No, you would not lie, not to your mistress, and not to me, either, would you?" Var Jerrol asked. He already knew the answer, so Elske did not need to say anything. "But I have something for your mistress," he said, his lowered lids hiding his thoughts. Unnoticed in the crowd of Vars, he put a purse into her hand. What it held was round, and flat, much larger than a coin, heavy. Elske could guess what it was.

Elske put the purse strings around one wrist. "The Lady will thank you." She added, then, because she liked the chance to use Var Jerrol for her own purpose, "There were also gold necklaces, and some coins."

"She scattered them around freely, as I hear. As I

hear it," he warned Elske, "your mistress was on an urgent errand, her spirits as desperate as her need."

Elske understood him and chose to say, "All will be well."

"When she is in your care, I think it may," he answered carefully, and bowed to the two Adels who approached Elske as the Var moved away from her. The two were bright-eyed with wine, and said to Elske, "We are brothers-in-arms, or we would be, Lady, if there were any enemy you would ask us to defend you from. We come to ask your name, so that when you send for us—"

"Why would I send for you?" She thought they must know from her wrapped hair that she was no Lady. And Var Jerrol must have meant to discomfit her by leaving her with them.

"In your need," said the second merrily. They were both dark-haired, clean-shaven and richly attired. "We would be your knights, and slay your dragons. We would dance and duel for your amusement."

"We would, in short, know your name, Lady," the first spoke again.

"I am Elske, serving maid to the Lady Beriel," Elske told them.

Either the wine interfered with their ability to understand, or they were dumbfounded to hear her deny herself the higher birth. There was a silence, and then they laughed into one another's faces, clapped one another on the shoulder, and stepped back from Elske. "You should be the Lady," the second one said over his shoulder, "and she the serving maid."

Perhaps they didn't recognize a Queen when she

walked among them. Or perhaps they hoped that Elske might prove gullible and be lured by them into her own ruin. But Elske was in no danger from them. She moved back to the rear of the hall and stood among the servants again, her hands clasped behind her to hide the heavy purse.

Before her, the scene spread itself out. The colors of gowns, tights, tunics and coats moved and mixed, like a school of small fishes darting through the water. Oil lamps washed everything with warm light, and the air was filled with music. The high, hopeful voices of the young women melded into the bold and hopeful voices of the young men; and like river-banks containing and guiding the flow of water, the deeper voices of the Vars could be heard, speaking in their more guttural northern tongue.

Elske stood back against the wall, watching. There was something of the beauty of spring wild-flowers in the scene before her, as if the room were a meadow with winds blowing over it, and she fol-lowed her mistress's slow journey around and around, among all the Adeliers but never one of them. She saw Beriel turn her head to listen to what one of the Adeliers said to her, courteously atten-tive. The young man spoke with a graceful gesturing of his hand. He was a pretty fellow, Elske noticed, although he wore no golden chain, nor rings on his fingers, so he was not rich. His light brown hair curled, shining clean, and a smile rested comfort-ably on his face. He said something that caused Beriel to shake her head at him, although with a slight smile of her own. At that he backed away, bowing; he was not disappointed.

Too soon for Elske, the Assembly was over.

Servants brought the cloaks to wrap around the shoulders of the milling Adeliers. The faces of their masters or mistresses—cheeks that were pink with excitement or pale with withheld tears or red with anger—told the servants how to greet them. Beriel's face had no expression, and Elske greeted her with equal dignity.

Outside, snow fell thick on the unswept stone steps, but Beriel didn't hesitate. The steps would be where she wished them to be. Her dainty boots would not slip from under her. Her servant would follow.

When they had returned to Beriel's chambers and a meal of stewed rabbit, Beriel sighed. "There are so many more such occasions to be got through," she said. "It seems forever before I will be done with them."

Then Elske asked, "The Adeliers, the young men especially, what did they say to you, and what did you answer?"

"It was nothing. There was nothing said."

"There were words spoken," Elske argued patiently. "I was watching."

Beriel told her, "They praised my beauty, as if I wished to hear my beauty praised, as if there were nothing but her beauty a woman might wish to speak of. Such words are nothing."

"And you responded . . . ?"

"Oh, I asked if they thought beauty a thing of substance if they thought men also had beauty if they believed that beauty of face predicted beauty of character." Beriel smiled then, as she had not during the Assembly, with pleasure and mischief.

"And they said?" Elske smiled, also.

"They praised my skin, or my hands. My eyes," Beriel added, and then her smile faded. "I, too, was watching. I saw you in conversation with two Adels. This was after the tall Var brought you out among us, and gave you a silver cup. I saw everything," Beriel said, as if she was not pleased to have seen this.

Elske answered with her own mischief, "They might well praise your eyes."

"Yes," Beriel agreed impatiently. "But they might better speak of more germane matters, of their own lands, for example, and how they guard against droughts, famines, fierce winters. If my eyes are blue tonight, they were blue yesterday and it is an old story."

Beriel did not command, so Elske volunteered, "Var Jerrol, the tall Var—"

"He has a snake's eyes."

"He returns this to you, my Lady."

When Elske put the purse into Beriel's hands, her mistress breathed out a long, soft breath. Unaware or unconscious of Elske, she opened the neck of the purse to slide out onto her palm a thick, golden disk, emblazoned with a wide-winged bird.

Beriel folded her two hands around the disk and brought it up to her heart. She closed her eyes. When she opened them, and looked at Elske, they were as bright and blue as if it were midday in summer, and the sun flecked the dancing sea with gold.

After a time, Beriel returned the disk to its purse. Then Elske told her mistress, "I asked about the chains, and mentioned the coins."

Beriel waved a hand in front of her face, as if waving away a cloud of gnats, to show how little the coins and chains mattered. "He is the eyes and ears of the Council," Beriel said. "What was it he wanted to know from you?"

"He asked if I knew the location of your Kingdom. He asked if you have the black powder there, or know of it."

"Did you tell him?"

"Why should I not tell him what I know?"

This was the same answer Elske had given to Var Jerrol, but Beriel heard it crossly, although, like him, she made no response. After a while, she asked Elske if Var Jerrol knew of her child that was to be born, and Elske answered, "I believe he does."

"Will I be punished? Can you guess his mind? Will he betray my secret to shame me?"

"I told him all would be well and he seemed satisfied," Elske reported. "The door will no longer be locked," she said, seeking to give her mistress some good news.

Beriel rose, then, and went to the window, and looked out. She stood there, with her back to Elske, as if listening to the snow falling; and when she spoke again her voice was low with anger. "I don't need your help. I don't want your help. All I ask from you is to be served as befits my station. Am I making myself clear?" she asked, in deliberate, slow Norther.

"No, my Lady," Elske protested, which displeased Beriel further.

"I don't know why I must put up with such a maidservant," Beriel remarked to the falling snow. "It must be that there are only stupid servants among the Wolfers."

"The Volkaric have no servants," Elske reminded

her mistress, not hiding her own displeasure.

"Leave me now," Beriel said.

They had to go together to the next evening's entertainment, a dance given by one of the Vars at his villa on Logisle. Before leaving her chambers, Beriel ordered Elske to remain that evening among the servants, and reminded her of the impropriety of any servant responding as an equal to any Adelier. "How these Vars of Trastad behave is up to them, but my maidservant must act as I would, and I do not engage servants in idle talk, as if we were equals."

"But you have no equal, even among the Adeliers," Elske said.

"I won't be flattered!" Beriel cried, openly angry now.

"It's not flattery but truth," Elske argued. "It was what all saw at the Assembly."

For the first time since the previous evening, Beriel looked at Elske with interest. She asked, "What is it that all saw?"

"A Queen," Elske said, "who must stand apart from all others. You might talk with servants, as you do with me—when it suits you—and remain a royal Queen. You might dine at your ease with the Emperor, because you are a Queen."

"Yet you don't fear me."

"Why should I fear you?" Elske asked. "Is it my fear that makes you Queen?"

And Beriel laughed then, but still she maintained, "As my maidservant, you must behave as would the highest servants in the greatest of palaces. Remember your place," she instructed Elske, and

Elske agreed to do so. "And do not speak openly to your Var Jerrol," Beriel instructed, but Elske answered, "I like to know his purposes for you, my Lady," and Beriel agreed that she, too, would prefer knowledge to ignorance. "But if you would not discredit me, you *must* remember your place," she warned Elske.

Elske's place that evening was back against the wall that ran the length of a ballroom. She stood with the other servants while the Adeliers danced, in lines and circles, to the music of lutes. Hanging cloths covered the darkness beyond the long, frosty windows. Chandeliers dangled over the dancers, their many candles giving a warm light; candles also burned in their holders in the wall and in many-branched silver candelabra on tables. The polished wood floor gleamed, two large fires burned warmly, and the servants of the villa set out silver goblets of mulled wine and silver trays of sweet pastries for the refreshment of the Adeliers.

Elske spoke to those who stood near her, and watched the Adeliers turn in answer to the music's turns. Beriel never lacked for partners. Adels who joked with other Adelinnes became dignified for Beriel, stood straighter and performed the steps of the dance with more studied grace. Beriel looked about her and was looked at by those about her, unless what her partner said caught her attention; and then she looked into his face so closely that he stepped back, as if in alarm, although he was flushed, too, with the honor of her attention.

A message passed down the line of servants summoned Elske out to the villa's broad entry hall.

There, Var Jerrol greeted her. "May we be well met," he said, and handed her a purse lighter than that which he'd brought the previous day. "And what more can you tell me of this Kingdom tonight?"

"Nothing," Elske said. "How should I tell you of the Kingdom, where I've never been?"

"You told her I inquired." He did not ask this but still waited for her answer.

"Of course."

"How did she respond?"

"She was angry."

Satisfied, Var Jerrol sent her back.

As Elske watched, Beriel moved through the measures of the dance, her hand held by her partner as she crossed places with him in the line. She did not dance like a girl with her shame bellied out in front of her. She danced in her pride like a boat under sail, straight-backed and stately.

A manservant moved along until he pushed between Elske and the maidservant standing next to her. He spoke softly into Elske's ear. "Which is your Adelinne?" he asked, and added, "That's mine." He pointed to a young man with dark, curly hair and bright brown eyes. "Var Jerrol," the manservant said, his voice like a breeze as it crossed her ear, "watches my Adel as he does your Adelinne. Mine he watches because of his father's armies, which have won him rule over five great cities in the south."

"The father is a King?" Elske asked. The Adel's face was delicately boned and he danced as if music came from within him to join the flowing sounds of the lutes.

"To be a King, a man must have royal blood in his

veins, which is why the son comes to our Courting Winter. The father looks for a royal bride, that the son's sons may be royal, as their warrior grandfather can never be."

"Did not those five cities defend themselves?" Elske wondered.

"No army can win without the black powder," the man whispered into her ear. "No city can build walls thick enough to withstand that weapon."

"Where does the father get black powder?" Elske wondered.

"I wouldn't want to speak aloud my thoughts about that," the manservant answered. "But our Trastader merchants—Vars and Councillors, the banking houses, aye, and the shipbuilders, too— they're as eager as a man with a new wife. Lively as crickets. Your mistress is much improved since the last Courting Winter. Is it you who have taught her manners?"

Elske laughed then, and shook her head. She knew nothing of manners and, even if she did, she didn't imagine Beriel could be taught.

"What use has Var Jerrol for her?" the manservant asked. "What does he use you for?"

Elske shook her head again. Ignorance, she decided, was the wisest gown to dress herself in, when this fellow questioned her. She wondered what *his* uses for her were, and then wondered if he was in Var Jerrol's employ. That last thought she chose not to reveal.

"Unless it is your face," he suggested, looking at her with a smile that hinted at some private under-standing, and promised that she would enjoy it were he to share it with her. "With your eyes the color of a wolf's pelt. Do you know, it is not only the Adeliers who are betrothed at the end of a Courting Winter. And I might marry you myself, Var Jerrol permitting."

Elske laughed, as if this was all a mischief. And it was a mischief, or at least misprision, if he thought he would gain something by having her for wife. "I do not choose to marry," she answered him. "Not you, nor any other man."

"You will," he promised her.

Perhaps she would, but first must come the business of the babe. When that was accomplished, then everything might change, but until that was finished, Elske—like Beriel—could only wait.

Chapter 11

ELSKE THOUGHT THAT she had guarded against every danger the child presented, but Beriel had a more cunning and suspecting mind. One evening, she called Elske into the bedchamber and gave her servant the dagger. "I can't do this, so you must," she said, and held out her left hand, palm upwards. "Take the dagger and make a cut, here—where the blood flows freely. Along the soft pads of my fingers, Elske."

Elske took the weapon, willing to obey, but she first asked, "Why, my Lady?"

Beriel lifted a soft cloth from beside her. "Do you know nothing of how servants gossip? If I never once have my woman's bleedings, do you think they won't notice, those washerwomen? And haven't you sent in your bloody cloths, and haven't they been washed and folded and returned to you?"

So Elske held Beriel's hand firm in hers and sliced deep across the fingertips, ignoring her mistress's quick hissing intake of breath. Then she took up a cloth, to catch the bright blood. They both watched red drops soak into the white cloth.

Beriel voiced their opinion. "It's not enough, it's not—"

Elske agreed. "If we were to mix it with some wine?"

"Or snow, we can get snow by the window, and melt—?" Beriel suggested.

In the end they did both. Elske sent to the kitchen for a second goblet of wine, and Beriel set her first goblet on the stove to melt the snow she'd filled it with. Also, Beriel cut across the tips of Elske's fingers, and they gained more blood that way, and shared the same pain, and took the same comfort from thrusting their fingertips into the snow. And in the end the results were satisfactory. Melted snow thinned out the liquorish smell of the wine and blood brightened the color of the stain.

"Now we have a few more weeks," Beriel announced, satisfied.

"And there will be blood in plenty at the birth," Elske promised. But that did not cheer her mistress.

"It has been too long," Beriel spoke in a low voice, "since I knew how things are for my land. I remember this from the last Courting Winter, how I am imprisoned in ignorance. Northgate gives generously from the storerooms when his people need, and Arborford, too, cares for his, but there are royal lands that can be gripped hard by winter, and my father is too sick and greedy to remember how the people starve, and die of cold on their holdings."

"These Trastaders know how to prepare against winter's siege," Elske observed, but Beriel was lost in her own thoughts and memories: "The people of the Kingdom fear the royal house, and fear not our strengths but our weaknesses. But they do not fear me. They long to have me for their Queen," Beriel said, proud and sure. "If I claim my rightful place."

"And your brother?"

"Guerric is like my father, greedy, and his appetites will not learn patience. His advisors use him for their own gains—"

"These are they who raped you?"

"No, those were—"

Beriel ceased speaking, studied her hands where they were clasped together now to halt their bleeding. "I will not think of that," Beriel said. "When the time comes for my revenges, then I will think of those cousins. And that brother. Leave me now," she ordered.

Elske withdrew to the antechamber. There, she added the bloodied cloths to the accumulated shifts and nightdresses left for washing, and considered her own plans.

At the next Assembly, Elske left the hall while the Adeliers, the overseeing Vars, and all the servants watched the antics of little dolls on strings, who moved and spoke like people, quarreling, fighting, playing tricks upon one another and stealing one another's prizes and women. She took her cloak and slipped out into the marketplace, where snowflakes floated down through the windless air.

She hurried down towards the docks and Var Kenric's storehouse, where she hoped to find Taddus, or at least leave word that she had need to meet with him. As it happened, Taddus was there that afternoon, walking about the shadowy warehouse with a long book in his hands as he counted up stacked bolts of cloth and recorded their number. He was surprised to see her. "Alone?" he asked, welcoming, but she answered him without pleasantries. "Is Idelle with child?" She could spare no time for niceties.

146

"No," Taddus said. "I've a barren wife. Barren, and grief-filled. If I'd known—"

Elske interrupted him. "If I were to bring you a babe?"

"Who has done this to you?" Taddus asked, and Elske shook her head, impatient.

"If I were to bring a babe, a newborn, would Idelle take it? Would you accept such a child, if I could give you my word that the blood in its veins was as good as yours?"

Now Taddus hesitated. This Elske gave time, however little time she had to spare here. Behind her, in the shop-front, people moved about and sometimes spoke, buying and selling.

"Yes," Taddus decided.

"Idelle will need to prepare for a babe, as if she approached its birthing," Elske told him. "It must seem to be your own child you raise. You will want a cow, for milk, or a goat."

"Not a wet nurse?"

"The fewer who suspect, the safer is your secret. If I can, I will bring the babe to you before the end of winter. I have heard," Elske told him now, "how a barren woman's womb may open up with the joy of a child to raise, not her own but as good as her own. I have seen her womb now welcoming to the man's seed where before it was stony ground."

That hope eased the last of Taddus's doubts. "My house will be ready," he told Elske. He asked, "And when—?"

"I can't be certain," she said. "I think between the next full moon and the moon after. I must return now, before I'm missed."

"Alone?" he asked again.

"I am safe, alone. For the brief distance, safe enough."

Elske had already decided to go out in man's clothing, when she went out alone, if she went out alone again, even in daylight. She would make herself a set of trousers, and that would be all the disguise she would need under her winter cloak, a shirt and trousers. She could tie back her hair, as many men did. Nobody would notice a solitary cloaked boy on the winter streets. But what if the child were wailing at the time?

How could she keep the child from wailing, when she carried it out of the villa on Logisle and across the bridge to Var Kenric's house on Harboring?

If it were night, Elske thought, there would be none to hear a wailing child, muffled as the cries would be beneath her cloak, against her breast. These winter days were mostly night, and that was in her favor. But if there were danger of discovery, then she must strangle or smother it. Lest Beriel be betrayed.

All of this went through her mind in a flash as brief as sunlight on water, as she wished Taddus farewell and he thanked her, and she returned to the Council Hall and the assembled Adeliers, and to her mistress's service.

Day followed day, each day growing longer in such small steps that it was impossible to be sure that there was any difference between them. Like them, Beriel's belly grew imperceptibly.

Beriel was impatient for the birth to be completed. Once the child was gone, done with, and the afterbirth burned away in the stove, "then I can think of my return," she said. "If I live." Anger burned in Beriel more brightly, and shone out of her eyes, too, the closer the babe came to its birth. The Adels stood back from her anger, asking her, "Why so imperious, Lady?" And their menservants sought out Elske to ask, "Little lovely, can't you sweeten your mistress's disposition?"

Neither Beriel nor Elske cared to answer such questions.

The questions Elske did answer were those Beriel asked. "How do I know when birth has begun?" and Elske explained about the waters, breaking and flowing. "And that is all? Why do women moan so about it?" Beriel asked, and Elske spoke of the slowly closing gap from one cramping pain to the next, through much of which a woman might continue at her daily life—until the end, when a woman could think only of pain, and the desire to push the child out into the world. "How do you know these things?" Beriel demanded.

"My grandmother—the women came to her for their births. Our house was the Birth House."

"Was your grandmother, like you, not so strengthless as she looked?"

"Do I look strengthless?" Elske asked.

"You look of such cheerful heart, people think you guileless, which they take for weak. You smile as if this was a world without cruelty, hunger, injustice, ill luck, a world with neither fear nor shame. You smile like someone who is not life's prisoner."

"When I can so easily die, how can I be thought a prisoner?"

"As the world sees things," Beriel began, and then stopped.

They had lingered at table after their meal. Beriel had eaten little and drunk two goblets of red wine.

Outside, a thick snow fell steadily. There would be no Assembly that day.

"As the world sees things," Beriel began again, and again didn't finish her sentence. She rose from the table and walked over to the door, opened it and for a long time stood with her back to Elske, looking out into the falling snow.

Elske sat still. She waited to hear her mistress speak the thought that had moved her to open the door.

When Beriel at last turned around, her blue eyes shone as if there were not a gathering darkness outside, and a confining snow. "It's starting. I think it is— Now it's gone again, but—You said, the pains would come wide apart at first, and these—but I am not at peace," Beriel said. "The King my father is an old man, ill, and if he should die while I'm sent away here into the exile of courtship—"

Beriel fell silent again. Elske could not know if it was a birth pain that silenced her, or her own thoughts.

"A dead woman is no danger to a living King," Beriel said. "I must be careful to live."

Elske gathered their plates onto the serving tray.

They returned to the bedchamber, but Beriel still did not sit. She paced slowly from door to window, and back again, and back again, as steady as the sea against its shores.

"The Wolfer women make no sound?" she asked once.

Elske nodded. If the labor had begun, then she needed to prepare for many hours of sleeplessness. The first child might curl up smallest against his mother, but he was also the most reluctant to leave her. The first labor was the hardest, longest; but not necessarily the most dangerous. Unless, of course, the baby lay wrong in its mother, lay feet down and head up, for example, or crossways; those births were the most difficult. Whether first or not, such births were often the last.

"This Guerric, this brother, is only a year younger than I am. A year and a little less, my mother having been in a great hurry to produce a son. And heir, as if she did not wish me to inherit the throne. They make no sound at all?"

"Mewlings, sometimes, like a kitten," Elske said. "Later, all panted—" She tried to remember everything, and was about to mention groanings when Beriel announced, "What any other woman can do, that can I do. And man, too—but that's not the question here, is it?"

"No, my Lady," Elske smiled. Then she thought to tell Beriel, "Among the Volkaric, to become King one must win the throne away from all others, in battle, after the Volkking dies—"

"And the Death Maiden with him."

"Yes, then. For the Strydd, the captains strip naked, except for their swords."

"Naked?"

"Clothed in their strength and courage, why should they need more?"

"The captains fight until one has conquered all the rest?"

"Yes. Then all serve the new Volkking, and all belongs to him."

Beriel paced, and every now and then stopped to lean against something, concentrating on her labor.

"They do then make some small sounds?" she asked.

"My Lady, if you will be soundless that will keep you safest. And the babe will—"

"I've told you, I will know nothing of this babe."

"Yes, my Lady," Elske said. She explained to Beriel, "I can tell them you are ill, but to keep you safe we must give no suspicion of what illness it is that keeps you in your chamber."

Beriel agreed without argument. She paced, and said, "In a battle for the crown, I would stand the victor. Against my brother. Guerric plies his sword as if he were a strengthless girl, with a girl's cowardly heart. He keeps his horse to a trot, lest he fall off. He loves sweet cakes better than his land. He isn't fit to be King, and yet he is the King's preferred heir."

"A man who brings others to rape his sister, that man isn't fit to be King," Elske said. "Even were he a brave and strong swordsman, he would not be fit."

"Neither, I think, is that man fit who drags a girl child behind him into death," Beriel remarked.

"It is the way of the Volkaric that the Volkking take a maiden to serve him in his death, and offer him her body for his comfort in Death's halls. Is it the way in your Kingdom that a Prince should lack heart in fighting? And seek to shame his blood sister?"

There was no answer. Beriel waited out a pain, then said, "I have another brother, and sisters, and they are not poisoned as Guerric is, with envy and fear of me. I have a good brother, Aidenil." Beriel smiled, thinking of this brother. "My sisters, too, are gentle and obedient. Only in Guerric does ambition rage."

"And in you, also, my Lady."

"Do you say I'm no better than he?" Beriel demanded, displeased.

Elske said, "I say nothing of better."

"And why should I not be Queen? And is not revenge the action of a Queen?"

"Whatever you do will be the action of a Queen," Elske said, and Beriel subsided. Later, in the deep night, as the pains came more swiftly, "My mother, who should have saved me, has always betrayed me," Beriel said. She still refused to sit, or to lie on her bed. Elske knew that soon it would be good for her mistress to take off her gown, and good for Elske to take the white linens from off the bed—lest either be soiled in a manner that could not be explained away. Elske had already called for a bowl of water, as if for washing, and set it on the stove to heat. She had called also for a jug of wine.

"I had no grandmother to save me, as you did," Beriel said. Then she stopped speaking, to place her hands flat against the window and stare out, as she breathed deeply.

There came the time when Beriel consented to take off her gown, and lie down upon the stripped bed, and then the time when she could think of nothing but the labor working upon her body. She opened her mouth, but made no cry. Elske wiped the sweat from her mistress's face and neck. That was all Elske could do as the long night wore on. She could sit beside her mistress and dry her sweat and later her tears. Elske's hands were bruised in Beriel's clasp, that long night.

In the morning, she waited by her own antechamber door until the house servants brought food, and drink. "My Lady is unwell," she told them, whispering as if Beriel slept at last behind her closed door, after a night's illness. "She must have quiet."

"Shall we send for the housekeeper?" they asked, well-trained servants in a well-run household.

"Not yet," Elske answered. "She is not so feverish for that. Leave her to me, and to quiet."

Elske knew that if darkness did not come before the babe, her own dangers would be multiplied. Climbing out of the window in daylight would increase her chances of being seen, as would crossing the snowy lawn and gardens into the woods by day; but waiting for darkness would increase the chance of the babe's presence being detected at the villa.

And if the babe were born in daylight and couldn't be quieted, then Elske would have no choice. She would take it into another room and silence it; and at dark she would walk out over the ice until she came to one of the fisherman's huts, and the fishing hole within, through which a newborn babe with its soft bones could be forced. No one would ever know.

Beriel was beyond caring if it was daylight or dark and Elske—sitting at her mistress's side, meeting Beriel's blue gaze with calmness—watched pain wash over her mistress's body until the girl wept, tears as silent as the cries that came mutely from her howling mouth. Elske couldn't take time to look away, to know what time of day it was, if dark or light. They were near the end, she thought.

Beriel drew her knees up and Elske—speaking

almost in Tamara's soft remembered voice—urged her to push.

The blue eyes were near wild, like some wolf brought down, struggling to stand and run, except its legs would not obey its will. Beriel closed her eyes and wept with the pain, and the labor, and the silence.

And so the babe was born, the head first and hardest, followed by the narrow-shouldered body, which slipped out. Beriel lay back, panting, emptied, out of pain's reach—then her body arched stiffly one more time, to expel the afterbirth.

Using Beriel's dagger, Elske cut the cord and tied it off. Bloody and wet with its own birthing, the babe started to cry. She wrapped it around with soft cloths, and that soothed it again. It was a girl child.

Beriel lay, chest heaving, her eyes screwed shut. Her hands were fists where they lay on her breasts. Her hair lay wet and straggled around her head.

Elske laid the baby on a cloak which she had set out like a small pallet near the warmth of the stove. She took water, and washed her mistress clean, giving her clean cloths to place between her legs and catch the flow of blood there. She covered her mistress with a clean bedsheet and thrust the afterbirth into the stove. She returned to Beriel, lifting her head to give her wine.

The baby stirred, fussed.

Beriel lay abed, her face closed away from everything.

"I'm going now," Elske said, pulling on the trousers she had sewn for herself, tucking her shirt half into them. Putting her stockinged feet into her warm wolfskin boots, she took up the baby and the cloak. She set the baby down on the windowsill and settled the cloak around her shoulders, then climbed up onto the sill and jumped down into the deep snow. She reached inside to gather the baby to herself, tucking it up against her breast under the cloak. If the child would stay quiet and warm there, as if she thought herself yet unborn, then Elske could carry her safely through the darkness.

For it was deep, dark night, and her luck held—this might be a lucky child—as Elske crept out of the villa grounds and hurried along dark roadways, across the bridge that arched over the dark ice of the frozen river, then down the familiar streets of Harboring until she came to Var Kenric's house, silent and shuttered. She knocked on the door, and waited, hoping that the snow muffled the sound that was so loud in her own ears, hoping that none but the people of the house might hear. A shuttered window above her head opened, and Var Kenric looked down at her. Then Ula opened the door to her and she saw Idelle's freckled face as eager as it had been before she had been married and childless. Elske gave the child into Idelle's arms.

"A girl," she said to Taddus. He had bent over the baby's face, and only looked up to nod.

"We thank—" Var Kenric started to say and Ula was wiping at her eyes with her apron, but Elske said, "I must return," and she would not stay for food and drink, for thanks, for anything. She had done all she could here, and she would be needed by Beriel.

Darkness hid her in shadows as Elske raced back to Var Vladislav's snow-covered grounds, and climbed over the low fence, easier now without a newborn held close against her chest. She moved through trees, past stables, around the kitchen gardens—slipping like the shadow of a bird along the walls—until she was at the open window to Beriel's bedchamber.

Elske climbed back inside.

"I didn't close the window, but I'm cold," Beriel said from the bed.

Elske pulled the window in, and went to the stove to remove her boots and warm her hands, after the bitter night.

"I'm bleeding, as if it were my time," Beriel said.

"That's the way of it. Did you sleep?"

"I couldn't sleep. I did well."

"You did well, my Lady."

"I want food," Beriel said then.

"Wiser to wait for the servants to bring food in the morning," Elske advised.

"I'm very hungry."

"It's the hard work of birthing."

"What have you done with the child, then?" Beriel asked.

"I can't tell you that," Elske answered. She held her hands out over the warm stove, but she could hear Beriel stirring behind her, sitting up.

"I command you."

"I gave my word," Elske reminded her. At Beriel's silence, she turned around—and fury crashed against her like a wave thrown by a storm against the rocky coast.

"You gave your word to me and I return it to you. I ask again, what have you done with my babe?"

Elske didn't speak. This was no more than Beriel herself had warned Elske of.

"My own child, which I endured the shame of getting and the pain of birthing. Where is it now?"

Elske kept silence.

"Will you at least tell me if it was a girl child or a boy?" Beriel asked, more quietly.

"My Lady, I cannot."

Fury rose again in Beriel's eyes. "Will not, more like. It's fortunate for you that I am in your debt," she said.

"Why should you be in my debt?" Elske asked.

"Sometimes—you are so—innocent—and ignorant," Beriel answered, and this added to her anger. "I know you lived among brutes, but—" She took a deep breath and gave the order more quietly. "I am hungry, and you are my servant. I tell you to find me food, and drink. It has been more than a day since I have eaten, and if Var Vladislav's housekeeper catches you at the larder, and punishes you, remember that a better servant would have had food ready for me."

"Yes, my Lady," Elske said. She turned to leave the room.

"After all, they believe I have been feverish. When a fever passes on, the sick person is often hungry, so why should they suspect anything? Unless, you've told them—?"

Elske knew that if Beriel wished to believe ill of her, nothing Elske could say would convince her otherwise. But why should her mistress wish to distrust Elske?

And when Elske returned, carrying a tankard of ale, and some cheese, cold roasted fowl, fish pudding and bread, Beriel said to her, "You also have not eaten, have you, Elske?" Then she adjusted herself back on her pillows, as if the bed were a throne, and announced, "We must both eat." At last Beriel said, "I am afraid for my land, and for my throne," and thus ended her quarrel with Elske.

Chapter 12

IT WAS HARD to persuade Beriel to keep to her bed for as long as the household would expect for recovery from a feverish illness. It seemed as if the baby had been a stone in Beriel's belly, and she had needed her best strength to keep it hidden there. Now, Beriel could use her best strength for her own purposes and those required her to be out of her bed.

Elske reminded her, again and again, that she must appear to the servants to be weak, although recovering as her good appetite attested.

Beriel argued, again and again. "I gave birth as a Wolfer woman, soundless, and I think such a woman would not lie abed. Did they, among the Wolfers?"

"They did not, my Lady," Elske answered patiently.

"They must have been proud," Beriel observed from her bed. "To have given birth, so, and perhaps to a son. Did I have a son, Elske? You might at least tell me that."

Elske had given her word, and kept silent. She did, however, point out to Beriel, "The women of the Volkaric were never proud. What could a woman do to be proud of? Not win treasure for the Volkking, not fight in battle. The women couldn't hunt, either. And even when they hated—for they were good haters—it was only among themselves."

"You are quarrelsome," Beriel complained. "Go and find me some book. If I can't read it myself, then you must read it to me."

So Elske went to Var Vladislav's library, where she unexpectedly interrupted him as he sat for a painting of himself. The High Councillor was not displeased at the disturbance. When she explained who she was and that she had permission from his housekeeper to go to this room, and her purpose there, he answered impatiently, "I know, I know you, Elske. Take what you will, but I would ask your mistress, will she spare you to me, to teach me a little Souther, perhaps to tell me of the Volkaric, so I can make a use of these inactive hours?"

Elske carried that request, along with a volume of animal stories she had sometimes read to Var Jerrol's daughters, back to Beriel, who had an answer quick on her tongue. "If I say yes, will you tell me about my child?"

"No, my Lady."

Beriel then asked from her bed, "And if I say no?"

"I will obey you."

When Beriel did not say yes or no, Elske turned to leave the bedchamber. At the door Beriel called her back to say, "Very well, I give you my permission. I will also warn you, Elske, as a kind mistress. Do you know what men use flattery for?"

"For rape," Elske answered.

Beriel laughed, her ill temper flown like a bird out

of the cage. She said, "We must find you some other word, in Norther and in Souther, too, some word that tells the bed pleasures a man and a woman have together. Did your Wolfer women never have pleasure of a man?"

"They had babies. They never spoke of pleasure."

"And the men?"

"They had their desire and—sometimes—they had sons."

"Among the Wolfers," Beriel said then, "if you refused to tell me what I wished to know, I would have you killed. Isn't that so? No captive among the Wolfers would dare refuse her mistress."

"Among the Volkaric, you would be but one of many women," Elske explained patiently. "You might ask one of the men to accuse me before the Volkking, but the Volkking might easily give the same justice to both, give both to the wolves and thus be rid of our quarrels."

Elske must sew, now, whenever she was in Beriel's apartments, to return Beriel's gowns to their original seams. This occupied her hands and so to save them both from tedium, also to practice her skill in Norther, Beriel read aloud from the animal tales. In the stories, the animals had speech, like men and women; like men and women they were vain, ungrateful and greedy. "This tale-teller mocks us," Beriel cried, but she was amused, not angered. "He mocks us from the greatest to the least."

When Elske was called to Var Vladislav in his library, Beriel used her to discover what the Trastaders knew about the Kingdom. As far as Elske could tell from the maps Var Vladislav collected and from the few questions he asked her, the Trastaders knew almost nothing of the Kingdom, only that Beriel claimed to be its Queen.

"As Queen, do you rule everyone in everything?" Elske asked Beriel one evening, her hands busy with needle and thread.

"I do, but also I do not," Beriel answered. "I will share rule with the law, as the Priests read it. Also there are two Earls, each given lands that together make near two-thirds of the Kingdom. The Earls have power over their lands and people, but must bend the knee to the King and serve as his vassals, just as their own vassals bend the knee to them, and serve them. But there are also royal moieties, greater than what any Earl possesses. The people serve each their own Lord, who awards them their holdings, and each Lord serves his Overlord, until it comes to the Earls, who serve the King."

"Among the Volkaric," Elske said, "all men serve the Volkking, with no other to stand between them and him."

"Among the Volkaric, then," Beriel said, "if a man is not the Volkking, he has nothing more than any other man."

Elske agreed and pointed out, "Thus each man's loyalty is to the Volkking only."

At the end of her enforced time in bed, Beriel had her plans begun. "There is only one moon of winter left to me here in Trastad, and I will use that time to my own advantage. I will have Var Jerrol to dine with me, as my guest. You will deliver my invitation, Elske, at the next Assembly. I will have him come to me two days after the next Assembly. I will not be gainsaid in this," Beriel warned. But Elske thought only to obey—except she wondered if she would find such another, master or mistress, to serve, and she wished that Beriel had not made her know how little time remained in this Courting Winter.

The next Assembly came not four days after.

New-cut greens freshened the air of the hall with their sharp, bitter fragrances, as they did at every first-quarter moon. The table was set out with ale and cheeses and breads, as well as sweet apple cakes. For entertainment, a ropedancer performed on a thick hawser hung down from one of the open beams. Held by his strong arms, his legs stiff and straight, he swung up and down the rope, turning, twisting, poising to balance weight with strength in a solitary dance as measured and slow as a ship docking.

Beriel entered to the Assembly altered in no way that could be seen, but everything about her was changed. Now everyone attended her, Adeliers both men and women, both betrothed and free, and all of the servants and the overseeing Vars as well. None could keep their eyes from noting Beriel's progress through the hall—even while each continued his own private talk and flirtations. All wished her to notice them and yet hoped also to avoid her glance. Adelinnes praised her dress and wit. Adels offered her plates of food, and their arms to escort her around the floor. These attentions Beriel received as if they were her due, and her custom.

"What illness did she have?" the servants asked Elske, who shook her head, to ask how such as she would know the name of a disease. "How is she to serve?" they asked, and did not dare hope to be answered. They pressed Elske with questions, but also now kept back a little distance from her, as if fearing to be in conversation with her. So that Var Jerrol could speak to her from behind without danger of being overheard.

"Has your mistress had a proposal, then?"

"No," Elske answered. "She wishes to dine with you."

"That likes me well. I'll send to invite her," he said, but Elske told him, "She asks you to be her guest, two days hence."

"Ah," Var Jerrol said. "So she has sent *her* servant to me. And what have you learned about this Kingdom of hers?"

"Of the royal house, something."

"Royalty doesn't concern me. And if I know the world, this girl—however bright she glows today— will not rule in her Kingdom. For haven't they sent her here to marry her away into some distant land and bury her there? To make some lesser marriage than a Queen on her throne could command? She might do well," Var Jerrol said into Elske's ear, "to take one of these boys. If she cares for her own safety. Does she care for her own safety, do you think?"

Beriel stopped walking, and freed her arm, so that her escort could reach into his purse for a coin to put into the soft hat the ropedancer was now handing around. Beriel spoke a word to the dancer, who bowed from the waist to her, without asking her for coins; when she had turned to walk away from him, the ropedancer followed her with his eyes.

"When your Queen has gone into whatever fortune may prove to be hers," Var Jerrol said to Elske, "have you thought how alone and helpless you will be?"

Now Beriel was surrounded by Adels, like a wolf in the midst of a pack of dogs, and she freed herself from their attentions with a single glance, like a wolf keeping a pack of dogs at bay.

When Elske did not answer him, Var Jerrol said, "Tell your mistress, I accept her invitation to dine. Var Vladislav's cook has a fine hand with fish, I hear, and with the sweet pastry his master favors. Tell her, I anticipate luxurious hospitality."

All of this Elske reported faithfully, when Beriel wanted to know how Var Jerrol had received the invitation. Hearing what his questions, and concerns, and opinions were, Beriel only smiled. "I wonder what future Var Jerrol has planned for *you*," she said. "Once I've gone, I doubt you'll escape his bed. Fetch me the cook, Elske. My time here runs out and my will scampers before it. I'll have a menu, first, and then the housekeeper, and then I'll be ready for your Var Jerrol."

When Var Jerrol entered Beriel's private dining room, he looked around with pleasure. Against the dark wood of walls and floor, the table shone with the whiteness of its cloths, and gleamed with silver plates and utensils. Oil lights burned in sconces on all the walls, driving shadows from all but the lowest corners. The air was sweet with the odors of dried spices which Elske had tossed into the fire. Elske stood beside the chest, ready to pour red wine into the waiting goblets and serve the soup, which was being kept hot on top of the tile stove. Her mistress had not wanted to confide her purposes for Var Jerrol, so Elske watched this dinner unfold before her as if she were an Adelier watching an entertainment at the **Assembly**. Her own purpose at the dinner, she knew, **was to** enhance Beriel's queenliness.

Beriel entered beside Var Jerrol, so tall that she came up to his chin. Her brown hair hung down loose, and they had made one of her golden chains into a coronet. She wore her grandmother's medallion on her breast. Beriel noticed neither her maidservant's readiness nor her guest's pleasure; she merely indicated his place and allowed Elske to seat her across from him. Elske served the soup and placed a woven basket of little breads between them. She set down before each a goblet of wine so dark it seemed like a red ruby disk set in a silver ring.

"Do you always entertain in such luxury?" Var Jerrol asked, and Beriel answered, "Always. But you aren't unaccustomed to being richly entertained. For you must often dine by invitation with the Adeliers, although perhaps not often with an Adelinne, and alone."

"Correct," Var Jerrol acknowledged, then reminded her, "You were less circumspect, when last you were our guest. I was led to expect something less . . . civilized."

"I would never think anyone could lead you, Var Jerrol," Beriel said, as amused as he was by their exchange. "And is it not fine weather we are enjoying?" she asked.

They discussed the spring melts, already begun, sending flat islands of ice floating out to sea. Var Jerrol explained how the fishermen in their little boats could avoid the dangers of ice, but said it would be a few sennights yet before the less agile merchant vessels would set out for the year's trading. "And to return our Adeliers to their own homelands, their futures now happily settled, as we hope," Var Jerrol said.

As the dinner progressed, soup and fowl, fish and roasted meat, plates of savories, Elske removed the empty plates from the table and exchanged them for trays from the kitchen.

"They might be enjoying spring already in your homeland," Var Jerrol said, leading the topic of the weather into a new direction. "It lies far enough to the south, doesn't it?"

"They might, but I have no way of knowing. And you will soon be opening your mines?" When Var Jerrol didn't respond, "In the Kingdom," Beriel told him, giving him something of what she knew he wanted, "spring is long and generous, a slow, sweet-smelling, soft-winded time upon the land."

"In the Kingdom, you say? Do you know, I couldn't find your Kingdom on any map?"

"And I could find my way there blindfolded." She was playing a game with him, as if he were a child.

"It is no great thing to find your way blindfolded when you travel on a ship another man captains," Var Jerrol pointed out humorously, playing his own game with her. "The ship must come to land, somewhere."

"At a small city," Beriel agreed.

"Celindon?" he guessed.

She didn't gainsay him. "I was there under close guard, to protect me from contact with its inhabitants."

"So you know nothing of it?"

"It is a city on a river."

"It must be Celindon," Var Jerrol decided. "You would have approached it from inland, traveling down that river."

"We traveled downriver for many days," Beriel agreed.

Elske didn't know what Beriel would need her to have understood, when they discussed afterwards what information had been gained in the evening. But she had to be careful not to let her attention to their talk lead her to neglect her duties.

"You traveled from your home on horseback? Or by boat?"

"On horseback," Beriel said. "The Kingdom is hidden away, as if we wished to be concealed from the rest of the world. Although merchants do find us, for the Spring and Autumn Fairs."

"Never Trastaders."

Beriel agreed. "It's odd, isn't it, that they knew to send me here for your Courting Winter?"

"To find yourself a husband," Var Jerrol said.

"What would I want with a husband?" Beriel asked, signaling for Elske to offer around the platter of fish again.

"Only if you had need of an heir."

They ate, and Elske served them, and they talked together, each maneuvering to gain much from the other, and to give little in exchange.

"If I wanted an heir, I would find myself one," Beriel told Var Jerrol.

"There are some things which, however much you desire them, you cannot be certain they wish to be found."

"Like the alchemist's stone," Beriel suggested, agreeably, "able to turn any material into gold, or like the storied black powder, or the fountain of eternal life."

"Black powder turns stone walls into dust," Var Jerrol said. "Turns living men into dead. Black powder is, I am afraid to say, easier to come by than any alchemist's stone, or waters of miracle."

"Who would desire such a weapon?" Beriel asked.

"Anyone who feared that his enemies might already possess it."

"Yes." Beriel was thoughtful. "I would give much to be able to protect my Kingdom from such weaponry. And then, a merchant might desire the weapon also, for the great profits to be made in selling it."

"A man who knows its formulation would grow powerful," Var Jerrol said, adding, "But that is a closely guarded secret."

"Oh," Beriel laughed now, as lightly as any Adelinne who had her Adel on his knees before her, "do you never think that there are too many secrets in the world?"

Elske offered Var Jerrol a platter of thick slices of roast meat, from which he served himself, with onions and carrots that had been roasted beneath it, catching up the juices as they dripped down.

"I am a great believer in secrets," Var Jerrol told Beriel. "I draw them to me, as flowers draw bees, as beauty draws the hearts of men."

"Are you here to draw my secrets from me?" Beriel asked, still teasing.

"Who would want to take anything from you, my Lady?" Var Jerrol returned the question. "Any true man would only hope to give you the choicest of his treasures, and if you were to reward him with a smile, he would count himself overpaid."

Beriel returned the smiling compliment. "As if a Var were like any ordinary man."

"Vars are but ordinary men," Var Jerrol said. "Unusual in their wealth but wealth cannot buy all you desire. Our Vars have disappointments."

"What could disappoint men of such substance?" Beriel wondered.

"You speak lightly. You think I speak lightly," Var Jerrol said. "Or perhaps, you think I speak falsely. Let me give you a plain tale, which none but I know the whole of, with a happy enough ending for a Lady's soft ears." He drank from his wine, and went on. "There is a young merchant of the city who married well—so well that he will become a Var while still a young man. In fact, now I remember myself, it was just this young man who accompanied our Elske to Trastad, and it was just his new wife she saved from attack by ruffians."

"I remember hearing something of such an incident," Beriel observed, with a glance for her maidservant.

"This young couple had no child, to their great sorrow. For she was the only surviving child of her father's house. She must have a child to inherit the wealth of the house, which otherwise must return to the Council of Trastad," Var Jerrol explained, as if this loss of wealth were the point of his story.

"To be divided among them? I can't think, then, that such a lack would be all grief to the Council," Beriel said, as if she were only hearing another tale of Trastader greed.

"That question is now moot, for the young woman has a child." Var Jerrol glanced carelessly at

Beriel as he said this, and speared an onion on his fork, and ate it.

"A great happiness for her," Beriel responded with equal carelessness.

He chewed, and nodded pleasure at her kind thought. "Yes. It is that. Were her friends and family, and the young husband also, not so gratified by this turn of events, they might wonder at so secret a pregnancy, so sudden a birth, but— All is gladness where before sorrow shadowed the house, and who would deny them their happiness? So you see, our Vars are indeed ordinary men."

"Did I doubt you, that you needed to give me such proof?" Beriel inquired.

Elske poured more wine. She kept silent, but she saw the direction of this intricate conversational dance. She saw its direction, and unease gripped her heart. Meanwhile, she gave their plates to the kitchen maid and sent the girl back to fetch the cold fowl. Meanwhile, she set out clean silver plates, one before each diner.

"I am ready to believe whatever you might tell me, Var Jerrol," Beriel continued.

"I tell you only the tale I heard," Var Jerrol concluded.

"What happiness for the young husband, this child. But I am still curious. Is it a girl child, or a boy child?" Beriel asked offhandedly, as she lifted her goblet to her lips.

So this was Beriel's purpose for Var Jerrol. Elske's heart grew chilly, to know why she had been kept ignorant.

"The child is a girl, as I hear, with a strong pair of lungs and a healthy appetite. The Varinne is already famous for her motherly devotion." Var Jerrol continued to eat, too clever to let Beriel see that he knew he had given her what she wanted from him, too clever to ask immediately for a favor in return.

"I wish her many children," Beriel said, with another glance at Elske. "And much joy of them all. But now I wonder, have they given their daughter a name?"

"I've heard that they call her Elskele, as if to honor Elske for her rescue of the Varinne, with that gratitude always fresh in their minds."

"As it should be," Beriel announced happily. "As my own gratitude would be kept fresh, should Elske have so well served me."

This wasn't gratitude, Elske knew, even though she knew also that she had served Beriel so well, and better. She stood with her back to the table, listening, carving the fowl. She offered the platter to Var Jerrol, first, then to Beriel. The silver platter was icy cold in her hands, from having been set out in the snow, lest the fowl grow warm in the heat of the dining chamber. If this fowl were to grow warm, Elske thought, it would be from the fury that burned in her, and from the hot grief for her sworn word, now a dead thing.

Why should Beriel take from her the worth of her own word, which was all that she owned? And which Beriel herself had given to Elske, by showing her that she did own it. Although Beriel had given it to her, she now seized it back, imperiously.

The two were talking now of trade, and how it served the well-being of Trastad, or any other land. Var Jerrol asked Beriel what metal ores were to be found in the Kingdom, and what crops grew there, and if they had coins and how they were minted, how sold, what cloths, blades, books and ales. He argued that understanding of letters was best distributed freely among all who wished to learn it, although Beriel feared that knowledge would lead to discontent. They spoke of law, and Beriel wondered how the Council could govern without written laws. But he assured her, "We have custom and tradition, to be considered during any judgement. We are well-governed."

"Yet the cells are full, as I hear it, and overfull."

"We build new cells as we need them," Var Jerrol said. "They are not overfull."

As they spoke, Elske stood in the silence of her anger; for Beriel had taken Elske's word and made it valueless. Elske felt as if Beriel had walked with her out to the hillside; and she had gone with her mistress, all trusting; and Beriel had left her there for the wolves.

Elske did not know which cut more deeply, her defenselessness or her solitude.

"I'd have thought you would be using Elske to translate for you," Var Jerrol said, and Beriel answered him that she had improved her knowledge of his language, under Elske's tutelage.

Var Jerrol asked, "Do you ever think to open the door to your land?"

"I think of it," Beriel said. "I think of sending out emissaries, and merchants, and even of sending my unruly cousins to the Courting Winter. I think of giving my Kingdom a place in the greater world."

"Why should your Lords and Princes not wed outside of your Kingdom?" Var Jerrol asked. "If you were to have a brother, for example, and I a daughter both richly dowered and gently reared, might not all profit from a union between them?"

Beriel agreed. "I have brothers, that much is true, and one a worthy Prince. I will think of what you have said, you who are the eyes and ears of the Council, and a man of wisdom."

Var Jerrol bowed his head, receiving the compliment.

Beriel told him, "Mine is a land of stories, not like Trastad which is a merchant city. I think often of Jackaroo, who with his sword and his great heart brought justice to a people oppressed by poverty and misgoverned by Overlords. Jackaroo rides out only when the land has need of him, then rests in sleep under the mountains until he is needed again, to save his people." Var Jerrol smiled tolerantly and Beriel reflected the expression back at him. "I always believe, however, that if my land needs saving, I must save it myself."

"Trastad makes a generous ally," Var Jerrol told her. "But is your Kingdom in danger?"

At that question, Beriel stood. Restless, she moved to the window, to look out at the ice-clogged river. She became again a young woman, sent into courtship against her will. "I do not know," she said. "I have no reason to think so, but my father was not in health when I left and—I have been too long away."

Var Jerrol watched her the way a snake might watch a mouse. "It is a moon yet before you will set out on your return."

Beriel turned around to face him, and she was a Queen again. "It may be," she said, "that it is time for we of the Kingdom to travel outwards from our own borders, and beyond the protection of the forests that surround us, and of the mountains that ring us. If it is that time, be sure I will remember you, and I will think of the skills of Trastad."

"You mean in trade."

"And carpentry, shipbuilding, too, in your paintings and goldsmiths, your spacious houses and the tile stoves with which you heat your chambers. There is much I value in Trastad," Beriel said, holding out her white hand, "as you know well."

Var Jerrol became gallant. "When you leave us, there will be a diminishment in that sum. And more, if you think to take Elske with you."

"What happens to my maidservant does not concern you," Beriel announced, to which Var Jerrol made no quarrel. "Escort my guest to the door," Beriel commanded. "See Var Jerrol safely away, Elske."

When Elske returned, she found Beriel in the dining chamber, at the window, and looking out to where a sky of deep blue shone over the moving water, which carried its cargo of ice down to the sea. A field of ice-crusted snow sparkled white down to the water's edge, and across the river more white fields held the dark forests back from little houses. Smoke rose from distant chimneys into the bright blue sky.

Beriel turned to greet Elske and her eyes shone like the sky, and her whole face was alight with her victory. "Now I, too, know where my child, my daughter, lives, and what child it is I had. Did you think you could keep a secret from me?"

Elske gathered up plates and goblets. She was expected to make her own dinner from whatever was left on the platters, but she had no appetite for this meal.

"Have you no answer?" Beriel demanded.

"None."

Elske attended to her task.

Beriel watched her, then said, "How could Var Jerrol know something so close to me and I not seek to find it out, since you must have told him."

"No." Elske denied what Beriel already knew was a false accusation.

"You need not fear my anger," Beriel promised.

Elske forced herself to respond. "I am not afraid."

"Then you're jealous. You thought that you alone could hold Var Jerrol's eyes and attentions. You thought that only your smiling ways could win him. I will not have a jealous servant, Elske."

"Nor jealous," Elske said.

Then Beriel did look long and hard at her, and Elske met the glance like a swordsman meeting a blow.

"No, you are not jealous," Beriel admitted. "But you would have kept me in ignorance about my own child."

Elske spoke her thought, "I gave my word."

"So you did, and you kept it."

"My word was made worthless."

"But you gave it to *me*," Beriel protested. "Can I not say when you must change your word, if you gave it to *me*?"

"I thought, it was *my* word. I thought, it was *my* promise."

"Not jealous, but proud," Beriel said then.

"Why should I be proud?"

Beriel answered impatiently. "I do not know,

177

unless it is for your charms and high-heartedness, which draw people to you. But what are those more than charms and high-heartedness? What cause for pride in these? Still, I am myself proud enough to recognize pride's face when I see it in a beryl glass. So. So." She stood taller even than before, her eyes still alight, and asked, "Are you grown too proud to be my maidservant?"

"No, my Lady," Elske said, for that was true.

"Give me your word for that," Beriel commanded.

"I have no word to give," Elske answered. "You've taken it from me, this day."

"Then I give it back, as a Queen can. Elske, you have never given birth, and neither had I when I asked for your promise. When I know that my child is cared for, named—a daughter—now I can truly leave her behind me. How could I have known my true will before she was born?"

"You could not have, my Lady," Elske said; and that, too, was true.

Elske thought, How could Beriel, who would be Queen, be asked also to know herself? Willful, imperious, unyielding—how could Beriel accept not knowing of her child, when with wit and charm she could win that knowledge? Even at the cost of Elske's word, Beriel would have her own way. Elske could not remain angry at Beriel, for how could Beriel have known how bitterly Elske would see her own little word gathered up into all the rest that a Queen possessed? As servant, Elske might have nothing but her own word and her own choices; but perhaps a Queen had no more—had less, even, if her royal word was not good, or her choices suspect. Elske would not wish to blame Beriel—but neither did she intend to give her word, her choices, into Beriel's keeping.

"And if I were to ask, would you come with me to the Kingdom? There will be others to offer you a more certain future here in Trastad," Beriel said. "If I am displaced, I cannot promise you anything but death, but still, I ask you to come with me."

"I need no promise of rewards," Elske said, making her own choice.

Chapter 13

BERIEL RECOUNTED the obstacles: A ship must be found and passage negotiated. It must be decided how they would leave Var Vladislav's villa undetected—not that she thought the Council wished to detain her, just that they would require her to travel at the time of their choice, not hers. There was the question of what essentials to bring, for if she was to travel unescorted, she must travel light.

But the greatest difficulty they faced was gold. If she wished to return to the Kingdom at her own will, Beriel needed gold to purchase berths on a ship, and then more gold to bribe the captain to set them ashore on the harborless coast close to Pericol. There, they would need yet more gold to purchase horses, food and safe passage from the cutthroat who ruled that city. And even when they had arrived in the Kingdom, who knew what preparations it would be necessary for Beriel to purchase. For Beriel couldn't know how her land would greet her.

"I know how my brother would like to welcome me. Guerric," Beriel spoke his name as if she had her foot on his neck. "He is no question. But the others? The soldiers, Priests and Lords—they will be divided, I'd guess, they'll be uneasy, fearful to choose the losing side and thus forfeit their high positions. Some are loyal, I think, Northgate and his heir, Arborford, probably. I can't know if my father still lives or what my mother might do after his death, except that she will not hope to have her daughter share the name of Queen. She is proud, and jealous. Oh yes," Beriel answered, although Elske had not spoken. "I am her true daughter."

"You have my purse," Elske offered.

"For which I thank you, and promise to repay you manifold," Beriel said. "If I live. The people will welcome me, I believe. My people, I think, know me. I trust my people," Beriel said, her chin high and her eyes shining blue.

They were in among the books and maps of the High Councillor's library, and in fact stood with a map open before them. Beriel's fingers traced the coastline between Trastad and Celindon. Elske could not find Pericol named on the map.

"All the baubles they've sent to me, these Adels, these boys, and for which I have been so grateful and smiling, a goldsmith will buy them—at his own price, but between his price and nothing my choice is easy," Beriel told Elske. "You must find the man, to conceal my interest. Wear those trousers you put on when you took my daughter—"

"You saw?"

"It was clever. In trousers, cloaked, your hair tied back like a man's, no one would take you for a girl, and unprotected. So you can move as freely as a man through Trastad, and carry these jewels safely. Take my dagger, against thieves—for danger stalks anyone seen leaving bankers or smiths alone, even a man." Beriel put her finger down on the map, on the coast north of Celindon, where a river entered the sea. "Pericol," she said. "They put me in the midst of a troop of horsemen to go through Pericol, have I told you?" And Beriel laughed at the memory. "With Guerric's hand-chosen captains in charge, and they did deliver me safely, so I have something to thank them for. I do not know if I can deliver us safely through that place," Beriel said. "But I think I might," she said.

"I can take us that far," Beriel said, and then added, without prologue or preamble, "If I have not already lost my Kingdom forever, and my people lost their chance of me, I must marry. For the heir," Beriel answered the question Elske had not asked. "Be it boy or girl, my first child will be named heir to the throne of the Kingdom."

"I will set about finding a goldsmith," Elske said.

"And a ship, too. But none must suspect us. You have a wide and loyal acquaintance in Trastad, Elske; what help can you offer me in the matter of ships?" Beriel asked.

"None," Elske answered, truthfully.

As it happened, however, after she had exchanged baubles for coins, she ran into Nido as she walked along the docks to see what ships were being read-ied for embarkation, to see what goods they were to carry and hear what destination they sailed for. Elske kept her head low to hide her face and her hands hidden under the short cloak to conceal the heavy purse she carried, but Nido had no difficulty in recognizing her. He insisted on walking with her, at least as far as the bridge that joined Harboring to Logisle. He hadn't seen her for so long a time and there was much he wished to tell her. Was it that she didn't want his company? he asked. He wouldn't give her disguise away, he assured her of that, and besides, wouldn't the disguise be improved when they were two young men, walking about together?

Nido had grown taller, and had the shadow of a beard. The labors of apprenticeship hadn't dampened his spirits. His great news was that he was to be sent out as the assistant to a ship's carpenter, on one of Var Kenric's vessels. "We are fitted and stocked, and the ice has broken up. Var Kenric wants to be the first to offer goods in Celindon—I'll see Celindon again, Elske. The other time I was just a boy, the time we met you, Taddus and Father and I, when we were returning. He's ill, did you know?"

"Taddus?"

"Not Taddus, Father. Taddus counts himself the luckiest man in Trastad, now that Idelle has given him an heir. They named the girl after you, did you know that? If Taddus were not Var Kenric's heir, now, Father and Mother would worry where they might find stock, for Father will not be strong enough to travel out this summer. But Taddus supplies their shelves, and I am now placed on one of Var Kenric's ships. In only two days, or perhaps three, I'll be gone. So it is good fortune that I saw you here. What do you think of that chance, after all this time, Elske?"

Elske thought it was a fair chance, and she decided to risk Beriel's anger and spend some of these coins taking that chance. "Will your ship take passengers?" she asked.

"Ships that will bear the Adeliers back to their own lands, and carry our merchants south, will await the fairer weather."

"What if I knew of two travelers who desire to commence their journey now and don't fear foul weather?"

"My ship has a stateroom, next to the captain's quarters. But the sea is still rough, they say—and storms not unlikely. Although, less likely as we move south," Nido told her.

"I do know of two such," Elske said. "What would the charge be, for your captain?"

"I'd have to ask him, and he would have to know he wasn't setting himself or Var Kenric against the will of the Council." Nido looked like a man grown now.

"These are two the Council will not object over," Elske promised him. "There is no criminal, no traitor, no one Trastad wishes to keep within its own territory. I give you my word."

Nido studied her face. They had arrived at the bridge, and stood talking there. "Have they the Council's permission to leave the city?"

"Can two women, neither of them Trastaders, one of them impatient to be back in her own land, endanger Trastad by leaving it betimes?"

Nido thought. "And the second is you?"

"Yes."

"Can you give me the fare now, to convince my captain?"

Elske opened the purse and took out four gold coins. She put them into Nido's hands.

"It's too much," he said.

"You can return to me what you don't need."

"Or it maybe will not be enough, if you cannot show the captain your permissions," Nido said thoughtfully.

Elske gave him four more coins, and so she had spent half of Beriel's purse.

"How will I find you?" Nido asked.

"I'll be here, in this place, at this time, every day until I hear from you," Elske said.

"You'll hear from me tomorrow," Nido promised her.

So it was that two days from that time, Beriel strode up the wooden gangplank and onto the deck of the ship. Elske followed behind, wearing her warm Wolfer boots, carrying the pack in which whatever clothing they brought with them was folded.

Nido led them down a steep ladder into the belly of the ship, then through a low doorway into a low-ceilinged, narrow, short room where two high, shuttered portholes let in light. With the three of them in the room, there was barely space to move, but Nido squeezed out past them, saying hurriedly, "The captain will send me when we're far enough from land." And he was gone.

The boat moved gently under Elske. The sound of feet came from overhead. When she opened the portholes, she could see the open sky, with a few wispy clouds hurrying across it.

Beriel sat down on the bunk, to wait. Her first fury, when Elske had reported to her of the meeting with Nido, and the coins spent, and the plan laid, had faded away under her desire to return to the Kingdom. She had left behind her a letter for the High Councillor, an elaborate apology for her hasty departure, citing unease about her father who had been in poor health when she had left him, thanking Var Vladislav for his hospitality, hoping that he had intended her to take Elske with her, for that was her will. "I take with me the maidservant, Elske," Beriel had written, and then offered a guileful compliment, "Your wisdom and good judgement in choosing me this girl for servant reveals how it is that Trastad has come to such well-deserved prosperity." So Beriel completed her affairs in Trastad, and Elske—who had no affairs of her own—now sat beside her mistress on the narrow bunk, listening to the sounds of a ship being readied to sail.

Eventually, the ship drew heavily away from the dock. Unable to see, listening, Elske heard the sails being raised and knew they were on their way even before the ship came alive all around them. Elske felt the quickening and asked, "Can we go up on deck, my Lady?"

"Now you're the impatient one," Beriel observed, refusing. "Remember, your little Nido will come to tell us when that is permitted."

"He is not little anymore."

"Will you marry him?"

"Why should I marry Nido?"

"Why should you marry any man?" Beriel answered. "But you will. You are like a flower for them, and they come around like bees to suck the honey of you, the happiness. But perhaps you will not marry."

"Why should I not marry?" Elske asked her. "When I choose. Who I choose, if he chooses me. When it's a good time for marriage, then if it is good to do, why should I not do it? Yours is the dangerous case, as I think, my Lady."

"I know that, Elske. I don't know why you trouble me with it now."

Elske fell silent.

The ship rocked beneath them, like a cradle, and they swayed on the bunk. The lamp which hung down into the center of the room stayed still. Elske's skin felt cold and her mouth dry, but when Nido opened the door to call them out she stood eagerly.

The floor underfoot—moving—made her stumble clumsily. Beriel promised, "You'll get your sea legs soon, Elske, but until then, be careful. Hold on."

Elske hung on, climbing up the ladder, and scurried to the side of the boat where she could hold on to the railing. The sharp wind blew away her own chills; the taste of salt water on the air moistened her mouth and cheeks. Beriel went off with Nido to look at the section of the stern deck the captain had set aside for her particular use, but Elske stayed where she was and saw the city falling away behind them as the river emptied its waters into the open sea. They sailed out into this open water, until the islands that hugged the shore blended into the mainland, and all together they lay like a flat grey cloud along one horizon. Off to the west the sea moved empty, endless, as the boat sailed southwards. But by the time the sun was lowering itself behind the shelter of land, they had come back close to land, and they dropped anchor in a small cove on one of the islands.

After eating they went below, to sleep. Beriel's bunk had a thin straw mattress, but Elske wrapped herself around in a blanket and climbed into a hammock. This bed swayed with the waters that rocked the boat, and Elske woke many times, and slept again, until at last she could see lightening in the sky outside. Then she rolled herself quietly out of the hammock and let herself quietly out of their small room, and climbed in quiet stockinged feet up the ladder.

The ship was getting under way. Long slow waves rolled under her, lifting her bow and lowering it. The ship was like some snared bird, struggling to rise, but falling.

Elske leaned against the railing as the ship rose and fell under her. The cook had a steaming cauldron set out on his stone hob, but her stomach disliked the smell of food. She would have liked fresh water, though. She walked off-balance over to the helmsman to ask if there was any water. "Are ye blind?" he asked, laughing at his wit.

Elske could only smile, and he relented. He pointed to a barrel at the boat's midsection. A wooden ladle was tied at its side, and she thanked him.

Water cooled her mouth, and moistened it. The wind blew from behind her, lazily, and clouds covered the sky. The deck rolled under her feet, and her legs felt weak.

Elske had just seated herself on cushions provided in their section of the stern, had just closed her eyes, when she was called to answer Beriel's summons. She went slowly down the ladder, feeling that if her feet slipped on the rungs her arms would lack the strength to catch and hold her. In the dark companionway the air was close, and in their cabin, too. Beriel wanted the chamber pot emptied. "Unbolt the shutter," she instructed, "and empty it out of the porthole."

The swaying rolling surging of the ship was stronger, below, and also slower. Elske felt sick, but not with fever; it was as if she had swallowed into her stomach something which it did not wish to keep. A cold sweat misted her face. She turned around to return the chamber pot to its hook under Beriel's bunk—but brought her stomach up into it, instead.

She knew she was vomiting. She had seen men at the Volkking's feast empty their bellies of honey mead and meat. But she did not remember ever having done so herself.

"Elske! Don't—! What—?" And then Beriel laughed. "You're seasick. I never was, not even in storms. Come, you have to get into fresh air. There will be no getting over it if you stay here below. Come," and she lifted Elske onto her feet, then pushed her out the door.

Elske hauled herself back up the ladder.

It was the same clouded sky overhead and the same wood decking underfoot, and Elske fell back onto the same cushions from which she had arisen when summoned. There she spent the long day. Sometimes Beriel was nearby, and sometimes Elske dozed uneasily, and sometimes she stumbled to the barrel for a mouthful of water, and often she leaned over the railing to vomit. In the afternoon, Nido came to sit with her. He had none of his customary liveliness and she knew that he, too, had caught the seasickness. When the ship rode at anchor in protected waters that evening, Elske felt more herself, although she did not eat. Beriel offered consolation.

"Seasickness only lasts a day or two in this gentle weather."

Elske waited for the named time to pass. Nido was his usual self again after only a day, and in two days had forgotten that he ever shared Elske's misery. Elske, who had never before had any such misery, had enough now to share with any who asked. She lived on deck, in the fresh air, and refused to go below, even in rain. She slept out on the deck, also, because even at anchor the ship swayed with the movement of the water. After a few days, she found she could keep some of the evening meal down. "That's a good thing, or you'd starve. The captain says there's some, the sea always brings up their stomachs," Beriel reported, scraping clean her own bowl of stewed fish.

Elske waited three days, then four, five.

Eight days, then nine, ten—

"Do you never complain?" Nido asked her. "You look like you're dying, all pale and greeny. How can you stand it?"

Elske endured. Beriel grew impatient with her, and restless, too. "This ship is twenty paces long, and I've walked it a hundred times. More than a hundred. I've explored into every cabin—although the captain was none too pleased to show me his, and he doesn't know I could find his strongbox where he thinks it's so well-concealed. I've counted every piece of cargo. Don't you want to know what we're carrying, Elske?"

"No," Elske said, but at the sight of Beriel's bored displeasure she found words in her throat to add, "Later, perhaps. Perhaps tonight."

"Tonight I'll be tired, sleepy not restless. I need

to tell you now. There are a dozen barrels—hidden away under the stacks of furs. Barrels the same size as they store ale in but marked by dustings of fine, dark powder. Do you know what I think we are carrying?"

"Later," Elske answered, and Beriel went off to join Nido at his work of repairing one of the chairs from the captain's cabin.

"You look terrible," everyone said to her, and Elske smiled weakly, and nodded her agreement, unable to speak. The times she felt well enough for company, most of the others were asleep, except for whichever sailors stood the watch; those men made her companions of the journey. The ship rode quietly at night, and by dawn Elske often felt entirely well. Now that she knew sickness, she could recognize and name this well-feeling, and take pleasure in it, too. Until the ship raised anchor and set sail again.

As they moved southwards, into spring, spring rushed northwards to greet them. When they were not more than a few nights from Trastad, the night air warmed enough so that Elske was never wakened by the cold. When they were at almost two sennights' distance, Elske could smell on a light wind, blowing off the land, the sweetness of flowers. In Trastad, when a flower came into bloom, if you bent over it you could just catch its perfume. Here in the south, the air itself was flowered. "Does it always smell so, the southern air?" she asked Beriel.

"It's only spring," Beriel answered, but this was Elske's fifteenth spring, and this was more than spring.

And then one afternoon, while sunlight poured

down over the deck of the ship and the sails thumped sullenly on their masts, she could see a cluster of buildings on the distant shore, where a wide river entered. Behind the houses, a dark forest spread backwards, so thick and heavy that it seemed to be pushing the little wooden buildings into the water. That day the captain lingered far out to sea, and it was almost full dark before he brought the ship close in, to anchor. Nido explained to Elske, "That town has no name, but all know to keep a distance from it. They're thieves, pirates—and they sell slaves. They can be bribed, sometimes, if your cargo means less to them than gold, but they always choose to board and take Trastader vessels."

"This is where I go ashore, Nido," Beriel announced.

"My Lady, you can't go to shore here. What kind of a man do you think my captain is, to leave two unescorted women here? What kind of a fool do you think him, to put himself in danger by lingering at this place?"

Beriel didn't hesitate. "Enough of a fool to transport barrels of what looks like ground charcoal into the south, but which someone might—or might not—guess to be black powder," she said to Nido's surprised face. Then she added, "I wonder if the Council knows what Var Kenric is shipping into the south, or why one of Var Kenric's near relatives has been given the position of assistant carpenter, when he hasn't completed four years of his apprenticeship and the requirement is for seven. I wonder if Var Jerrol—who is the eyes and ears of the Council— can have been kept ignorant of this merchandise or if it isn't, instead, his own, alone or in partnership with Var Kenric, and the Council kept blind and deaf on this matter. Tell your captain this, if he objects, and tell him that I require to be delivered onto land in the morning. Your ship is safely south of Pericol and we will make our further way by ourselves. Isn't that right, Elske?" Beriel asked.

Elske agreed. She would have agreed to anything that marked the end of this terrible journey.

Chapter 14

WHILE NIDO WAS rowing them to shore in the morning, Elske watched the ship fall back, and away. The curved wooden sides rose high out of the water, and the tall masts stretched up into a pale sky. Nido's oars dipped and pulled in the water. He tried to persuade Beriel to sail on to Celindon, to make a safer journey from that city, but his words affected her no more than the slapping of the waves affected their little boat. When he'd pulled the little boat up onto a narrow beach, Nido gave Beriel his hand, still making his quarrels. "Leave me," Beriel answered him, and he obeyed.

Beriel was impatient. "Come along," she commanded Elske. "What are you doing?"

"Looking back," Elske said. She had looked back over the distance to flames, leaving the Volkaric, and now she looked back to sails being raised, leaving Trastad.

"It'll take us the better part of the morning to reach Pericol and I'd like to be far from that place before dark has fallen," Beriel said. "Take up the pack."

But Elske had started to undress, letting her overskirt fall to the ground.

"*Now* what are you doing?"

"Putting on the trousers. I can make you a pair, in a day; we could delay that day. It would be safer to travel as a pair of young men, wouldn't it?"

"I doubt anything could keep us safe from these citizens of Pericol who try everything—rape and robbery, and there are some who enjoy torture, or we might be sold into slavery. I know them. If Josko is still their King, I've dealt with him before, but if he has been killed—"

"Who would kill the King?"

"Any one of these cutthroats who thought he could get away with it. But Josko is strong, and cruel, a madman in a fight they say. Also, he makes fair judgements, and even thieves and pirates prefer some order in their lives, in their home city. Even thieves and pirates like to keep their possessions and women to themselves. So they allow Josko to rule over them."

"None would have dared to attack the Volkking."

"Josko has his protections. He has Wileen, and although a man might leave Josko sitting in his own blood, he knows he must then deal with Wileen— who would take revenge."

"Why would you know such people?" Elske tied her trousers at the waist.

"He held me captive the first time I came through Pericol, to go to Trastad. But Josko enjoyed a bold child. Who was a girl child. Who paid her own ransom. Who claimed to be Queen, and could make him laugh."

"Perhaps then you *should* wear trousers, my Lady, now that you aren't a child."

"A Queen," and here Beriel paused, as if troubled

195

for the way to speak it, "must always be seen to be a Queen. I will never be otherwise." She looked at Elske, in trousers and the Wolfer boots, her shirt hanging out loose and her cloak draped over one shoulder. "You'll do for my escort, perhaps; and it is well for you to try, for I've never treated with Josko and not had soldiers nearby. Tie your hair back, and now can we go?"

They scrambled along the land's edge, which was sometimes stony outcropping, sometimes stony beach, and every now and then a shallow cove with a narrow pebbled beach at its heart. Elske followed Beriel, her feet too warm in the boots but too softened by the years in Trastad for barefooted comfort. She had the pack slung across her back, carrying Beriel's clothing as well as the maps Beriel had copied from those Var Vladislav kept. What wealth they had, Beriel carried in three purses. The lightest purse was at her waist. She had one not quite so light hidden under her skirt, at the side. The third and richest purse was in fact the hem of her skirt, which Elske had sewn up in little pockets for storage of coins, and golden chains, and the heavy medallion, the best of her wealth. Before leaving Trastad, Beriel had purchased a knife for Elske, and she carried her own; they wore their weapons sheathed, but only half hidden.

Beriel had said it was unwise to show weapons too openly in Pericol. That might be taken as a challenge, or a threat, or even a game; but games in Pericol were as deadly as challenges and threats. Also, it was unwise to appear helpless, if you wanted to reach Josko safely.

"We will have to see him," Beriel said, picking her

way over the stones which the withdrawing tides had left damp and slippery. She held her skirts up, but they were still wet, and dark with mud. "Only he can offer us the mounts we need and make it easier for us to supply ourselves at a fair price. That is," Beriel laughed, "fair price in Pericol. Even the profit-mongering merchants of Trastad would be ashamed to take what the tradesmen of Pericol demand for their goods."

"Do they receive what they demand?" Elske wondered.

"It depends on how desperate the need. It's cheaper, often, to murder than to purchase; and the tradesmen know this, too."

Like the Volkking's stronghold, Pericol had no outlying farmlands, although there were a few huts—small gardens spread out before them, fishing nets spread out to dry on straw roofs—huddled together at the shore. Then there appeared a dirt path.

Beriel led Elske along this path, which kept them to single file through dense and overgrown woods before it became broad enough to walk abreast on, as it ran between crowded wooden buildings and became a muddy street. Branches and logs had been scattered along the street to make it firmer underfoot. There were no fences, no flowers, no trees in Pericol. Pericol was mud streets and log houses, two stubby docks and a single well; they could have crossed the city in no more time than it took the sun to rise.

It was midday by the time they entered the city, and the citizens were just stirring awake. Shutters were thrown open, and men called to one another from doorways, rubbing their faces and urinating. The sky had filled with clouds but the air was still warm. Elske followed Beriel.

Beriel walked without haste or hesitation, her shoulders high. Some of the men in doorways called out to her, but they did not approach. Women called out at her from windows, hooting and mocking; they called to Elske, too, as if she were a young man. Elske walked behind Beriel, as unresponsive as her mistress.

The muddy street twisted down to a broad river, where low, marshy islands floated on glassy water. On the opposite bank, more log houses could be seen. Some coracles were tied up to ramshackle docks, and some masted boats as well, such as a fisherman might take out into the sea. A sign with two gold coins painted on it hung over a doorway, and there Beriel entered.

Elske followed.

The room they entered was lit by many candles, some in lanterns hung on the walls, some standing in a pool of their own wax on wooden tables, some set into wooden rings, like the wheels of wagons, hung down from the ceiling. The air was thick with the smell of ale mingling with smoke from the open fire, odors of roasting meat, sweat, cheese, privies and damp riverside mud. The room was crowded with people, mostly men, lounging on benches along the walls, or gathered around long wooden tables.

At Beriel's entrance, the noise ceased and every eye was fixed upon her.

Beriel ignored this greeting and moved into the room, winding between tables. The noise rose up again like waves around them as Elske followed.

Beriel crossed the room towards a closed door. Following, Elske looked around at drinking men and women with their breasts half pushed out of their bodices. In a back corner, three men looked with hatred across the table at a fourth; but he was not uneasy. Near them, a man and a girl leaned back against a wall; he offered her a coin. In the shadow of the balcony, two men held a third with a knife to his throat and a hand over his mouth. The third man's eyes wept with fear and fury; his hands couldn't reach to the sword at his side, for they were pinned back behind him; his booted feet kicked out, and his captors backed away, mocking. He was a young man, bearded, and his red hair shone like fire out of the shadows in which he struggled to save his life. At one of the tables in the center of the room, a grey-haired woman—looking like one of the distinguished Varinnes of Trastad—dealt out cards to narrow-eyed men, who tossed their wagers into a bowl she had set before her. At another table, two women sat on the laps of two men and all four laughed openmouthed, and drank from tankards.

Beriel was observed, but not questioned. She was watched, but not accosted. Everything about Beriel declared that she had a purpose and a right to be where she was, going whence she went. Elske followed in the wake of Beriel's passage, looking all about her.

The door opened before Beriel had raised a fist to knock. A man stood framed in it, his face bright with greeting. His thin brown hair was tied back, his grey-brown beard was trimmed short, and his smile showed brown teeth. He held out a hand and Beriel put hers into it.

The room behind watched all of this.

The man wore a dark tunic, not clean, and tights. A sword hung at his side and he had a pair of knives in his belt. He wore golden rings on his fingers and golden hoops in his ears. Raising Beriel's hand to his mouth, and bowing over it, he watched the room behind her.

"Welcome, my Queen. I welcome you to my humble manor," he said. His voice was rich as red wine, and loud, to carry all around the tavern. "You honor me with this unexpected visit. Please, enter." He stepped back to let Beriel pass. Elske followed.

When they were through, he closed the door behind them and asked, "Was that greeting enough, Queenie? Was that the honor you looked for?"

This chamber was as large as the room they'd just crossed. A curtained bed stood at the rear, beside another closed door. Two chairs with cushioned seats and backs, and carved arms like thrones, were set out near to the fire. In one of them sat a woman, a jeweled pin in the yellow hair that tumbled in curls down onto her shoulders, her dress a bright woven blue and her stockinged feet resting on a pillow. The woman glanced at Elske without interest. It was Beriel who commanded her attention.

"I am flattered that you come to me without soldiers," the man said. "This—boy—not being, as I take it, much of a soldier."

Beriel didn't answer the man. Instead, she returned to the door through which they had just entered. She opened it wide and stood in the open doorway until the room outside fell silent again, and then she raised her arm and pointed. She motioned with that hand, and waited.

Elske could not see past her mistress. She could see only the fall of Beriel's cloak and her brown hair, hanging in a long braid down her back, and her arm raised, imperiously.

The red-haired young man, his face still wet with tears, stepped into the room, a hand on the hilt of his sword, his eyes fixed on Beriel's face as if hearing words she did not speak.

"What do you—?" their host said, but Beriel interrupted his thought.

"Did you permit the slaughter on your very doorstep, Josko? Had you given those two louts permission to take this fellow?"

"I have nothing to steal," the young man protested to Josko. His beard might be soft, and his eyes might weep, but he was no coward. "Why do they attack me? I have not a single coin."

"Oh, well," Josko answered, and a smile returned to his face. "You have youth, and good boots, that's a sweet piece of steel you carry even if it is plain-hilted—"

"They would have killed me," the young man insisted, indignant. "What kind of law do you have here?"

"As little as possible," Josko answered lightly. "What regulation there is exists to protect our own citizens. My own people, I should say, for this place is *my* stronghold."

"And it's not much of a place, neither," the young man said. He might have a fox's hair, but he did not have a fox's cunning. "You ought to warn strangers."

"But would that work to my advantage?" Josko asked, patiently. "For then my people might have to turn against themselves for their livelihoods, and eventually they would have to turn on me. No, we welcome strangers to Pericol. They are our lifeblood."

The woman, who had been silent at the back of the room, rose then, and came forward to them. "This is tiresome and you are only teasing," she said. "Get on with it, Josko."

"Beriel must tell me, then, what she wanted with this fellow," Josko answered. "He's handsome enough, if you like pink cheeks. Do you think he's pretty enough for Beriel, Wileen?"

Nobody responded to this jesting.

"There's a door at the back of the room, boy," Beriel said. "Anyone who leaves through that door has Josko's hand over his head until the next daybreak. After that, you'll be fair game again. Go now," she commanded, putting up a hand to silence whatever he might have said to her, and he obeyed.

"You're in my debt now, Queenie," Josko said. "To the measure of one life."

"I have owed you a life for years now," Beriel answered, "and I begin to hope that you will never call that debt in."

"This is the gratitude of a Queen?" Josko laughed, and beside him, Wileen smiled approval.

"And I have another favor to ask of you," Beriel said. "Two favors, if you keep careful count, and that makes three, if we include the life just granted."

"By all means let it be included," Josko said. "May I offer you refreshment, and to your man, also?"

"No, but we thank you," Beriel said.

Josko and Wileen seated themselves in the two chairs before the fire, and Beriel stood before them with Elske at her shoulder, but several paces back.

Elske was overly warm now, in her cape and fur boots, so close to a fire. Beriel stood in the petitioner's position, but she seemed to be granting rather than asking.

"I ask to purchase two horses from your stables, and a supply of food, too."

"You aren't going to stay with us until an escort arrives? The first ships are expected to pass within two sennights, if the weather holds. Your own escort is looked for daily," Wileen said. She leaned forward to ask, "If I were suspicious, I might think that you wished to evade the company of your own soldiers."

"Why should I trouble my soldiers when I can ride to meet them?" Beriel asked.

"I might wonder if you intend to return to your home," Wileen asked.

"There I can reassure you," Josko said. "Queenie would never give up her throne, not of her own choice, not of her own will, not alive."

"She's not the crowned Queen," Wileen pointed out. "For all that her father is dead, and buried, and she the eldest—"

"The King is dead?" Beriel demanded. "When?"

"Word reached us at winter's end, with the first who came out from the Kingdom," Wileen said.

"The King is dead, long live the King," Josko added.

"My brother is crowned." It was not a question. Beriel looked over her shoulder at Elske, for once indecisive, for the first time since Elske had known her, unsure.

"Perhaps he's not yet crowned," Josko said. "What will you do?" he asked Beriel.

"Claim my throne," Beriel said. "So I ask you for

horses, and food, and I will pay you twice their worth if you can answer me speedily."

"If you can pay so much, why should I let you go?" Josko asked. "When your pockets are so thick with gold—more than you offer, I'm sure. When there might be a King in the Kingdom who would be glad to sit unopposed on his throne, why should I give you what you ask?"

"Because the gratitude of a true Queen is a treasure," Beriel answered him, "while the thanks of a false Prince come stuffed with adders. Because the King of Thieves might someday need a deeper hiding place than Pericol, and a friend to help him live comfortably there."

"A Queen's word being law in her own Kingdom," Josko observed.

"As long as the man seeking sanctuary abides by the laws of the land," Beriel answered.

Josko turned to Wileen then, to ask, "It has value, don't you think?"

She agreed, and asked, "Do we need a pass? Some written word?"

"Well thought, queen of my heart." He gave Beriel paper, ink and quill. While she wrote he asked Wileen, "But what if Guerric should be King and this paper prove worthless?"

"He'll kill her for certain, then, if she has made a public challenge, and we'll be out two horses and some food, plus the life of a nondescript young man. A bearable loss," Wileen decided.

"No; too unequal," Josko announced. He stood up. "You," he said to Elske. "Come to me."

Elske looked to Beriel, who nodded. Elske

approached the man until she stood not two paces before him.

"A life for a life," he suggested. "This life for that young man's. What do you say, Queenie?"

Beriel was shaking her head. "I say, this is my proved servant, when there is no other I can trust. I do not wish to be parted from this servant."

"I do not wish it, either, Josko," Wileen said, but she spoke as if this were some small and careless thing.

"And do I obey your wishes?" Josko asked Wileen.

"You know the answer to that," she said to him.

He walked around Elske, looking her up and down, and answered Wileen. "You know that you are not my wife."

She answered him, "I don't need to be a wife to keep a man at my side."

Beriel said, "I will take my chances in the streets of Pericol before I will part with this servant."

"You would have no chance," Josko told her, amused.

Beriel said nothing, for a long time. Then she spoke. "I would have a chance."

"Leave the lad be," Wileen said to Josko.

"Lad?" he asked, and in one swift move he had a knife from his belt and with his free hand shoved Elske backwards, until he held her pinned against the wall. The point of the dagger was at her throat as sharp as a needle, and the man looked down into her eyes.

He meant rape. She could see that. There was nothing she could do against him. But he would not live long afterwards. That she promised herself, staring back into his mud-colored eyes.

And Josko released her. He lowered the knife and took his hand from her shoulder to take her by the hair at the back of her head. "This is no lad." He pulled her around to set her in front of Wileen. "Haven't you got eyes? This is a girl, and she's dangerous. I think she's even more dangerous than you are, Queenie," Josko said. "But if you want to be a lad and you can't grow a beard—I'd better cut your hair for you," he said, bringing his knife around.

"If I were you, I'd settle for stripping the girl of her boots," Wileen said with laughter in her voice. "They're worth at least one life, if you ask me. Wolfskin, is my guess, and warm enough for Wolfers in their snowy caves. How would a girl get a pair of Wolfer boots?"

Josko shoved Elske back towards Beriel. "How indeed?" he asked, and "Do you refuse me the boots?" he asked Beriel.

Beriel raised her hand, in a gesture of command, and Elske bent over, pulled off her boots one after the other, and gave them to Beriel. Beriel presented them to Josko, who set them down beside his feet. They looked like a child's boots there beside his heavy leather ones, so he picked them up, and laid them in Wileen's lap.

"I'm honored by the gift, Josko," she said. "And yes, pleased, too. You're in a generous humor to let these two pass safely."

"And horses? Food?" Beriel asked.

He held out his hand, and she gave Elske the light purse from her waist, to hold, while she reached up under her skirt to take out the heavier one. This she gave to Josko, without even counting the coins in it.

He weighed it on the palm of his hand. "Two horses from my stables, and tell the men to fetch you bread and cheese for a sennight's journey."

"How *did* you get the boots?" Wileen asked Elske.

"I am Wolfer born," she answered.

"Wolfer?" This interested Josko. "How do you know she is not a spy?" he asked Beriel.

"But she is a spy," Beriel answered him, and now she was the one laughing.

"So that's how you plan to do it," Josko said. "You'll use Wolfers."

Wileen disagreed. "Beriel wouldn't betray her own people."

"She's ambitious for the crown," Josko answered her.

"Beriel is a Queen," Wileen said. "She would never give her land over to Wolfers."

"What do you wager me?" Josko asked her, and she was thinking of her answer when Beriel interrupted their game to ask, "Do I have your leave to go?"

They both stood up, then, stood side by side. "We give you leave, Beriel, Queen that may be. And you have given us your word for safe passage, safe keeping, in need."

"You have my word," Beriel affirmed.

She left the room without looking back, and Elske followed in her stockinged feet. Beriel hesitated at the doorway, to let Elske hold it open for her.

Outside, late afternoon light filled the air and painted the river gold and red where it flowed past Pericol and out into the sea. Beriel hesitated on the covered wooden porch. The steep muddy bank fell away below them; if they had wished, they could have climbed up on the railing and jumped into the water, to join all the other men and women who had fallen out of the world from Josko's porch.

After taking a little time for thought, Beriel descended the staircase to a path along the high riverbank, with Elske following. Something stirred under the staircase and Beriel had her dagger out before she had turned. Elske also had drawn.

A man spoke as he emerged, crawling and cob-webbed. "Lady." He brushed dirt from his face and red hair, and his knees, too. He straightened up, then bowed clumsily from the waist. "My Queen. I owe you my life."

"You *are* one of my people," Beriel said. "Your name?"

"Win. I am the third son of the innkeeper at the Ram's Head."

"In Hildebrand's demesne."

"Yes, under Northgate's banner."

Beriel wore her royalty as naturally as her own skin and as she drew close to her own land, her queenliness intensified, or so it seemed to Elske, but now she turned to Elske like any girl in her delight at her own cleverness. "I thought he was. I *knew* he was mine. Tell me, Win," she demanded, turning back to where he stood red-cheeked, eyes shining. "Why have you come to Pericol, and without any coins to buy food or safety? Do you flee the law? Has winter been so harsh in Northgate's lands that younger sons must find livings outside of the Kingdom?"

"I came to protect you, my Queen."

Beriel asked no more. "Then you must travel with

me. Stay hidden while we get horses and food. I'll look for you just within the forest."

He bowed, and Beriel walked on along the path, without another word for him, or a glance to see what direction he chose. Elske followed Beriel.

At the stables, the men gave Beriel a wide-backed grey palfrey and a livelier chestnut, and one seat and tack, but said that her manservant would have to ride barebacked. Beriel insisted that they find some kind of bit and reins for Elske, and they did. She insisted that Elske be given a blanket, folded, to sit on, and they found one. She insisted that the stable boy be sent for the food Josko had ordered, and he was. She required the men to find a pair of boots, of a size for her servant, and one of them ran after the stable boy to tell him that, then ran back to face Beriel.

Beriel refused to step out of the sun and into the shadowy stables, and so the two men brought the horses out for her inspection, and got them ready. Through all of this, Elske said nothing; she was a sullen lad accompanying his mistress on her willful way, a lad who could not be bothered even to raise his eyes to watch the dealings his mistress conducted.

"You'll want hobbles," the stable men told Beriel. Their greedy eyes had noted the purse at Beriel's waist. "Otherside, if these two get loose they'll come back to us like calves to their mothers at feeding time, and don't think our Josko doesn't know that."

Beriel thought hard about the question, her brow wrinkled, her mouth frowning. At last, she offered two silver coins, for two hobbles. The men were pleased. The boy returned with heavy round loaves of bread and a wheel of cheese, two strings of onions, and also a pair of heavy, much-worn boots. Elske stuffed straw into the toes, and shoved her feet into them, as she thought a boy might who resented wearing another man's boots. She put the food into the pack she carried.

"That's a fine seat Josko has given me," Beriel remarked to one of the men, and he smiled to show his three remaining teeth and tell her, "That 'tis. It belonged to the widow of a tanner, from the south, fleeing Wolfers. Josko let her pass through—in exchange for a horse and its gear, and a handful of coins, and a certain necklace of twisted gold that Wileen fancied, set with bright blue stones, as I was told. Whether she made it to the safety of Trastad we don't know. That would be up to the captain of the boat, wouldn't it?" he asked Beriel, smiling.

She didn't answer him.

"There's worse than Wolfers, to sniff out a fat widow," he said. "Or a proud young woman, ill-attended."

Beriel stared at him until his smile faded, and his eyes lowered to elude her gaze, and he bowed his head to her as she walked past him. "We'll walk the horses out of Pericol," she announced, "as Josko has given us safe passage through." She took the reins, and led the chestnut, which followed her without hesitation, as did Elske, leading her own mount and carrying their pack on her back.

Pericol the city ended abruptly, muddy streets becoming a thin dirt track at the last log house. Then they were on a narrow path through forest, with the river somewhere nearby but hidden from sight. Elske could smell the river, sometimes, and when Win stepped out onto the path to join them, his boots were damp from clambering along its bank. He hailed them, cheerful as a robin.

He gave his hands to help Beriel mount and held the reins while she settled into the seat, her legs to one side. Then he gave his hands to Elske. There was no way for Elske to ride comfortably or safely unless she rode astride, which suited her trousers. Win said he could trot along behind them and catch up when they halted, but Beriel did not allow that. "You would slow our progress," she said, and ordered him first to tie the pack onto her own mount and then to ride seated behind Elske.

While they traveled, they listened closely but could hear only forest sounds. It was midspring here, leaves unfurling and birds restlessly nesting and the quick quiet animals on their daytime hunts. Nobody trailed them out of Pericol. Josko's hand was over them, for the day.

They used what was left of that day to move north, putting as much distance as they could between themselves and Pericol.

Chapter 15

AS THEY TRAVELED northwards, leafy trees and thick undergrowth separated them from the river, for the traders who used this path hoped to remain hidden from the river and its pirates. As they traveled, the sun lowered into the west, until the trees were black silhouettes against an orange sky, and still Beriel did not rein in her horse.

Win told Elske that it was seven days' journey on horseback from Pericol to the Falcon's Wing, the inn at the southernmost point of the Kingdom. "At a horse's walking gait," he said, adding, "It took me longer, but I was on foot." As they rode on into the evening he started to sing. His songs told stories: of the young hunter who chased a white doe into the forest, where she turned into a beautiful Princess, and he stayed with her forever, and was never seen again; of the soldier glad to die in battle for his King, although he also thought sadly back to his wife and children, in the village he would never see again; of Jackaroo on his winged horse, and how he disguised himself as a puppeteer and went from north to south with the fairs, to see that all was well in the Kingdom.

"And if he sees that all is well?"

"Then he goes back to sleep under the mountain, and is never seen again."

Elske laughed. "All of your songs come to the same ending—'never seen again.'"

Win was merry. "Is that not life's ending, also?"

Beriel looked around then. "This singing and chattering," she said. "It displeases me."

Elske asked, "How can it displease you?" but Win said, "I apologize, my Queen," so seriously that Elske quelled her own high spirits. After that, Win would only hum, the melody repeating and repeating, to pass the time.

Elske thought of Beriel's queenly imperiousness, and kept her thoughts her own. Beriel in desperate need in Trastad was not the same companion as Beriel riding to claim her Kingdom. And how could she be unchanged, whatever Elske might wish?

The air grew murky, thick, purpled with the shadows that were closing in around them. Still Beriel rode on, and even when night cloaked them so they could barely see one another, she did not stop. So at last Win called ahead to her, "My Queen, there is a clearing, with the firestones set and a fire built. We're a safe distance from Pericol, and it's not wise to ask the horses to walk on when none can see what lies on the path."

Beriel reined in her horse. "Here?"

"Soon," Win said, and it was no time at all until he said, "There."

In the darkness, the clearing could be felt more than seen, until Win took a tinderbox out of his purse and struck it, to start a fire. When the dry twigs and grasses had infected the sticks and logs with flame, they could see the circle of stones and the tall ring of trees that fenced a flat space, grassy underfoot. Win had hobbled the horses by then and Elske had opened the pack to remove bread and cheese. "There is water in a bucket. On one of the trees—here. I had only half of it, less than half."

Beriel had seated herself on a log, her cloak gathered around her. Elske lifted down the bucket and read, in the restless light from the fire, a notice that hung above it. "To who comes after me, Fill this for who comes after you: that none go thirsty." She carried the bucket over to Beriel, who dipped her hand into it, and drank.

"Why didn't you fill it again?" Elske asked Win, as they awaited their turn to drink. Win looked surprised, as if she were asking him some unlikely question, so she explained, "The notice asks you to refill the bucket for whoever comes next."

"You can read?"

"You cannot," Elske realized.

"He's not a Lord," Beriel explained to Elske. "Only the Lords are taught letters, and some of the Ladies if they ask to learn. As I did," she said. "Come, sit and eat. There are things I would ask you, innkeeper's son."

Win sat on the ground. Elske cut off chunks of bread, offering them to Beriel first, and then the young man, then she cut hunks of cheese. They kept the bucket of water where all could dip into it. The fire crackled and burned, the horses grazed and stamped, and all around them the forest whispered in the wind. A disk of dark sky above was filled with stars, as thick as daisies scattered in a field.

"Who are you?" Beriel asked. "Who are you, really?"

Elske had difficulty remembering that just that morning she had awakened on a ship, on the sea, all the air salty.

"I am just what I said, my Queen, the youngest son of the innkeeper at the Ram's Head."

And she had long forgotten the smoke-choked air of Mirkele's little house, and the wide skies that spread out over the treeless land of the Volkaric.

"Why would a son of the innkeeper at the Ram's Head be sent to protect me?"

Elske had no part in their talk. She was content to sit, and chew on the thick bread, and watch the skies, and listen.

"But nobody sent me, nobody knows—I don't know what they think happened to me."

"Then what have you to protect me against?"

"A plot. Against you, against your life, if you were to return unwed. He said—"

"Who said?"

"The King. Your brother. King Guerric, who was crowned at the end of winter, thirty days after his father's death."

Beriel rose, then, and walked away from the fire to stare into the thick black forest. At last, she turned, and returned to her seat. She asked then, "Said what, Win? What did he say? This King."

"It was whispers," Win answered uneasily. "I do not believe them."

"Speak it."

"They said, that you had formed a shameful alliance and were with child."

"And the man?"

"He'd been put to death, as would you have been were you not a royal Princess. Guerric said . . ." Win stopped again. "Lady, there is truth in me, even if it angers you to hear what I tell you. There are many of the people who believe you should have been crowned, and I think there must be those among the Lords, also. What I speak is treason against the King, I know, and if you tell me I must die for it, then I will."

Beriel waited.

"The land trembles, my Queen," Win took up his tale, after waiting for her silence to end. "This is more than fear of change. The new King has taken two cousins for his advisors, making the eldest his First Minister and giving the younger rule over the Priests and laws. The new King keeps the army under his own hand. The soldiers are restless—the King's courage is untested and they doubt his generalship. The Priests complain that young Lord Aymeric lacks foresight and judgement; moreover, he cannot even read the laws, having lost whatever knowledge of letters he once had. The Lords are angry when Lord Ditrik stands between them and their sworn King, to whom they owe their allegiance, and who owes them honors in return."

"And the people?" Beriel asked.

"The people are frightened. Their few coins are squeezed out of them, like cider from apples, and those who have no coins are set deeper into servitude. The people think of Jackaroo, and some dare to speak aloud of him. They hoard food in their own cellars, for themselves and their families; they begin to look on their neighbors with untrusting eyes. The people say you have forgotten them. Some say you have married the Emperor of the East, leaving the Kingdom to the ravages of your brother, and some say you have blessed the Kingdom by leaving it to its rightful King, and these two factions distrust one another. All agree that you have abandoned your Kingdom. But I knew you would not," Win said.

"How would you know that?" Beriel asked.

"You are our Queen," Win answered. "You could not abandon us. I saw you once—when you were a girl, a child—"

"How can that be, when you are yet so young?"

"My Queen, I have two or three years more than you. Do not mistake me, for all that I look young, and soft. Let others overlook me, but do not you. I saw you the once, at a hanging offered your father and his retinue for their entertainment, when they visited Earl Northgate."

"The man did not die well," Beriel remembered.

"No, not bravely. And he was a murderer who struck his victim from behind, and we all knew that of him. But his wife asked mercy for him—"

"I remember."

"For the sake of his children. The King refused it."

"Do you question the King's judgement in that?"

"No. And neither did you, except—"

"Except?" Beriel demanded.

"You sent one of your maidservants with a purse of coins for the family, so that they would not starve, so that the widow might have a dowry to attract another husband for herself and father for the children. You asked only that the gift be kept secret."

"What was the woman to you?" Beriel asked.

"A woman of the village, only that, but she had made an unthrifty marriage. I have a troublesome heart," Win smiled, his teeth showing in the firelight, "as my father and brothers will tell you, mother and sisters, too. My heart was troubled for the woman, and her children."

"What was the woman to you?" Beriel asked again, patient.

Win lowered his head. "The man was my uncle. None from the inn offered kindness to his wife, because they were shamed by him. He was a villain and a coward, as we all knew. But his deeds were not done by his wife, nor by his children. Were they? You knew that they were not, my Queen, even when you were a child yourself."

"So I had sealed you to me, and I never knew your face," Beriel said, not displeased.

"So it is with many of the people. You are our hope."

"Which is why you came to warn me."

"And save you, if I can. He plots your death, this Guerric, whom I will not call my King."

"It is not for you to choose who rules," Beriel reminded him.

"I choose who I serve," Win said, proudly.

"So might you change your loyalty, should you be displeased."

"I think I am loyal," Win said, so simply that Elske knew he could be trusted. "You are the firstborn and the heir under the law, unless you renounce your claim. Do you renounce your claim? If so, let me go with you, to serve you in whatever foreign land you like. If so, let us turn around now, because Guerric will not leave you alive five days within the Kingdom."

Beriel brushed aside that danger. "He cannot murder me."

"My Queen," Win said, rising up onto his knees.

"You must believe me. Your safety lies in believing what I say. I am a man often trusted with another's secret joys, or fears. The short of it is that I have friends among the soldiers. They have told me this: The King has formed an escort to meet your vessel when it lands."

"As there was an escort to see me onto the ship last fall."

Elske didn't know why Beriel thwarted the telling of Win's tale, as if she needed to test Win's loyalty. So although she longed for sleep and rest, Elske kept herself awake, lest her mistress need her.

Win argued, "This escort will be different. Each soldier will be a stranger to all the others, because each man comes from a different village or city, each serves in a different company. Their orders depend on what they find when you step off the ship. Should you have a child with you, they will bring you back in chains to stand trial for your misconduct; and Guerric has ordered the Priests to prepare a case to try you by. If you have no child, then you must not arrive back in the Kingdom alive; and each soldier will be given a purse of gold. Gold is the prize the King offers to rid himself of this shamed sister. Should you bring a guard of your own hire, then it will be battle, until you and all who are with you are dead, as if by robbery."

"This is known?" Beriel demanded.

"Only by the soldiers of the King's chosen escort."

"No soldier questions the order?"

"There are enough who say that where smoke rises, there fire burns, and there are those who would save a civil war, and always there are those who wish to continue the gold that flows into their purses while Guerric rules," Win answered.

"Having less to lose, in wealth, in lands, in reputation, the people can see farther into the truth," Beriel said. "The people will support me."

"Think you?" Win asked. "Having less to lose, in wealth and lands and reputation, don't they guard their little more jealously?" But with the dangers defined, Win settled back, leaning against the log on which Beriel sat. He asked, "What will you do, my Queen?"

"I'll sleep," Beriel said. "I'll consider what you tell me. Then, sleep and waking, I'll consider further. We leave at first light," she told them.

This was the permission Elske had been waiting for, to slip down onto the ground and close her eyes.

It seemed to Elske that she had barely rested a moment when Beriel was shaking her by the shoulder, dragging her up and away from the comfort of sleep. Win refilled the bucket with water from the river and they loosed the horses. "We'll eat as we go," Beriel ordered. They were mounted and on their way before the first yellow beams of sunlight came tumbling down through the trees.

Once again Win rode behind Elske, his arms around her waist, and Beriel carried their pack behind her. Win rode silently, or sang softly to himself and Elske. There were more tales of Jackaroo, how Jackaroo dressed the bride, and how Jackaroo brought the three robbers to hanging. There was the song of a fisherman, calling to the fish as if he wooed them, and the song of an old woman after her man had died. There were children's songs in plenty. The Kingdom was a place where stories grew as plentifully as apples on a tree, Elske thought; Tamara would have been at home in the Kingdom.

On this sunlit day, far from Pericol, Beriel sometimes rode beside them and joined Win in his singing, her displeasure of the previous day forgotten. So the day's journey, although long, passed pleasantly.

That second evening, once again Beriel and Win talked about Guerric and his rule over the Kingdom, until Win said, hesitantly, "Also, my Queen. Also, there are tales from the northernmost holdings."

Elske pictured the map Beriel had shown her, the northern borders of the Kingdom up against high mountains.

"Where at the northern borders? The royal lands? Hildebrand's?"

"In Northgate's lands, under Hildebrand, but— it's cruel, my Queen."

Elske wondered what this news could be, if Win was more reluctant to speak it than he had been to tell of Guerric's plots.

"I have stomach for the cruelty of truth," Beriel said.

"A band of—wild men, thieves, monsters—"

Then Elske knew the end of his tale.

"They came out of the forests at the end of summer. They fell upon isolated holdings, one village, too. One boy glimpsed them and he ran home to tell his father of the strangers, but he found his father's holding in flames and all his family slaughtered, except for the youngest child, a girl of seven winters, and she was gone. Lord Hildebrand sent out his soldiery, and they found a number of holdings so destroyed, but they could find no battle. The enemy slipped away. The soldiers brought back one old woman in jabbering madness, who said it was the northern wind, howling, taking human form. They burn their victims like logs on a fire, while they eat and drink in its warmth."

"Do we know what they are?" Beriel asked.

"At the inn, merchants have told stories which we dismissed as the talk of men who enjoy frightening those they think simple, as fathers like to frighten their children. The merchants spoke of warrior bands, swooping down to take anything of value, gold, silver, food, clothing. They kill for the pleasure of killing and take prisoners—dark-haired women, a few men—only rarely. Although why they keep some men and slaughter others, nobody knows."

"For Wolfguard," Elske explained.

"Wolfers," Beriel said. "I thought so. I hoped not."

"These wild men speak gibberish," Win said.

"They speak Norther," Beriel told him, and said to him in Norther, "I thought the Kingdom was hidden away, safe from this danger. I hoped."

"Lady?" Win asked, uncomprehending.

"She spoke in Norther," Elske explained. "I'm Wolfer born," she explained.

"No." The firelight washed over his face like water, making shadows of his eyes, and then revealing his hidden thoughts. He stared closely at Elske, a sudden stranger. He asked Beriel, "How can that be? When you trust her."

"With my life."

Beriel gave this gift to Elske carelessly, as if to be trusted were the common fortune. But Elske opened her heart to take the gift into her care as if it were a babe.

Win made his decision. "If my Queen trusts you, then so will I," he said, and held out his hands to her. "I give you greeting, Lady Elske."

Elske took his hands in hers. This was another true servant to Beriel. "I give you greeting, Win," she said, while Beriel protested, "Elske is my servant."

Win's surprise spoke. "She can read. You trust her with your life. Her dress, hair—this is more than servant."

"If you cannot be a servant, then who will you be?" Beriel asked Elske but answered herself, "I will think who you must be."

Win knew who he was, for Beriel. "I am in your debt for my life," he said, "so it is I who am your servant. And your soldier, too, if you need me, against your brother, against Wolfers. I am your man against any enemy who offers you harm."

"At the moment, you are my eyes and my ears in the Kingdom," Beriel said, and smiled at Elske, then asked, "But what is this Wolfguard you mentioned?"

Elske could tell her. "When the Volkking's warrior bands return in the fall, they must cross lands where wolves roam. So pairs of prisoners are bound together and set out, each night. These the wolves devour, leaving the warriors unharmed."

"The prisoners don't escape?" Win wondered.

"They're hobbled," Elske explained, and at the expression on both of their faces she added, "As we do with our horses."

"But they are men, not animals," Win protested.

"For the people of the Volkaric, they are human animals who cannot speak and have little courage,

223

Fruhckmen. Would you never stake a goat to draw wolves away from your houses?"

Win said, "These Wolfers are fearless, the merchants say. They go into battle armed only with long knives, clad only in animal skins."

"I do not call it battle to attack an undefended holding," Beriel said.

"No human force can stop them," Win said.

"They were stopped in Selby," Elske told them. "My grandmother was a girl in Selby when they fought off the Wolfers, all the men of Selby standing together. The Wolfers can be turned back," she assured Beriel. "At cost," she added. "With courage."

"The merchants say—" Win started, but then didn't finish the thought.

"What do they say?" Beriel demanded, so Win told her this, also. "When you hear their cry, your heart freezes within you. Men have gone mad with fear, from just the Wolfer cry."

"And such enemies have come into my Kingdom?" Beriel cried out, as if she had taken a wound. "How will the crops be put into the fields so there will be food next winter?"

Win agreed. "Fear is plowed like salt into the farmlands of the north."

"And Sutherland?"

"The south feels far from danger. Let the wild men feed off the north, they say, thinking that will guarantee their own safety, with the rivers running between them and danger."

"Wolfers do fear water," Elske told her companions.

"And so we have Northgate's people for a

Wolfguard of our own," Beriel observed bitterly, then said, "I will sleep now."

The long days of the journey passed slowly, in sunshine, clouds or rain. Evenings were spent with whatever news from the Kingdom Win could remember, or guess at. Days held the steady thump of the horses' hooves on the packed dirt pathway and more stories, more songs, more questions from Beriel.

Elske did not need to be told when they had crossed the borders into the Kingdom. Beriel shone with it, like a sun, the Queen in her Kingdom. It was as if each breath she drew increased her pleasure, breathing that air. It was as if each hoof the chestnut planted onto that earth increased her strength. Beriel looked about her, to the broad slow-flowing river and the thick-trunked trees. She looked to the sky, less blue than her eyes.

By midday they had come to an inn, the Falcon's Wing, sleepy grey stone soaking up the spring sunlight. Beriel rode up to the doorway, and dismounted.

"My Queen," Win protested. "They will know you here."

"As they should. I must send messengers to the Earl Sutherland, my uncle, and to the King in his palace, to say when they may expect me."

"My Queen," Win said. "Do you think how this forewarning places you in harm's way?"

"I do not fear the King," Beriel said. "Rather, he should fear me."

"My Queen," Win said, "I think he does."

Beriel smiled up at him then, and offered him a

hand to aid in his dismounting. "So you are more than the country onion you pretend," she said.

The three stood together, looking at the blank stone face of the building before them, and Beriel gave the order. "Announce me, Win. Tell the innkeeper of the Falcon's Wing that I have returned, and have need of messengers, and have need of fresh mounts. Tell him that we require also food for three, with his best ale. I will tell you, Win, since you concern yourself with my safety, that I will be safest riding openly to Sutherland's castle. If all know that I have set off, then all must seek out treachery should I not arrive."

She looked around her then, at the grey stone inn backed up against the tree-clogged forest, at the green meadow stretched out before them and the blue curve of river beyond; all under a bowl of sky out of which a warm and generous sun poured its light. "Is it not beautiful, my Kingdom?" Beriel asked Elske.

Chapter 16

THE MESSENGERS RODE off at the gallop, but Beriel's party rested at the Falcon's Wing. Elske and Beriel walked across the meadow, down to the river's edge and out onto a dock, and when they returned, the innkeeper had set out a platter of baked fish for them, and bread, and onions, and tankards of his own ale. Win was fed in the inn kitchens.

At Beriel's command, Win brought their fresh mounts around. Elske, at Beriel's command, changed her garments, wearing now a dress so that she also must sit her palfrey sideways. Her hair, like Beriel's, hung loose, with only a broad ribbon to hold it back from her face. Win walked behind them until the inn was out of sight, and then once again Beriel took the pack while Win and Elske rode together at her side. As they traveled the King's Way east, Win reported what he had learned in the kitchen and the stables:

Beriel was rumored dead. Where the rumor had started, none could say, but all had heard it. A maidservant had declared that the soldiers would be bringing a dead body back for its burial, not a bride to her wedding day nor a Queen to her people.

There was sadness in her telling, and in the hearing, too, for Beriel had been well-beloved.

There were rumors of a terrible army attacking the north, Wolfers, wild men; but Sutherland's domain was in no danger as long as Earl Northgate's farms and villages satisfied their blood lust. The Wolfers were a destruction from which none escaped. Lands they crossed lay barren—choked with blood, blackened with fires. People lay slaughtered, and worse. Lest they lay hands on him, and his Kingdom founder, the King had taken his court and his soldiers into Arborford, where two armies would give him twice the might, rumor said.

The King had fled for his own safety, the cook muttered over her pastry.

Another rumor reported that the King had a weapon that could spit out fire like a dragon, and when he turned this against the Wolfers they would be driven back. This new weapon burned hotter than fire, and had teeth that could rip a soldier into pieces of flesh that even his own mother wouldn't recognize. With this weapon, the King would preserve his Kingdom, and the people in it. Only King Guerric could save them, rumor said.

Thus, a groom reasoned, if this Lady of Win's was Beriel, Beriel alive, she would cause civil war. The Kingdom would be split over the question of King or Queen. Its men would be taken off into armies, and killed or crippled, the crops would suffer, all would go hungry—and the wonderful new weapon would be turned on its own people. Wolfers from without and the royal family from within: Destruction threatened at every turn of the wheel.

But if this Lady was not Beriel, then there was

hope. And how could this be the Princess, and her dead in that far city where she had gone to seek her husband, since none in the Kingdom could satisfy her proud heart? No, this was not the Princess.

"What did you say to that?" Beriel asked Win.

"I said only that I rode with my Queen, who would separate rumor from fact, and deal with these Wolfers."

"You promised much," Beriel remarked, not displeased. She turned to Elske to ask, "Do you think Guerric has the black powder?" but it was Win who answered, "I think not. I think nobody in the Kingdom knows more of the black powder than— What is it? What? My Queen, what have I said to offend you?"

"What do you know of this weapon?" Beriel demanded.

He reminded her, "Merchants come to an inn. However quietly men may talk among themselves, he who serves them will overhear."

"You serve the inn's tables? But you are a son of the house, not a servant," Beriel protested.

"Among the people, as among the Lords, however different the labors, a son does the work of the house."

Beriel accepted this, and now wanted to know, "What do you hear of the black powder?"

"They say that in the cities of the south, there are those who possess it. They speak of a captain who has made himself a Prince over many cities by its power, and none dare oppose him, for the destruction he can visit upon them. He aims to give his son a royal bride—"

"I have danced with this son, I think," Beriel said.

229

"I did not know he was to be such a King, but if he rules as stupidly as he courts, he will lose all that his father has won. Do my people fear the black powder?"

Win answered apologetically, "Your people fear everything, my Queen. If it is not the terror of the black powder, then it is dread of the consequences of Guerric's crowning or the dread of the consequences of your return. Fear spreads like a plague, and especially in the north where the Wolfers have struck." Then his face grew thoughtful, quiet, and he added, "Or perhaps fear is least in the north, for there they know what dangers they face. Imagined terrors are more fearsome than known, think you, my Queen?"

"I think I will see what awaits us at Sutherland's castle," Beriel decided, and urged her horse on, leading them.

Elske followed her mistress. She knew little of the Kingdom and its ways and had not been sent among the women of the inn, to gather their rumors. She didn't know how she might now help her mistress. There was that in Elske for which this was a gall, and she felt like a sail bereft of wind, a useless thing.

They traveled quickly, not stopping except for what quick refreshment an inn might offer, for fresh horses, for a few hours of sleep out under the open sky, to awake damp with dew. A little more than a day from the Falcon's Wing, they skirted a walled city, and then the King's Way took them across gently rolling lands, through the occasional village. Everywhere, the fields were being tilled and household gardens were being dug over. People came to the roadside to see them pass, as they rode north to

Earl Sutherland's castle. None cried out in welcome, but their eyes were fixed on Beriel.

Beriel looked neither to right nor to left, but she saw everything and later would ask Win if he drew the same conclusions from the same rows of brown earth—"Is it not late for the crops to be going in?"—and the same faces—"Were they not used to be more merry? When I was a child, I thought them carefree."

Elske's impression was that nobody need go hungry here in the Kingdom, with its farms and herds, and Win told her that in his own northern lands there were lakes filled with fish, as well. There was room, and food, for all who might be born into this rich land.

And Beriel, riding always ahead, always now at a canter, was born to be Queen in the Kingdom. Even the horses she rode, which neither tired nor stumbled, seemed to take from her the strength to travel on, day after day, until at last they rode between the high stone gateposts into Earl Sutherland's castle.

They were expected there, and escorted across the yards, and welcomed on the doorstep by the Earl himself, a tall, broad man, grey-haired, with a kindly expression. He looked with brief curiosity at Win and at Elske, then gave his full attention to his niece. He took her by the hand as she stood before him, to say, "Beriel, I give you greeting."

"Sir, I give you greeting," she answered.

They met as equals, not as Earl and niece, neither as Queen and vassal. There was no bowing of the head or bending of the knee from one to the other, although Beriel wore her travel-worn cloak and the Earl a green shirt with a golden falcon stitched onto it, on his breast a medallion like the one Beriel now carried in her pack.

"Welcome to Sutherland's castle," he said. "You are welcome into my home. The servants will bring in your chests. Where are your chests?" he asked.

"I travel in haste, for I have heard much to disturb me," Beriel answered him.

"Will you not rest a night under my care?" the Earl asked. "Will you not take a meal with us? For you look travel weary and travel stained, Niece. I promise you your safety, here in my castle," he told her. "Also," he said, and his face looked suddenly tired, "I would have your advice on some matters of importance. To the Kingdom, Niece, for the Kingdom. You are right to think that these are parlous times."

"More even than you might yet know, Uncle," Beriel said, as if in warning, but gently.

"May we not advise one another, Niece?"

Beriel assented, and turned to Win, telling him to see to their horses and refresh himself against their continued journey. Then Beriel summoned Elske to her side. "My handmaiden," she said. "Elske."

"I give you greeting," Elske said, and curtseyed—as she would have to a Varinne—and the Earl answered her courteously, "I give you greeting, Elske." She was close enough to see relief in his eyes, and she thought she could guess what need Beriel had for a handmaiden. Her spirits lifted, when Beriel had a use for her.

"I am glad to see you decently attended, Niece," the Earl said. "I had heard rumors that the situation was otherwise."

Beriel acknowledged neither the warning given,

nor the offense offered. "My man will wait out here, after he is fed," was her response. "I need fresh horses. Can you supply us?"

"Of course," the Earl answered. He summoned servants and sent them ahead, while he escorted Beriel through the arched doorway into the castle, with Elske at her mistress's shoulder.

Bathed, wearing fresh clothing from shift to dress, they joined the Earl in a large dining hall. Chairs were set around three sides of the table, which had been drawn up close to the dying fire. Elske was seated beside Beriel, and next to Beriel sat a Lady who must be the Earl's wife, for she, too, wore the medallion. The Earl was catty-corner to his wife, and down the length of the table from him sat a young man, his son. While the servants placed food and drink before them, nobody spoke.

The Earl's Lady, her faded hair held back from her face by golden combs, looked from Beriel to the Earl, as if she sensed trouble there; and the young man—tall and slim, with his mother's fine face—watched only his own hands, which rested beside his plate. They ate of smoked pig meat and onions, carrots, a cold fowl and some bitter greens. When their plates had been cleared from the table, the Earl asked, "Well, Niece?" and drank from his goblet of wine.

"Guerric is crowned," Beriel began.

After some thought the Earl remarked, "You ever were desirous to be the Queen."

"I am the firstborn, the eldest."

"But not male."

"In the history of Sutherland, as was made the law of

233

the Kingdom, the firstborn inherited, be it woman or man. This was my own mother, your sister, who gave the Earldom into your inheritance when she chose instead to marry my father and be his Queen."

The Earl nodded, agreeing.

"The Priests allowed my mother her inheritance of the Earldom, and gave her the power to name her successor."

The Earl pointed out, "You have not been named successor."

"I should have been," Beriel argued. "Until my father lay dead, none ever dared name Guerric, for fear of the law."

The Earl nodded, but "Will you have a civil war?" he asked.

"I will have my crown," she answered.

"To do that, you must turn traitor to the crowned King."

"A usurper is himself a traitor. It is no treason to take the crown from him."

The Earl considered. Elske, watching the faces around the table, thought that the Earl's son was troubled, uneasy, although not about the question of King or Queen; and she guessed she knew what he had to trouble him. The Earl's Lady listened, and often leaned forward, with her mouth moving as if to speak; but she uttered no words.

At last the Earl said, "You want troops. But, Niece, I have bent the knee to Guerric and am his vassal. Even if I accept your claim, I cannot, in honor, send troops against him."

Beriel considered this. She decided, "I will not ask dishonor of you."

"I will gladly give you troops to go against the Wolfers," the Earl offered.

"Hasn't the King already sent an army into the north?"

"Guerric orders Northgate to defend his lands as best he can, and has left those royal villages unprotected that lie in the north. The soldiery Guerric has, he keeps close about him, and he has taken his army eastwards, to bring Arborford under his will."

Beriel asked, "Lord Arbor refuses the King soldiers?"

"Arborford goes its own way, and ever has."

"Yet, is not Lord Arbor your vassal?" Beriel asked.

"He is," the Earl said.

"You have not required him to give Guerric his soldiery?"

"Arbor's vow is to me, to protect me in need. I have no need," the Earl pointed out.

Beriel considered this. The room was still, except for the Earl's Lady restless in her chair. Elske could not think what Beriel was planning, except there would be a revenge on this young man, with his shining pink cheeks, who could not look at his cousin's face.

Beriel changed the topic of conversation, then. "My brother plots my death, as I hear."

At this the young man told his father, "This is what I reported to you."

The Earl nodded at him and told Beriel, "It is for this reason our Aymeric has been sent home in disgrace—sent by his own brother, who is now the King's First Minister. Because Aymeric won't conspire to your murder."

Beriel stared at the young man, then, until his

whole face burned red. It seemed to Elske that shame sat on his shoulders like the Volkking on his throne; and it seemed to Elske just that Aymeric should carry that weight, for all that it crushed and crippled him.

Beriel spoke boldly then to her uncle, "You will have heard rumors that I was with child, last fall, when I left the Kingdom."

"I see no child," the Earl answered.

"You would not have known whether to believe the rumors," Beriel said. "Aunt?"

The Earl's Lady looked at her husband, who awaited her answer. She said nothing.

"I ask you, Aunt," Beriel repeated.

"I must speak, when this—girl—requires?" the Lady asked her husband. "When I must keep silent about important matters, of Kingship and the promotion of my son into a rank higher than I had dreamed, of—"

Beriel interrupted the complaint. "I have asked you."

"If I must speak, and speak truly, I did think you had the look. Last fall. I wondered. And you were—you were often angry, when you were a child, impatient, but last fall you were uncontrolled. I did wonder if you were with child. But who in this Kingdom cares for what a woman thinks, what a woman knows? So I held my tongue—and begged the maidservants to overlook your spitefulness. It was not too soon for me when you rode out of my gates, with your guard—although none asked me if your visit was to my taste, not before it happened, nor after."

The Earl looked as if he wished to silence his wife, and their son was almost smiling at this tirade; but

Beriel remained courteous. "I thank you for your silence, Aunt. But I have a story to tell, and it is not a tale to lighten your hearts. May I speak of it?" she asked the Earl.

"You may," the Earl answered.

His wife said, "No." His son's chair scraped on the stone floor.

Beriel addressed her uncle. "In the spring of last year, a year ago—or perhaps a little more than a year— In the spring," Beriel said, pale but keeping her eyes fixed on her uncle's face, "there were men let into my apartments. At the palace, and the door was locked behind them. So that I couldn't escape them. Night after night, they came. And raped me." She kept her eyes on the Earl when she asked, "Is this so, Aymeric?"

"Yes," he whispered.

Silence settled over the table.

Beriel watched her uncle. Elske, that she might report what she observed, watched the other two, both as still as deer, startled into fear. The fire whispered to itself.

"I don't—" the Earl's Lady started to say but her husband interrupted her again to inquire, "Who would have wished such disgrace on you?"

"My brother," Beriel said. "Guerric," she said. "The King."

"She accuses our son, our Aymeric, of this—vileness," the Earl's Lady said, and warned Beriel, "I will hate you forever if you accuse my son."

Beriel gave Elske a troubled glance.

"I would not wish your hatred, Aunt," Beriel said.

But it was not the hatred that troubled her, Elske knew.

"Then that's an end on it," the Earl's Lady declared. "I will forget what you have said."

Elske saw what troubled Beriel: The Earldom would be divided by the hatred of the Earl's Lady for Beriel, if Beriel were Queen and had accused the Lady's sons of rape. Beriel could not speak openly without risking a necessary ally; and that was what troubled her.

"I will accuse Aymeric," Elske said.

All turned to her.

"I will accuse both of your sons," Elske said, to the Earl.

"I cannot credit it," he said, but Elske could see that he half-believed her.

"Why would Beriel lie about such a thing?" Elske asked.

"To be Queen!" the Earl's Lady cried.

"In the Kingdom, must a woman be raped before she can be Queen?" Elske asked.

"She has always hated my sons, with a jealous hatred."

Elske said, "She has hated Guerric thus, and he her. But not your sons."

"Why doesn't she accuse her brother, then?" the Lady demanded, furious.

"She does," Elske said, and turned back to the Earl, who was studying Aymeric's bent head. "If I had a son," Elske said, "I would not wish this shame on him. I would not wish to leave him in his shame."

The Earl nodded.

"If I had a daughter," Elske said, "I would wish to keep her safe from such shame." The Earl's Lady said nothing.

At last, the Earl spoke. "Aymeric," he said. "My son. I ask you if this accusation is true. I ask you to tell me only what is true, because I will take your word in this."

"Tell him it's not true," urged the young man's mother.

Aymeric raised his unhappy eyes to Elske's and said, "Lady, it is true. I did that thing."

"He's just a boy," the Earl's Lady explained to Elske.

"And your brother?" the Earl demanded.

Aymeric looked at Beriel for the first time. "Lady," he said. "I would give an arm not to have used you so. If I could, I—" His words stumbled, halted.

"You cannot, Cousin," Beriel answered him.

"Whatever revenge you wish," Aymeric said, "even my life—"

"No!" cried the Earl's Lady.

"And your brother, Ditrik?" the Earl asked again, more sternly.

"I cannot speak of my brother. I have given my word," Aymeric told his father.

"Which means he extracted a promise from you," his father said, "and that means there was need of a promise. But I can at least be glad you were stripped of honors and sent home. I can know that my heir is not such a villain as to become another man's hired murderer."

"Aymeric cannot be your heir," Beriel announced.

"Who—?" the Earl started to demand.

"Have you no other sons? I think you have one other, and daughters, too, although they are young."

"Who are you to say who cannot—or can—be Earl Sutherland?" the Earl demanded.

"I am your rightful Queen," Beriel answered. "Aymeric has shamed his name, dishonored it."

"He has shamed *you*," the Earl's Lady said. "And you wish revenge."

"But he has not dishonored me," Beriel said quietly. "The dishonor is not mine, for all they wished it so, and tried to make it so. As to revenge," Beriel said, in a voice that turned her aunt's face pale with fear, and respect. Beriel took a breath, and said it again, "As to revenge, I think his own heart has been taking my revenge upon Aymeric. I need no more."

"And for Ditrik?" the Earl asked.

"Ditrik has sought my death," Beriel answered. "He is a traitor."

Elske remembered Beriel locked into her chambers in Trastad, as if she were a criminal. She remembered Beriel standing naked in her pride, in the bath, in her shame, with the child pushing her belly out. She remembered the silence of those laborious hours of birth. "He is *Fruhckman*," Elske said.

The Earl sighed deeply, accepting. "The word is foreign, like the lady, but I know its meaning. We must lay what plans we can, Niece."

"Yes," Beriel agreed, and she spoke in a new voice, ready to make her plans with the Earl. "Your captains have sworn their allegiance to you, as I think. If I can win them to my cause, will your vow to the false King be broken?" she asked.

But before the Earl could answer this, the doors into the hall burst open and a young man strode into the room. He wore leather armor and carried a long sword, sheathed, at his belt. His dark brown hair clung to his forehead and neck, wet with sweat. Beardless, he had not shaven, so his face was shadowed. His strides, in booted feet, carried him swiftly up to the table.

"My Lord Earl, I must speak with you," he said, noticing none of the others in the room.

The Earl rose and the younger man bowed slightly, impatiently, while the Earl said, "I give you greeting, Lord Dugald. What brings you—?"

"I need troops," the man interrupted. "Forgive me the lack of courtesies, but—my father has sent me—he sent first to the King, who has denied us. Wolfers are poised to pour down into our lands, like crows circling over a wounded bear, and our people are— *Can* you give me any soldiers? I must be answered, and quickly, for I have been away too long, and I would not have my men defend the holdings and villages and my sword not raised with theirs, and my life not given with theirs, if needs must. What say you, my Lord?"

"I will give you soldiers, and weapons, horses, and supplies, also," the Earl said.

The dark-haired man went down on his knee, then, in gratitude. He was white-faced, and trembling with fatigue, Elske saw. She rose from her chair, so that he might sit. He accepted this place, without thanks.

"Do you not greet *me?*" Beriel asked him. "Am I so much changed, my Lord Dugald?"

He turned to her, surprised. "Beriel? And alive? Why did you leave us to this fortune?"

"The fortune of the Wolfers?" Beriel asked. "Or the fortune of this King?"

He did not hesitate. "Both," he said, "and one as ill as the other. I take it, then, that the rumors were

241

false?" This was a blunt man, and privileged to speak plainly.

"Are not rumors most often false?" Beriel asked him, teasing. "I am as you see me, Dugald," she said, neither lying nor telling the truth.

"I see little, blinded as I am with tiredness and hunger," he answered, with a little upwards lifting of the ends of his mouth, to make it a pleasantry. "And it's many days' ride before me, back to my own lands, where . . ."

"But first you must rest," Beriel told him. "You'll be of little use to your soldiery if you ride so exhausted." He opened his mouth to argue but she raised a hand to silence him, and he obeyed her command. "Moreover," Beriel announced, "I have need of good counsel here, as I determine how to make my claim on the throne. So I ask you to sit, take some rest, take refreshment, and give me the benefit of your counsel. Grant me this, Lord Dugald."

"It is granted, Beriel," he said. "But I will not deliberate overlong," he warned her with a smile.

The Earl's Lady rose then, to give order for food, and the Earl asked Elske to take that empty seat before he turned to the newcomer, to explain where they had arrived in their talk. Elske could feel Beriel's anger at being left out of the men's talk, as if she had nothing to contribute, as if it didn't concern her. The newcomer was too engrossed to even notice Beriel's growing fury, as he leaned in front of her to hear what the Earl was saying. Elske couldn't help but smile, although she *could* help laughing where any might hear it.

When Elske smiled, the newcomer turned his head to her. Quickly, she made her expression solemn, but his stone-brown eyes stayed on her. "Has our Aymeric brought home a bride, then?" Lord Dugald asked. "And the stories of the King's dissatisfactions with you, are they then also false? Will you, too, come to my aid?"

This man would not long be diverted from his own purposes, Elske noted.

"She is not my wife," Aymeric said, "although I might do much worse than such a stranger. For you are a foreigner, aren't you?" he asked Elske. "From the great city of Trastad, I think, for that was a Norther word you spoke, was it not? *Fruhckman?*" he repeated it, with a sad smile.

Lord Dugald did not smile. He put a hand on his sword's hilt, as if Elske had drawn on him. "It *is* a Norther word. Who are you?" he demanded of Elske.

She did not look away. "Elske," she said.

"Wolfer?"

"Yes."

She studied him as closely as he studied her, and thought she could trust him to see into the truth of her.

He shifted in the chair. "Are you not afraid I will slay you?"

"Why should I fear you, when your care is for your people?" she asked him.

"And my lands, also—for I am the Earl that will be," he told her, then, "How came you here?" he asked.

"I am the Queen's handmaiden."

"Oh—ho—Beriel, so that is how the river runs," he laughed. "So you will be Queen?"

But she would not be jested with on this point. Solemnly, she answered him. "I will. And will you bend the knee to me?"

Lord Dugald, too, grew solemn. "My Queen, I will. Whom even Wolfers serve, she has my sworn loyalty. As you always did, from when we were children. Northgate is ever for the law, and thus for the Queen."

Beriel rose then and placed her right hand on his left shoulder. "I accept your sword, Dugald, heir to Earl Northgate. Now, then," she said, and turned to them all, taking her place once again at the head of the council of war, "let us lay our plans. For we waste time here, while the Kingdom is being wasted around us. What is your choice, Uncle? Will you let me speak before your soldiers to win them to my cause?"

It didn't take long for the decisions to be reached. The Earl's soldiery was divided into three parts. One part would remain where they were, for although the Earl didn't think his own lands were in danger, Beriel would not have him defenseless. The second part was given for Lord Dugald's use. The third part of the army—those who chose so, if any did—would ride with Beriel, to confront Guerric at Arborford, to ask him to bring the question of the succession before the law or, if he required it, to do battle with him. Beriel expected battle, although the two men chided her for bloodthirstiness; she argued that she knew her brother, knew what he was capable of, and would trust him only when she had buried him.

It did not please them to hear her speak so. The Earl told her she did not mean the words she spoke, but Lord Dugald only looked at her thoughtfully. Elske believed Beriel, and hoped to ride into battle before her mistress, or beside her, and wondered which place would enable her to better protect the Queen.

Aymeric would ride with Beriel, as her herald. He

would bear letters to the First Minister and to the King, ordering the two before the law to answer certain charges. "If I die in this, then the dishonor I have done you, my father, and you, my Queen that will be, and to myself, also—then all will be paid," Aymeric said, as if he almost hoped for death.

With them also, to his dismay and deep pleasure, would go Win. When he protested to Beriel that he should ride with Lord Dugald to the Ram's Head, to stand with his family and his neighbors in need, she reminded him that he had vowed to serve *her*, and argued that she needed his service now even more than when he first pressed it upon her. If he chose to go home she would not bar his way; but her own will was to have him at her side, someone she could trust absolutely. Hearing her will, Win did not hesitate to promise his life to his Queen.

A brief speech won many of Sutherland's soldiers to her cause. Elske watched from the background how Beriel stood up tall on a mounting block to look over the men, and pick out their captains with her glance. She said only: "I am the Queen that will be. I am the rightful Queen under the law, and I ride to place my claim before this cowardly false King. Who rides with me?" Her voice carried easily as a falcon in flight over the assembled soldiers. She stood high-shouldered and unafraid. There was that about her that all recognized, and trusted, and wished to follow.

To her surprise, and chagrin, Elske was sent with Lord Dugald and his soldiers. "You must," Beriel told her. "I order it. You will understand the Wolfers more than our own people can. At least you can speak their tongue, so that if it comes to treating, you can speak for us."

"The Volkaric do not make treaties," Elske said. "If they have sent war bands, they will overrun what they can and avoid those places that can defend themselves. Like wolves, they disappear into the safety of the forests and hills and come out of hiding to attack where they are least expected and will be most weakly opposed. Once they have entered your land, all you can do is warn your people to flee the danger," she told Lord Dugald. "In the autumn, they will carry their booty back to the Volkking, and then you will have time to arm and train your people, for their own defense. But there is nothing I can do at this time against the Wolfers, my Lady. Let me ride with you."

Win added his voice to her pleas. "Aye, and whatever Elske undertakes goes well. For did you not come out of this castle with an army to ride behind you and the Earl's own son in your service? Take Elske with you."

At his words, Beriel's blue eyes grew hard and she would not be persuaded. So Elske rode out of Sutherland's castle at the side of Lord Dugald, with an army at their backs. Beriel had already left, for Arborford.

Watching that army take one broad roadway while she herself rode with another army down the other, Elske felt what must be fear curl its wolf claws into her heart. For what if Beriel were to die, in claiming her throne? In battle or by treachery, what if Beriel's life were lost? What if they were never to meet again?

Chapter 17

THEY MARCHED AWAY from Sutherland's city with two bands of soldiery, the smaller loyal to Lord Dugald, the larger serving the Earl. The two soldieries camped separately from one another, strangers and mistrustful. Each ate from its own supplies and tended to its own animals, and arms.

Dugald gave Elske the use of his own tent and himself slept on the open ground, with his soldiers; but they shared a fire, and food, and they rode side by side, all the days of the march.

He was a good companion for a journey with urgent business. He might talk or he might ride silent, but he never complained nor did he forget to ask after her comfort, thirst, hunger or desire to rest. While he did not sing and jest, as Win had, still the hours in his company did not drag. He spoke of his father's land, which he would inherit, and the people of it—less pleasure-loving than those of the south but staunch, and true-hearted. "There are those who say that the land in the north, with its dark forests and icy lakes, its rocky soil, too, is not hospitable, but I have ever found it kind." He spoke of the history of the Kingdom, its treacheries and disasters, its great Kings and Earls, and Jackaroo, too. He explained its laws and described the great wheel of the year with its plantings and harvestings, its fairs; they discussed how a Lord could assist in the well-being of his people.

Elske enjoyed the company of this Lord. But when he called her Lady for the time that made it too many times, she asked him, "Do you not remember I am no Lady?"

At that, he gainsayed her, for all around to hear. "My Queen so calls you when she names you her handmaiden, which is her Lady-in-Waiting." And he smiled, to ask her, "Will you set me against my Queen?" He smiled, making his courtly request, and she saw no falsehood in his smile. Also, there was a different request in his eyes, asking her to trust him in this, and follow his lead, as if they were moving through the steps of a dance, together.

Elske had neither will nor reason to quarrel with Lord Dugald, and so she acquiesced.

During the day, Dugald and the countryside they crossed diverted Elske, but at night, even in the privacy of the tent, she could not rest for long. Tired from the day's exertions, she'd fall immediately asleep, but in the dark of night she would awaken, and think of Beriel. Her thoughts made her restless, so she'd wrap herself around with her cloak and leave the tent.

Sentries grew accustomed to her, and watched for her. They greeted her. "A cool night, my Lady, sit here by our fire." She learned their names and the names of their fathers, too, mothers, sisters, sweethearts. She asked after their brothers. She learned about the cities or villages where they had lived, and the work of their fathers' holdings, shepherd and pigman, blacksmith, weaver, farmer, fisherman. "The lakes of the north are as full of fish as a goodwife's stew," they told her, when she was surprised to hear of fish, here, so far from the sea. They were surprised to hear that there was a way of smoking fish, as if it were pig, to preserve it. Most of these soldiers were younger sons, ambitious to be named sergeants so that they could take a wife, and be given one of the little houses the cities of the north kept for the particular use of a soldier's family. The one thing they never spoke of was the battles ahead. Elske guessed that the depth of their silence reflected the depth of their dread.

Eventually, Elske also wandered into the camps of Earl Sutherland's men, and they also welcomed her. These southern men worried less than their northern counterparts about doing battle with the Wolfers; they spoke of it carelessly, jestingly, as confident and eager as Adels before a ball, as if the Wolfers were a game.

The soldiers looked out for Elske, and Dugald often brought their well-wishes back to her from his twice-daily inspection tours. Lord Dugald was a useful man, Elske thought; and she had never met with such a man before. He carried messages gladly, without any pride of place to interfere, whether the word traveled from captain to captain or soldier to soldier. He could deal with the stone caught in a horse's shoe or set a broken bone as easily as he detailed men to gather fuel or encouraged them at the arduous march. The soldiers came to him with their quarrels and their desires, and he answered their needs. Elske had seen his dark brown head bent over a needle and thread, mending a tear in his own blue tunic—on the chest of which Northgate's bear, standing, had been emblazoned. Like his soldiers, Elske came to trust the Earl's heir in all things; and Sutherland's soldiers, too, soon followed him confidently.

All this he achieved without—apparently—even thinking of it. He did not make his own cleverness known, or his strength, power or position. Those who served Lord Dugald did not so much follow him as find him at their shoulder, ready to assist or to give succor or just to hear them. Thus it was he listened to Elske, as if he wished to understand even that which she could not put into words. However, his thoughts did not always march with hers, as when he pointed out, "There will now be another Death Maiden, won't there?" The grim sorrow in his voice caused her to turn her head so that she might see his face. But he was staring ahead, towards the hills they approached. So Elske, who had never thought of her, must remember this next, unknown Death Maiden, without Tamara to protect her, and must feel a sorrow that matched his own for this unmet child, and for herself, too, as she had not known herself to be.

Dugald was like a beryl glass, showing Elske herself. "You have been so many things," he once exclaimed, "and seen so much of the world. Do you never think how wonderful it is, what you have seen and done, all that you know? And now you are here to make a lighter time of this strenuous march, and help us know what awaits us. For which I thank you, Elske. My soldiers are less fatigued of body and fearful of heart than they would have been were you not with us. Me, as well.

You have shone in my days like the sun in the sky," he said, and she laughed, then, at his courtly extravagance here in the rough life of a marching army, and at her pleasure in his good opinion.

They had forded the great river and were camped on its western banks the evening that Elske unknowingly risked the loss of that valued good opinion. It was a mild evening. They had just set up camp, the fires lit, refreshing water taken by men and animals; they had not yet eaten. Dugald was conferring with the captains and Elske walked to the riverbank, where the water rippled golden under a burnished sky. Some of Sutherland's soldiers were about to wade into the water and she asked them if they knew how to swim.

"Aye, Lady," they answered, so she asked them if they would teach her. "Nay, Lady, why should you know that?" they said, answering her neither yes nor no as they stood barefooted, wearing only shirts and trousers, halted in their undressing by her arrival, wary as foxes.

"I wish to know," she said. "The Queen that will be, Beriel, was taught it by fishermen."

They looked at one another, and thought to say, "What would you wear, Lady? If you try to swim in those skirts, you'll drown for sure, and what Lord Dugald would do to us I don't like to think. It would be a quick hanging, if we were lucky."

"Can I not wear what you do?" Elske asked.

"Lady, we swim without clothing."

"Naked?"

"How else?"

Elske could not answer, never having seen a man either unclothed or swimming.

"I'll give her my shirt," one of the soldiers volunteered.

"How can we watch over her, when we are naked? Not watching, how can we be sure of her safety?" they asked one another.

"And why should our Elskeling not learn to swim, or have anything else she wishes?"

So they took off only their shirts and stood in a circle around her, with their backs to her, while she removed her own clothing until she wore only a shift. She put on the soldier's green shirt, which reached below her knees. Then she moved down into the water among her guard of soldiers.

This was a sandy-bottomed river and Elske stepped barefooted into the water, which rose steadily as she walked out into it, cool against her ankles, then calves, then knees. The green shirt grew heavy with water, and what was cool on her feet was cold enough on her belly to make her gasp.

They walked her out until the water reached her breasts and then told her, if she was not afraid to try, that she might lie down on it. "Lie on your belly. Lift your face," they advised her.

Elske bent her knees, but could not persuade her feet to leave the river bottom.

"Push off," her teachers advised her, laughter in their voices, and eagerness for her to learn. "Push yourself towards the shore where the water grows shallower."

Elske filled her chest with air and pushed off. Almost, she stayed on top of the water, before she began to sink, and her feet scrabbled beneath her to stand on firm sand again. But her *almost* had given her a sense of it, and soon she floated easily, and even rolled over onto her back to look up into the sky while she floated on top of the water, swimming.

The soldiers were pleased with themselves, and with her. "Our Elskeling can do anything she sets her spirit on, can't she?" they asked one another. "Now, Lady," they told her. "You must learn how to paddle with your hands, and kick with your feet, so that—like a boat with its oars—you can steer yourself whither you will. And then you will know how to swim."

"Yes," Elske said, and smiled so widely, to know that she had thought she already knew what she did not, that her mouth filled with water, and she coughed so hard to get it out that she forgot to keep her chest filled with air, and she had to stand up, and stop swimming as she choked, chest-deep in the river, her wet hair plastered to her shoulders.

This was what Dugald saw, as he came searching for her. Seeing this, he rushed down to the water's edge, bellowing orders to the soldiers, bellowing orders to Elske, his anger whipping out in all directions.

The soldiers scurried out of the river and gathered up their clothing. "We only—" "It wasn't—" He would deal with them later, Dugald promised them, and would not hear their protests. "My Lord, you know we wouldn't—" He sent them back to their captains, at a run.

When the soldiers had gone, he called again for Elske to get out of the water.

She, too, protested. "But I can swim."

"Just obey me," he commanded. He waited on the shore with his boots on and his cloak held out to wrap around her. He scolded her, even as she walked through the water towards him. "It isn't decent for a Lady to be so undressed among men, and the soldiers bare-chested—"

"They told me, usually they swim naked but they didn't today, because of my presence. They gave me a shirt so I wouldn't be naked. They've done nothing wrong," Elske said as she accepted his cloak. She picked up her own clothing from where it lay folded on the long riverside grasses. "And I've done nothing wrong."

The man at her side was dark-faced. "I don't know what is permitted in Trastad, how their women behave, but in the Kingdom no Lady would see men bare-chested, nor would she let them see her so unclothed—"

"I am neither a Lady nor a Trastader." He had no reason to speak so to her, and she had no reason to be courteous to his anger.

"Neither would any woman of the people," Dugald went on, ignoring her. "You are as blind and willful as Beriel."

"Beriel is not blind," Elske answered him. "She is no more willful than she must be."

He escorted her back to their fire, and neither one of them spoke to the other. Elske withdrew into her tent, to change into dry clothing, but she did not remain there. Instead—being careful to tell one of the soldiers in which direction she would go, lest Dugald think she had been cowed by his anger—she walked away from the river, along a path out into the countryside, until she stood beside the dark furrows of a plowed field.

The sky was darkening from the east but still glowed blue gold in the west, where a horizon as uneven as the sea's showed hills, rising up. The mountains, she knew, lay out of sight, beyond; if she could see them, they would be covered still with snow. It was as if Dugald's troops were the army of spring, hurrying to catch up with her and escort her safely through the land from which winter's troops were retreating.

He spoke behind her. "Lady, I give you greeting."

Elske turned around, and found that her ill humor had left her. "I give you greeting, Lord Dugald," she answered. When he stepped up beside her to look out over the fields, she saw how dark his eyes were, as dark as the deep rocks in the land of the Volkaric, as unchanging as earth.

"This is my father's land," he said to her. "It will be mine, in my time, if I live. The soldiers call you Elskeling. Does that offend you?"

"Why should it offend me?"

Dugald smiled at her then, and said, "And I, if I were to request it—with courtly flourishes, with songs and flowers—could I ask you to teach me to swim? Not now, but at some future time, when the men have forgotten how they trespassed against your dignity."

"The soldiers would make better teachers," Elske said, and with a teasing smile of her own reminded him, "You would all be men together as is proper."

He shrugged.

"But," she said, then stopped, then decided to speak, "Why should you ask me to teach you what I barely know myself?"

The steady eyes looked down into hers and he told her, "Because I am afraid to learn, afraid to drown learning it. But I think you are someone I would trust to show me how to enter the water and not die there. I think my fear and my life would be safe with you. Because I think that when Beriel left us last fall Guerric didn't expect her to return. I think," he said again, his eyes now on the distances of his land so that whatever was written on her face might go unread. "Perhaps, if there is any truth to the rumors of a man in her bed and a baby in her belly, that Beriel has trusted herself to you, and you have served her well. So I think that what we call *proper* doesn't signify to you. Although this freedom could make you dangerous, especially to those whose secrets you keep, it is difficult for me to believe that you are a danger to me, or my land, or my Queen. On the other hand, it could make you a true heart. I can believe that your heart is true."

"I think it is," Elske agreed, accepting his arm and the apology of his request, and—most gladly—his good opinion.

With the army stretched out behind, they left the river. The King's Way ran north between low fences, through rough, brown fields. Dugald asked Elske about the Wolfers, telling her, "I've chased after one of the war bands, and raised my sword to its rear guard, and I have fought against those who buy the time for their fellows to escape. They don't fear death as we do."

She agreed. "They fear only the Volkking, and the shame of cowardice."

"And what do you fear, Elske?"

Elske considered, to give him the true answer. "I fear for the safety of Beriel."

"Not for your own safety? Not for mine?"

Elske considered. "No," she answered.

His shout of laughter caused the nearby soldiers to fall silent, so he spoke more quietly to tell her, "When we are at Hildebrand's city, there will be a council of war. I think, I would wish people to know you are Wolfer, so that we can hear your advice about our enemy. I give my pledge for your safety," he promised.

The army traveled at some speed along the King's Way, passing solitary cottages, farmhouses with their outbuildings, inns and villages. Sometimes, people gathered to watch them pass, and all their faces seemed stilled by fear. They feared even to hope, Elske thought. The green shirts of the soldiers from the south at least earned a look of surprise, and a man might whisper into his neighbor's ear, or point out to a child Northgate's heir.

At the Ram's Head Inn, Elske slept under a roof, in her own chamber. She dined with Dugald, waited on by the redheaded innkeeper, Win's brother.

Their host could not speak four words without putting in "my Lord" or "my honored Lord." His wife bustled in and out, as he apologized for the simple fare—"Had we known, my honored Lord, that you would dine with us, my Lord"—but dared to hope that the inn's wine, "made from the family vineyard, would please my noble Lord." He offered clean napkins, his wife offered a chair to make Lord Dugald more comfortable, until finally Dugald tried to divert his hosts by saying, "I have news of your brother, if you would hear it."

They stood with their hands folded in front of their aprons, to hear, and what they heard gave them unease. The innkeeper pulled ruminatively at his red beard, but his wife could not hold her tongue. "He ever did seek to serve that Princess," she said, to her husband. "She magicked him that summer, over the hanging of your uncle, and you know how Win is. Stubborn-hearted."

"He's ever been too quick to pity," the host agreed, sadly.

Elske spoke up. "Win is loyal to his Queen."

"Aye, and it'll be just that loyalty that will get him a traitor's death," Win's brother said. "And if I know my brother, he'll say she's done him fair."

"If that's what he gets, I'll be hanged beside him," Dugald told them and their host asked uneasily, "What mean you, my Lord?"

Dugald answered plainly. "I mean that if a brother seizes the crown from his sister who is the firstborn, then *he* is the traitor, as are all who follow him."

"Aye, and I know nothing of that," the wife said. "But I know they're cowards who follow Guerric into the safety of Arborford, and leave their own people undefended."

Her husband tried to shush her. "Here is Northgate's heir," he pointed out, "and he brings soldiers from Sutherland to join his father's army, to protect us."

"Aye, and there's no protection against these Wolfers," she lamented. "They move secretly, and in packs, they never stand to fight. And it is the worse, now, for now they take revenge, too." She turned to Dugald, "They eat the flesh of children!" she cried. "Women who fall into their hands go mad with pain, and shame, and fear, before they die. You must promise me, you'll slay me, Husband—I'll slay my daughters, I can do that—if those—"

"Hush," he tried to soothe her frenzy. "I'll not keep you here if they come close."

"You fool! They give no warning. Do you think the pigman would not have sent his daughter away? You saw the bodies, Husband. It's you who are the dreamer and fool, not Win. His enemy fights honestly—and speaks his language. Maybe he was the clever one, to leave you here without his arm at such a time—"

"She is afraid," the host apologized. "My Lord, I ask you to remember that our children are young, and she is afraid for them. We'll leave you, my honored Lord, to your dinner."

"Don't tell me there's nothing to fear!" his wife cried.

The host bowed to Lord Dugald, and bowed to Elske, too, as he drew his wife out of the long room, leaving them alone.

Dugald lifted his spoon and dipped it into his bowl of meat stew, but he didn't eat. Elske did not even lift her spoon.

"I need a map," Dugald said, but not to her. "Hildebrand will have one."

He took a bite then, chewed and swallowed. He drank a swallow of the wine. "I've let myself make a pleasure journey, and my people in danger."

He drank of the wine again, and poured more from the pitcher into his goblet. Then he did raise his face, his eyes as mute as boulders, to ask Elske, "How could you be as you are and have lived among Wolfers?"

Elske shook her head. She could not answer his question.

"Tell me," Lord Dugald insisted.

If he wished to insist, then Elske wished to make the attempt. "I was a girl," she said, "and among the

Volkaric—" but he interrupted her, "Who are these Volkaric?"

"Those whom you call Wolfers. Among the Volkaric," she began again, and this time he did not interrupt her, "women are nothing, useless in battle, useless to win treasure. They remain near their houses—as do the women of Trastad, both the great Varinnes and their servants—to sew and scrub and cook, to care for children. Among the Volkaric, the best of a woman is to bear sons. I lived among the Volkaric as women everywhere live," Elske told Dugald. "Except Beriel," she said. Then she added, "All women except Beriel, who would be Queen."

As she spoke, Dugald looked into her face, and looked still into her face. "How could they ask your death of you, being who you are?" he asked, but it was a protest, not a question. "And how could they ask you to know what your death was to be?"

"If it were kept a secret," Elske explained, "there would have been no revenge on my grandmother. I was their revenge on her. Whenever anyone saw me, they remembered how my death would come and so our life was better when all knew what my death would be."

"It was ill done," Dugald said plainly. He asked her then, "So you would have no secrets?"

"My Lord?"

"It is a simple question, a simple policy: Do you believe secrets should be kept, and that the people should be kept in ignorance?"

Elske considered what secrets she had known, and kept, and which she had spoken of, before she said, "I believe that there are some secrets danger- ous to their possessors, should they be known." She was thinking of the secret of the black powder, which she held unbeknownst to any other, not even Var Jerrol, who had assumed she could not comprehend what she had heard; for otherwise—this she knew—he would have had her killed. "And surely those who do not know secrets can live most easily, in this world. For the day, at least."

"For the day," he echoed, doubtfully.

"It is not a simple question," she told him.

"You've heard of the black powder," he told her.

Elske didn't wonder how he knew that of her. She just answered him truthfully. "Yes."

"A deeply kept secret, and no man knows where it comes from so that he may get it for his own use, even against Wolfers," Lord Dugald said.

Elske corrected him. "Men know where it comes from, and where to buy it, and even how to make it. I learned how to make it," she told him, trusting him, "from a man who revealed the ingredients and their proportions before he died. He gave up his secret so that he would live, but he died because he no longer possessed it. This was among the merchants of Trastad."

Lord Dugald looked into her face again. "Is this a secret that should be kept?"

"I think, no," she answered.

"But the people," he said, and waved his hand in the direction of the door through which the host and his wife had withdrawn. "If the people are so afraid of Wolfers—who are only men after all—how much will they be crazed by fear of the black powder, which is a hundred times more heartless than any Wolfer, and is moreover magic?"

"It is not magic," Elske told him. "Any man might make it."

"Can we? Have we the time?" Lord Dugald asked,

and when she shook her head he smiled ruefully. "Well, it's too dangerous a weapon to take lightly up, as if it were no more than a pretty dagger. And the Wolfers do not stand as still as city walls, so it could not serve against them. Yet I would like to be so strongly weaponed."

"Beriel also wishes to have it," Elske said. "Ask of me what help you need, for the Wolfers must not come killing here. In Beriel's Kingdom. In Northgate's lands."

"Can they be stopped?" he asked. He answered his own question, "How can I know unless I make the attempt? Are you willing to die in this cause, Elske?"

"Yes."

"Because it is Beriel's cause," he said. "Well, so am I, although I cannot be so willing for *you* to die. On some Wolfer blade or at the end of a traitor's rope, we may all die in Beriel's cause."

Elske had never seen a man hanged, but she saw in her mind Dugald so dangling, dead, and her heart twisted in her chest.

"Elske?" he asked, watching her face. "What is it? Did you not know the dangers you faced?"

"I knew my danger," she said, "but—"

"As Beriel knows hers, I promise you. It is in Beriel's cause, and that is a good one," he reassured her. "Few understand this of her, but I have known her from a child and seen how she masks her true heart. I know that if one of her people bleeds, Beriel bleeds. If fire scorches the land, Beriel has the scar. Can you ride through the night, Elske?"

"Yes," she said, and he was not surprised at her answer.

262

Chapter 18

THE LORDS AND THEIR CAPTAINS gathered together
in Hildebrand's great hall, where the long table had
a map unrolled onto it. The Lords were seated in
high-backed chairs, and their captains stood behind
them. Lord Dugald had Elske seated beside him.

A fire burned in the great fireplace, taking the
chill off the air, and the stone walls of the hall were
hung with woven carpets. Through the unshuttered
windows a mild blue sky shone over the low roofs of
Hildebrand's city. The army waited beyond the city
walls for the decisions being debated now, in this
hall, and Elske would have felt more at ease among
the soldiers.

Lord Hildebrand was an aging man, his thin hair
silvery, his cheeks sunken; he coughed, and drank
wine to soothe his throat, and kept his eye on
Dugald, to learn the younger man's thoughts.
Hildebrand's heir, a square-jawed man of middle
years, sat the length of the table from his father, and
kept his eyes on the map as if only his vigilance kept
it flat on the table. One of Dugald's brothers,
Thorold, had been sent by the Earl, and with him
came four other Lords, all younger sons, all bringing

troops in response to Northgate's appeal.

The map showed the whole Kingdom, and the men discussed how they might defend it. Troops were kept in plenty to guard the cities, but there was no protection for the villages, nor for the isolated holdings, all easy prey. The map showed these habitations and villages, as well as the cities. Northgate's demesne spread between the river to the east and the foothills to the west; mountains bordered the northern parts and thick forests guarded the south. Lakes were plentiful among the wooded foothills. The map did not mark the cities of the south, Celindon and Selby, nor the northern city of Trastad. Pericol was only a phrase: HOUSES HERE. It was as if in all the world, there was only this Kingdom.

White pebbles marked the places where the Wolfers had struck at the end of the last summer, and these were all gathered in the southern and western parts of Northgate's lands. For each homestead or village looted, burned, destroyed, there was a white pebble on the map. There was no marking for the lives lost. The men studied the map to see where a fortress might be built, to be garrisoned to patrol and guard the western and southern borders; or wouldn't a line of walled castles make a stronger defense?

Looking at the map, Elske could guess that the Wolfers had entered the Kingdom from the south, although she didn't know how they had found their way to its borders, whether they had been led by some trader who hoped by the favor to gain his life, or if some Wolfer bands, lost and wandering homewards, had stumbled into this unknown land. She guessed

that there had been at least three Wolfer bands entering together and then, when they saw what lay before
them, separating, each to pursue its own chances.
They would have joined up again where they had
parted, to return together to the Volkking.

None of the men asked her thoughts.

In any case, her thoughts were more with Beriel
than here in this hall. Messengers from the east had
told of two great armies moving towards one
another, and war declared between the King's army
and the Queen's. They said a battle was only a few
days off. Dugald had told Elske how armies fight:
The troops formed into lines, to dash against one
another until one or the other mass of men yielded.
Elske had thought of the seawalls of Trastad, and
the waves rolling up against the great cut stones,
and breaking themselves upon the walls; except that
there was no victory or retreat between the seawalls
and the waves, and in battle men die. In battle,
Dugald had told her, the air rang loud, as the soldiers cried out to one another to ask or promise aid,
to warn, to threaten, to curse their enemies, to curse
their luck. The air rang thick with the sounds of
fighting, steel clanging against steel, the pounding
hooves of the war horses, the men's shrieks of fury
and fear and pain.

"Have you been in battle?" she had asked him.

"No," he said. "No, I have not. But I have asked
those who have, or their fathers; we have few battles
in the Kingdom, although there have been occasional rebellions. I asked because I like to know
what might lie ahead to unman me at the very time
when I most need my courage. Knowledge blunts
the blade of fear," he said.

"Yes," Elske had agreed.

"Although there are those who would prefer to run blind into danger. But you are not one of those, are you, Elske?" he had asked, as if his mouth could taste honey in her name, and Elske had felt confused, as if she had stepped from darkness into blinding day. It took a little time for her to ask him, "How are men persuaded to enter such battles?"

Dugald shrugged his shoulders. "They fight to defend their homes or keep their vows, to gain revenge. Men will fight for profit, too, and also to stand for a Queen whose throne has been usurped. Do not your Wolfers go into battle? And are they not men?"

"Wolfers swoop in, seize, kill, then return into their hiding places," she had answered him. "They fight no battles. They are war bands, raiders—not armies."

"They are cowards, who attack only the weak."

"Not cowards," Elske had told him.

Now, seated in this long hall while the men debated how to do battle against Wolfers, Elske could only wish that Beriel was facing a Wolfer war band, and not the army of trained soldiers led by her brother who hated her. The Wolfers would know Beriel's quality, at one glance, and their choice would be quick—either to take her back to the Volkking, or to cut her throat across. They might not know the word but they would respond to Beriel as to a Queen.

But this brother did not have a Wolfer nature. He feared Beriel, that she was the Queen; and what he might do, in his fear—

Elske felt her heart race at the unfinished thought.

Beside her, quietly, Dugald asked, "What troubles you, my Lady?"

"I think of Beriel," she told him. If Beriel lived, Elske would serve her, but if Beriel were dead . . . Elske would not abandon Beriel's Kingdom to this false King. She thought, imagination as swift as a falcon falling onto its prey, that she would become Jackaroo, riding to free the land of its King, or perhaps she would find her own army. There was this younger brother, Aidenil, and he could be placed on the throne. Her own future decided should Beriel not survive her war, Elske could attend to Hildebrand's son asking, "Who is this girl, Lord Dugald? Why does she sit with us?"

"To give us counsel."

Hildebrand shifted in his chair, and let out his breath in a *pfftt* sound. "Women at a council of war?" he asked. "Go call your mother, my boy, and you might ask your wife, too," he laughed.

Hildebrand's son had already started to rise and obey when his father laughed, at which he sat down, red-faced. Hildebrand coughed, and when he could speak again turned back to Dugald. "My Lord, you are too young to remember—but your father, the Earl, he could tell you. This is one of those ideas out of the south, a Sutherlandish notion. In my father's time, there was a woman who advised the Earl Sutherland in his council; and they said she had an equal voice. I suppose it might have been possible in those earlier days, when there were no real dangers to face. But if my mother had had a voice, during the droughty years of my childhood when there was such unrest among the people, and armed robbers in the forests and hills—if there had been a woman on my father's council, I don't like to think what evil might have happened. It was hard enough times as it was, without a woman's voice to make quarrels. So, despite your bright eyes, my dear, and the pleasure a pretty girl always gives me, I must ask you to leave us."

Dugald put a hand on Elske's arm to hold her beside him.

"Lord Dugald," Hildebrand protested. "What does she know of war?"

"Nothing," Dugald answered. Then, with a glance at Elske, he explained to the gathered Lords, "But she is Wolfer born and Wolfer raised."

"A Wolfer? The enemy—" "Wolfer? A spy—" "Witch—"

The words were whispered around the room, and answered by the name "Elskeling," spoken reassuringly by Dugald's captains, that she should not be afraid. But Elske was not afraid of what might happen in this room.

"I give my word for her," Dugald said, in warning and promise.

Lord Hildebrand spoke to Elske, then. "Would you betray your own people?"

"They are no longer my people," Elske told him.

He made the *pfftt* sound again and asked her, "Who are your people?"

"I have a Queen. Beriel," she answered.

"If she lives," one of the young Lords muttered.

Dugald reminded them, "We have our own dire necessity. We have a Kingdom to preserve, if we can."

Elske could speak to that. "They will go no farther than this," she said, and traced the two rivers that divided Earl Northgate's lands from the King's holdings, and Sutherland's. "It is only this countryside the Wolfers will attack."

"How can you know this so surely?" a doubting Lord demanded.

"Wolfers fear deep water, and never cross it nor go out upon it," Elske said.

"This is true?" Dugald asked her, although he already believed her.

"True," she promised, promising every man there.

"So King Guerric need never have fled into the east," someone said, and "He could not have known," another answered.

Lord Hildebrand announced his plan. "We have the numbers to overwhelm them. They are only bands of wild men, and we have trained soldiers. I say, Lord Dugald leads the army into the west to engage these Wolfers in battle."

"I say, we make a line of our soldiers, along this border," Thorold suggested. "So many soldiers will make a wall of men to keep the Wolfers out."

"I say, we divide our troops, and let them roam as Wolfers, to fight and destroy the enemy wherever he might be found," said another.

"Elske?" Dugald asked her.

She shook her head, and tried to explain. "The war bands are as hard to track as a pack of wolves. They move separately, each going its own way under its own captain, except when they first enter a land, and make the camp at which they will gather again, to leave the land together. You might stand in a castle with your soldiers at the ready all summer long and never see a single Wolfer. Yet if you stretch your soldiers into a thin line, each of your men will be weak and alone—and those the Wolfers will attack."

"If the enemy will not engage us in our numbers, how do we fight him?"

"If you know where they gathered together last fall, before leaving the Kingdom—do you know where that is?" she asked.

"Isn't it too late?"

"Have you had word of attacks?" Dugald asked Hildebrand, who shook his head; there had been no word. "How early in spring do they leave their own lands, Elske?" he asked.

"The land of the Volkaric lies northwards from the Kingdom, and they will leave in early spring, but not so soon as to be caught by a late winter storm. Then they must travel into the south, to find again their way into the Kingdom, through the forest, as I guess."

In her mind, she could see the long-bearded Wolfers, knives at their sides, racing up through the thick forest into this newfound land. She could see their speed and eagerness, how they hungered for the slaughter and the stealing. How each captain hoped to carry back to the Volkking the richest treasures, and give to him the greatest honor, and gain from that an eminence over all the other Volkaric warriors. Elske never doubted the boldness of the Wolfers, and their willingness to die in the chance of standing proud before the Volkking. She didn't think these bushy-bearded soldiers of the Kingdom had that same wild courage.

These people of the Kingdom did not know the enemy they faced. Elske drew her attention back to the questions Hildebrand's son asked. "Lady," he began again, "these Wolfers—" He looked about him, as if hoping some other man would ask it. But no other man offered. "Their cry freezes the heart, and— What can we tell our soldiers? To keep them from cowardice, which will not only defeat but also shame them. Do you know the cry?"

Elske did.

"Do you know how we might guard ourselves against its power?"

"What can be so fearful in a sound that comes from men's throats," Elske asked, "any more than a dog's bark? But you might ask your soldiers to answer in kind. The Wolfers give themselves courage, following their own voices into battle. If your soldiers have the same voices, why should they not find the same courage?"

"Can you teach us?" one of the captains asked, and "Yes," Elske agreed.

One of the young Lords had been studying the map. "They gathered here," he said, now. "In my father's lands, beside this lake. Lady, following their spoor we found campfires—" There was something in his eyes that sorrowed Elske, as if he had seen that which would never leave off troubling him, every day of his life, and every night. "Lady," he asked again, "these men had taken— We found a creature, like a doll, at one of the holdings, only . . . It had been made out of the family, the limbs of children, the woman's body. Lady, these were goatherders. Not soldiers. Not armed." He had placed his memory out on the table before all of them. They wished to look away from it, but knew they had to stay and face what he had seen. They were angry at him, displeased. The silence in the long room grew heavy, the air cool despite the warming fire.

A captain asked, "What kind of men are they?"

"Not men at all," another captain answered. "They are animals."

"Lady?" they asked her, as much fearful as furious.

Elske shook her head. She could not answer, did not know.

The young Lord insisted. "As if death were a game."

So Elske answered him. "When men have drunk too much honey mead together, as the Wolfers love to do, or wine, or ale, and more so if they have passed some danger together, then they will do such things as they would otherwise not think of. Even Wolfers, accustomed as they are to battle and blood, can be made more wild by blood and drink and the fear with which their victims look at them." She looked around at the smooth-shaven Lords in their blue shirts, the bearded captains wearing metal breastplates.

They did not wish to meet her glance, and their faces were wiped clear of any expression. So she knew they had seen men behave so, and had perhaps themselves done that of which they would not willingly speak.

She turned to Dugald, to his rock-grey eyes. "Yes," he said. "They do. We do."

Around the two of them, the other men breathed out, and each might have been thinking to himself that whatever he might have done in the past, which he would never tell, he would not act so again in future. Dugald, by his words that did not deny, freed them, as from the spell of their own actions. As if their own actions were the enchantress and it must take Dugald to break her spell.

Thorold asked then, "What do they want, these Wolfers? Why do they deal so cruelly with our people, who are not soldiers and must, I think, surrender as soon as they see the Wolfers come?"

Elske did not know how to explain the people of the Volkaric to the people of this rich and pleasant land. "They want victory in the fight, to prove their courage. They want to take treasure, to please their appetites for food and drink, to rape women. They are as much children as men. They are as much animals as thieves, and murderers. They are like wolves, except for the treasure they seek, coins and jewels, swords and knives, cloths, dark-haired girls."

"If it is treasure they want, why don't they attack the cities where they'd find booty in abundance? These holdings are poor and the cities, especially the castles of the Lords, have greater wealth, so why don't they go after those places?"

"They will," Elske promised.

This caused another chilled quiet, until Lord Hildebrand asked the question of the meeting, again. "Can you tell us how to stop them, Elske?"

Beriel had sent her here, to protect this countryside. Elske had few sword skills, and she was no Queen to hearten men for their own deaths. She could fight beside the soldiers, and that would be her choice, but more help than that she could not give them. The rest they must find for themselves.

"You know where they had gathered together before they left the Kingdom?" she asked the young Lord.

"As I said." His finger pointed again to the map. "It seemed the Wolfers had rested there several days."

"Then that is where they will enter the Kingdom," Elske told the men. "That is where you will find them massed like an army."

"And there we can use our own army on them," a captain said, his voice glad. "If not when they enter, then when they leave the Kingdom. Just let them be gathered together, and we'll be on them like wolves on sheep."

The hall was suddenly lit with hope. The men pointed out routes, arguing, and made requests of Hildebrand for supply wagons, and Lord Dugald promised that the treasury of Earl Northgate would stand open for this cause. "That's the way, then," they said to one another, and "My men are ready to move out," and "All haste, my Lord," they said. Until Hildebrand raised his doubting eyes to Elske and asked, "So, we must trust you to betray your own people?"

"Not her people," Dugald's captains said, but Hildebrand insisted, "How do we know that? She has a plausible face, granted, but do we thus put all our lives in her hands?"

Again, Elske needed to explain what they could not understand. "I cannot betray the Wolfers. I can only betray the Volkking. The warriors are only his arms and fingers and hands, each man belonging only to the Volkking, and ruled by him. He is the spider in the web; if you take off a strand of the web, the spider only spins another. The web traps moths for the spider to eat, not for itself. I cannot be a traitor to these people and I have already betrayed the

Volkking. You have no need to doubt me."

But they wanted to know just how she had betrayed this Volkking, so she explained about the role of the Death Maiden, and her grandmother's revenge on the people of the Volkaric. And from that, with the days of the journey into the hills to polish and improve it, came Lord Dugald's plan of battle.

Chapter 19

IN A SILVERY dawn, mist floated on the glassy surface of the lake and rose up into brightening air. All around, forests darkened the sides of the encircling hills. In the far meadow, the night's campfires were black circles and the sleeping Wolfers short, black lines.

Soldiers of the Kingdom slipped among the trees, invisible, horseless, wordless. Silently, they circled around the lake, approaching the meadow from both sides.

Across the black and bottomless water, a small boat moved. Elske sat in the bow. Dugald—with his back to her—rowed. He had wrapped the oars in cloth, to muffle their sound. He himself and Elske, too, were wrapped around with long cloaks.

The air was damp, chill. Those birds that woke before the sun sang their brief songs, their voices cutting sharp as knife blades through the still air.

Elske's boat glided with only the tiniest ripples of sound, through the still water.

The sun rose up into the sky behind the eastern hills and the lake's surface turned pale gold, and the mists rose up gold and white.

The night before, as they stood in the short reeds, the coracle at their feet, Elske and Dugald had looked across the black surface of the lake to the many, many campfires—almost a reflection in yellow of the many, many white stars scattered across the black skies above—and they had spoken in whispers to one another, "At halfway, do you think?" It was at that point, they'd agreed, that Elske should stand up in the bow of the boat, and make herself visible.

Dugald, her ferryman, would be hidden behind her.

Their hope was to distract the Wolfers. They hoped that the sight of Elske—some of the men might think they recognized her—gliding towards their camp across the surface of the water, would seize their attention so that the Wolfers would not discover the approaching army until it was too late to do anything more than stand, and fight. They hoped that by the end of morning the soldiers would have driven the Wolfers out of the Kingdom. Elske—and Lord Dugald, too, who would let no other man take his part—would alarm and attract the Wolfers by gliding right up into their midst.

When the time was right, Elske would give the signal for the attack. Until they heard that signal, the soldiers were under the strictest orders of silence. It was Dugald who would tell her when the time was right, another part he would let no other man take.

"The Queen put her into my care," he said, over and over. "Elske is mine to guard."

Neither he nor Elske spoke aloud what they both knew, and all the others also understood: The two in the little boat would be alone in the midst of the enemy when battle was engaged. Elske was the staked goat, to draw the enemy out, and Lord Dugald perforce staked with her.

The boat drew the sun's gold after it across the wide lake, as a Lady would the train of her fine gown. The boat moved forward through the fading mist, so that it would seem—when Elske stood— that she floated upon mist, not water.

Halfway across, at a whisper from Dugald, she stood up. The round-bottomed coracle rocked under her bare feet and she heard Dugald's intaken breaths, his unspoken fear, before the boat rocked itself into safe balance again.

Balanced, Elske dropped her cloak. This was what she had told no one. As naked as the Death Maiden entering to the Volkking, Elske stood in the bow of the boat. Her dark hair flowed down over her back.

Dugald rowed steadily, quietly. His back was turned to her, so he could not see Elske, nor the beginnings of movement among the men on the shore. The men stirred. Their voices sounded, clear across the water, groaning, laughing, quarreling.

Elske stood motionless and the boat glided under her feet.

A few of the Wolfers rose. She was not close enough to see their faces and know if she knew them. They rubbed at their arms and looked about them. One man pointed, at her, and his neighbor responded by turning around to look. A muffled wave of voices rolled towards her, almost a greeting. Slowly, the Wolfers drew together in their numbers. Slowly, gathering, their eyes all fixed on her, they approached the water's edge.

They could not believe their eyes.

They were there in their hundreds, twenty and more of the raiding parties, come to scour this fat land clean of its goodnesses. In their hundreds they drew towards the edge of the lake, as if towards the Volkking's carved throne on the day he distributed the year's takings. But on this day, they faced not the man on the throne but a naked girl, her arms at her side, being carried magically towards them on water.

And on this morning, they drew their long knives out of the scabbards. Their long beards hung down narrow from their chins and their wolf eyes were wild.

The boat glided forward, towards them, towards their center, and the boldest of them stepped out into the water.

Elske stood with her dark hair loose over her shoulders.

There was a time of absolute silence. Silence hung over the scene like a knife. And then the sun broke free of the hills, to rise up into the sky as if it were a ball of flames, ignited, lighting everything.

"Now," Dugald said quietly, and Elske opened her throat.

The Wolfer war cry rose up out of her chest, out of her mouth and into the air where it twisted, and clawed its way up. Her cry howled out over the water and into the trees.

Before that sound had left the sky, an answering, echoing cry from the throats of hundreds of unseen soldiers rolled like a fog out of the trees.

On the shore, the Wolfers looked to one another,

unable to know, undecided and leaderless. The motionless Death Maiden approached them, coming ever closer.

Their eyes were on Elske, wild with confusion and doubt; then their faces turned from her to the trees, out of which soldiers emerged, howling endlessly as they marched into battle, attacking in orderly lines.

Turning to face the soldiers on their left and turning to face the soldiers on their right, turning to face Elske, turning back to see soldiers, the Wolfers turned their backs to the lake, the Death Maiden, and the army. They fled.

They ran in packs across the meadow grass, faster than the more heavily armored soldiers could go. They crossed the meadow and melted into the trees, as fleet as wolves.

The soldiers hesitated, unprepared for this response. Elske raised her cry again and—trained to this—they answered her, louder and more clear here in the open air. Then their captains ordered them after the enemy in his flight. Giving the Wolfer cry, the captains led their men in the pursuit.

Then it was that the coracle scraped its bottom on the sandy lake bottom.

Elske lost her balance, and stumbled forward. Clutching at the rounded side of the little boat, she tumbled sideways and the boat rocked.

Dugald leapt out of the boat, then, and in the same motion turned, drawing his sword to fight—as he expected—to his death. But he could see no enemy to engage. He could see only his own soldiers, some alert and watching on the meadow, some racing into the distant woods, and then he saw Elske crouched naked in the bow of the boat.

"What—?" he asked her, as he covered her with his own cloak. "Where—?"

Elske climbed onto her knees, and then—the cloak wrapped around her—out of the boat and into the shallow water.

"Elske! What has happened?" he demanded. The water rose almost to the top of his leather boots, and he clambered quickly onto dry land. There, he reached out a hand to her, if she might need it.

Shivering from excitement, her teeth chattering with victory and with fear dispelled, as if she stood barefooted in a snowstorm before the lighted doorway of her grandmother's little house, Elske felt laughter rise up in her. "I said, they are children. I said, I think—" She shivered violently.

"Bring drink for the Lady," Dugald called to a group of watching soldiers.

She was given a leather flask filled with a liquid that burned down into her stomach, and warmed her. She drank it eagerly, and coughed, and laughed out loud.

"As if I led troops of dead men against them," she told Dugald. He understood her immediately, and looked off towards the trees into which the Wolfers had fled.

"What shall we do, Lord Dugald?" a captain asked and Dugald gave the order, "Pursue, and do not take prisoners. Let me march with you, to see how the battle goes."

"There is no battle, my Lord," the captain pointed out.

All the morning, Elske waited alone beside the quiet lake, while those soldiers left on guard there rested on the ground behind her, joking and jovial now. She could hear complaints that they had missed their chance to prove their courage and skill, matched by rough reminders that they had also missed their chance at death and wounding. "To be prepared for bloodshed, and know you have the courage for it, but not to be put in the way of it—now there's a soldier's dream," more than one said. "This is our Elskeling's way of war," they said and called out, "Lady, I'll be your soldier on any cause."

"The battle won and not a man lost," they rejoiced.

It was midday before Dugald returned to break her solitude. He'd left a troop of his own soldiers following the Wolfer trail as the war band dashed headlong, stopping neither for drink nor food, back into the south, fleeing the Kingdom. "They're not likely to come back against us," he decided. "We can sleep easy upon the question of Wolfers."

"Unless they have changed their natures, I think we can," Elske agreed.

"And you did not guess what they would think?"

"How could I guess more than that seeing me they might be stunned with surprise, and therefore taken at a disadvantage? You know that was my thought. How could I guess that they would run from me?"

"I think it was the armies in the forest they ran from."

"Thinking they were armies of dead men, and deathless."

"Did you know that you would be naked?" he asked her then.

"I knew I must be. As the Death Maiden is, when

282

she enters to the Volkking." She also knew he would have forbidden it and so she had kept silent. Just as she had known his fear of drowning when he insisted on being her boatman, and kept silent. Now she waited for his sentence on her.

"You did not tell me that you would be naked."

"You would have stopped me, I think," she said.

"I think I would have tried to stop you, and you would have persuaded me of the need," he corrected her. "Elske," he said, and then said her name again, "Elske. I never tire of your surprises. You know that."

That, she hadn't known.

"I can warm my hands in the grey of your eyes, as in the warmth of wolf fur. I warm my heart at the sound of your name. Elske, if I have my way, I will have you with me every day of my life, as long as I live," he told her, and added, "Also, in my bed."

Elske had not known that, either.

"Will you have me?" he asked, and before she had time to say yes, he said, "For husband, I mean. Do you want me for your husband?"

"How could I not want you?" she asked him. "For husband, but—"

"Why?" he interrupted.

This she could answer easily. "Because you are true-hearted," she explained, "and brave. And useful—in many ways—and you desire to be useful to people. Because"—she didn't know how to say this in the more delicate southern language, in a way that would be decent to him; the feeling being so unfamiliar to her, and confusing to her, and understanding as she now did how rape was not the right word for her feeling—"because I would be in your bed with you, and both naked, even if it is not decent," she said and then, when he shouted with laughter, she remembered, "because of your laughter."

When he wrapped his arms around her and lifted her up into his embrace, the soldiers around them looked away, mumbling to one another, shuffling their boots into the dirt, coughing and spitting, before they gave way and stared.

When Dugald set her apart, it was only to hold out both his hands to her and say, "I offer you my heart, Lady, my hand, my title and my lands. Give me your word that you will take them."

"I promise you," Elske said, almost unable to breathe for gladness, almost as if she were drowning, with his hands held in her own strong grasp.

Chapter 20

THE ARMY UNDER Lord Dugald returned woundless the way they had come. At every village and inn they were greeted by welcoming crowds, for their story preceded them. Elske grew accustomed to hearing her name called out, perhaps by the children near a farmhouse, "Elske, Elskeling!" or by villagers gathered near a well, "Elskeling!" She rode at Dugald's side, once again dressed as a Lady must and riding sideways. Elske could wave, and smile, and be glad of the victory. She could be glad that through the victory, the shadows of fear had been lifted from this land, with its stony fields and the flocks of sheep and goats which grazed on its hills, with its dark-eyed sturdy people, who cheered for the soldiers as they marched past in file, and cheered for their Earl that would be, and called her by name, "Elske!"

Dugald chose not to disband his army until he knew the outcome of the royal contest, so he sent messengers out ahead, to find what news they could, and received them without delay when they returned, and questioned them closely. For these interviews Elske was with him, although, "Beriel does not concern me as she does you," he remarked.

"Beriel is your lawful Queen."

"And I will be her loyal vassal," he said. "But if she dies in battle, she cannot be my Queen and I must be vassal to another, and that with a good heart—if my lands are to prosper. She rules you almost as a sister, bound in blood. Let us hope she will approve our marriage."

"How could she not?" Elske asked.

"Beriel's is a Queen's royal will," Dugald said. "But first, there is the question of the throne to be settled, for if Beriel is slain or taken—"

All along the King's Way, messengers met them with news, in Hildebrand's city, in inn yards and at the ford of the river. The reports of these messengers sometimes echoed and sometimes contradicted one another:

There was to be joined a great battle, with many soldiers risked on both sides.

There was to be a duel, because Beriel had challenged Guerric, offering a fight to the death. Her brother would not accept her challenge, claiming she mocked him, being a woman, claiming that a victory in such combat would be shame.

A later messenger told them the armies had taken up positions on opposite sides of a broad valley, where the sleepy little river meandered lazily through grassy meadows.

Dugald rode on towards the King's City, encountering the messengers who rode to tell him that a fierce battle raged, the green grass turned into mud by the booted feet of the soldiery while the little river turned red with men's blood. They told him, Guerric delayed the start of battle, and delayed again, while Beriel chafed at the postponement of the chance to prove her claims. They told him, Beriel was slain, taken captive, hanged as a traitor without her royal privilege of the ax.

No, it was Beriel's army that had won the victory. The number of dead exceeded the number of those left alive, including the wounded.

No, King Guerric had set an ambush for his ambitious sister, and trapped her and all of her royal guard, too. Thus the battle ended in victory for Guerric.

No, the Queen had found and slain her brother and enemy. She rode now at the head of those who had survived her victory. She carried the severed head of Guerric on a tall pole, that all might know her power and her right.

All the messengers agreed that many lives had been lost. Most reported victory for Beriel so Dugald and Elske moved forward with hope.

Their way led them now beside the river, and they set up their camps in the sweet spring evenings, the army around them. "You have not taught me to swim," Dugald reminded Elske, who by then knew enough propriety to answer, "When we are alone, my Lord. When we are alone and by one of the lakes, for didn't you promise me that I would have a house at the lakeside to be my marriage gift?"

"I did, and you will." They were watching night settle gentle as falling snow down over the silver river and the green land. "Let Beriel be Queen," Dugald said, then, "and I will ask no more for my perfect contentment. And did you ever think you would be an Earl's wife, Elske?"

"No," she said, for she had never thought of being any man's wife.

Dugald was in a robust pride that evening. "Has another man—any other man—asked to give you the honor of his name?"

"Yes," she said.

This surprised him. "Who was he? One of the Wolfers?"

"The men of the Volkaric have no wives," she explained, meaning to tease him. "Besides, I was the Death Maiden, and belonged to the Volkking."

This reminder drove the pride from Dugald, who took her naked hand in his own bare fingers to say, "Then who was this other man? Must I be jealous? Or were there many men, and I must be jealous of them all?"

"Be jealous of none," Elske reassured him.

The river nuzzled into the long grasses at its shallow banks, and Elske's skirts swished in echoing sound. From behind them came the voices of their soldiers. "In two days' journey," Dugald told Elske, "we'll be at the King's City and know what fortune awaits the Kingdom."

"I'll be glad when the cheering's done," Elske admitted.

But when the two armies met together and joined into one on the jousting field outside the walls of the King's City, the cheers of the citizens for their soldiers and their Queen, and the cheers of the soldiers for their victories and their Queen, for Northgate's heir, and Elske, too, choked the air. Beriel stood on the King's pavilion, where all might see her, tall and high-shouldered, one arm bandaged close to her chest, this being one of the deep wounds she had taken in battle, and leaning on a carved wooden stick for the other. She turned and turned, showing her face to all in the crowd that surrounded her. Her eyes shone blue, and her bandages shone white as she stood before her people. She wore no crown, not yet having been anointed; but Beriel had never needed any crown to be the Queen.

The soldiers of Dugald's army, both those of his father's house and those of Sutherland's, lifted Elske up onto the platform, that she might stand with Beriel, but the two could not say any words to one another, for the roar of voices. They clasped hands, once, before the voices called them apart. "Beriel!" the people cheered, and the soldiers, too. "Long live the Queen! Long life to our Warrior Queen!" Voices of men and women and children, Lords and people, all mingled together. "Elske!" they cheered, "Elske of the deathless battle, Elskeling!"

At first, Beriel and Elske stood back-to-back, like Wolfguard. With Elske to balance against, Beriel could drop her stick and raise her good arm up into the air.

Louder cried the crowd, in its joy at the double victory and in honor of these two. The two were filled with the cries of the people as the sails of a ship fill with wind, and Elske, too, raised an arm in answer to the people's joy in Beriel, and honor to them both.

When they turned to face one another again, each with her own name and the other's ringing in her ears, Beriel stepped back. She held out her right hand to Elske, palm down. She wore on that hand the royal signet. Her eyes were like the blue sea when it reflected back the light of the midday sun.

This was Beriel in her full power. This was Beriel, Queen.

Elske took the hand in her own, and when the crowd saw that it cheered more loudly, and gladly, "Elskeling!"

Beriel's hand pressed hard down on Elske's. "Kneel," she commanded. "Kneel to me."

But why should Beriel need Elske kneeling before her? Still, Elske sank down to her knees before her Queen, and pressed her forehead to the hand which she held, to show loyalty, to give honor, in servitude, and all gladly.

Now the crowd cheered Beriel's name, over and over, tirelessly.

Before Elske could rise, Beriel signaled to five men who stood close by the pavilion's steps. They were richly dressed, and two were also bandaged; they came forward to surround her. This guard, with the Queen in their midst, descended the steps and stepped into the crowd, which parted to give the Queen passage.

Win was not one of this close guard. Left on her knees on the pavilion floor, Elske wondered what had befallen the young man, wondered if he lived. She had just stepped back onto the ground, when one of the guard returned to tell her, "The Queen requires your attendance, my Lady. With no more time lost, my Lady. That is the Queen's will."

"I obey and follow," Elske assured him, and he was away to rejoin the Queen.

Wide wooden doorways opened to let Elske enter the reception chamber where Beriel was holding court. A tall-backed throne, with carved arms and legs, stood on a raised dais at the far end of the room, and there Beriel sat.

Beriel saw Elske enter, but made no sign; she was giving public thanks and praise to the captains and Lords of Northgate's army, who were called up one by one to receive her hand and swear their allegiances.

Elske looked around her, while she waited her time to be called forward. The wooden floors in this hall gleamed with polish, each plank fitted tight against its neighbors. The long windows were unshuttered, letting fresh, sun-warmed air fill the hall. But Elske did not see Win among the courtiers gathered in this room, nor among the soldiery.

Beriel called for Dugald, heir to Earl Northgate. He knelt before her and she thanked him for driving the Wolfers out of her lands, and she proclaimed him first among her loyal Lords. Then she rose up from the throne and asked him for his arm so that he might escort her through a doorway behind the dais, thus ending the ceremony of thanks.

At the opened door, Beriel sent one of her hovering Ladies-in-Waiting to Elske, to tell Elske that she, too, was required in this private conference with the Queen. Elske followed the woman's broad skirts and stepped through the door held open for her. Elske hoped to find Win waiting within. But Win was not there in the small paneled room. Dugald and Beriel sat across from one another at a table, and there was no one to occupy the fourth chair.

"Be seated," Beriel told Elske. "Now, Dugald, give me your report. Tell me how we stand with the Wolfers."

"We stand free of them," Dugald told her. "They think they were met by the Death Maiden and her army of the deathless dead. That at least is our

291

guess, my Queen, and if that is so, Elske tells me it will be many years before they dare the Kingdom again, and maybe forever."

"I don't think you should promise us forever, Elske."

Elske protested, "I have promised nothing, my Lady."

"I can offer you no honors that would equal your worth," Beriel said to Dugald.

Dugald answered her. "I seek no honors."

"Sought or unsought, you have gathered honors about you," Beriel answered. "Rumors unsaddled their horses in my courtyards before you dismounted your own, tales of a bloodless victory, of a naked maiden before whose brightness Wolfers flee. My own wars don't make such a pretty story."

"Nor such an easy one," Dugald agreed. "What of Guerric, what of the battle? For we, also, have dined on rumors."

At the question, Beriel leaned towards Elske with a mischievous smile, as if they were back in Trastad and she the Fiendly Princess again. "Guerric put a price on my head—a fortune in gold coins and land rights, which he offered for my capture alive. If dead, then only coins. But many coins," Beriel announced, as if that pleased her.

Her next thought did not please her. "He would have suborned his own soldiers into murderers. He hoped to corrupt those who had pledged their swords to me. He was a fool."

"Ah, he *was?*" Lord Dugald asked, seizing on the clue, but Beriel would tell her own story in her own way.

"I had an army to defeat, trained and weaponed,

led by experienced captains. I had my own men to use—and not to waste. Our battle plan was to attack at three points, in three equal parts, two at their flanks—where they were spread thin, not expecting attack there; and I led the third party of my soldiers into the waiting center of their line."

"On horseback?"

"At first, but after the first clash I dismounted. Sideseated is a weak position from which to wield a sword. So I fought among my soldiers, beside my own men. Elske, I think I am more of a Wolfer than you."

"I think you are," Elske agreed.

"I have walked into battle," Beriel told Elske proudly. "I have had soldiers ready to follow me to their deaths, and many did die in my cause. I have had a man's heart at the end of my blade, and watched the life leave his body, and pulled my sword free for the next enemy. And my courage did not fail me," Beriel announced. "I have had my revenge," she told Elske.

"On Guerric?" Dugald asked.

Beriel told Elske, "I was too late to be the man who slew Ditrik. But I watched him fight, and lose, and lie open-eyed as the sword came down into his throat. He knew I watched. He died bravely, which I will be able to tell my uncle, the Earl Sutherland, that harmony may grow between our houses. And I return Aymeric to his father, his honor restored as much as it can be, earned back to him by his sword. So that is finished."

"What of Guerric, the crowned King?" Dugald asked again.

"The usurper," Beriel corrected him, then told

him, "Guerric surrendered his sword to one of my captains. Of course, when he saw he could neither defeat me nor escape me. He was ever a coward— what was the word, Elske? The Wolfer word, like spitting."

"*Fruhckman*," Elske said, and could wait no longer for her own question. "But where is Win? I would have thought to find him here. Is he dead?"

"Not dead," Beriel answered. "Win was at my side throughout the battle, and took wounds—although none deep. He was at my side afterwards, when I visited the wounded and walked among the dead of both armies. And Win was at my side when they brought Guerric to me, my wounds freshly bound and my cheeks still wet with grief. Guerric offered me the ring, and the throne, and asked in exchange for his life. He asked only for his own life. The lives of all the others he gave into my hands. He offered me only what was mine by right, and my lands still wet with the blood of our soldiers."

"Where will you send him for his exile?" Dugald asked.

"I took our father's ring. I had already won the throne. What need to treat with him? Guerric ever hated me as much as I learned to hate him, and he knew I wished him dead." She stood up from her chair and went to the window, leaning heavily on the stick, to look out over her city before she turned to tell them, "So then he thought to make my men doubt me. He accused me of being possessed by insatiable appetites for the men around me. To have them in my bed— Why do you smile in that insolent way, my Lord?" Beriel demanded.

"Anyone who knows you must know the falseness

of that charge," Dugald answered. "I know you from childhood, and you have ever been more quick to quarrel than to kiss—and if ever you did kiss any man, even as a willful girl, it was not me. And yet," he said, "I'd swear you were my fond cousin."

"As I am," Beriel smiled. "As you are mine, I hope. But Guerric claimed to know of his own experience men I had called to my chamber, and claimed to be one of those himself, and he said he could prove by his knowledge of my private body that he spoke the truth. He called me unworthy, and would have said worse, except that Win cut his throat and silenced him forever."

Nobody spoke in the little room. Almost, they might not have been breathing.

"Knowingly," Beriel said slowly, as if they could not understand it spoken otherwise, "Win slew the anointed King."

"High treason," Dugald said.

Elske didn't understand them. "Can it be treason to defend the honor of your Queen?" she asked. "Can it be treason to slay a traitor? Guerric was the usurper, wasn't he? And he had sought your life, Beriel, in battle and before, also, as Win told us."

Dugald and Beriel spoke as if Elske were not present. "The Priests will have to read the law over him. My Queen, will you lose your throne?"

"I gave no order for Guerric's death," Beriel answered.

Elske cried, "Will Win die for taking your revenge?"

Beriel told Dugald, "Guerric's death Win's own loyal heart offered to me."

"You will speak to the Priests for him?" Dugald asked.

"Can your Kingdom's law condemn the man who defends his Queen?" Elske protested.

"I cannot speak. The Queen cannot. The Queen must not attempt to influence the Priests, as they apply the law."

"What will happen to Win?" Elske demanded, and at last they looked at her.

"She wouldn't let him be hanged," Dugald said.

Beriel answered precisely. "If I could lawfully save him, I would. He has given me the only cheer I have found in all of this bloody claiming of my throne. If I can lawfully save him, trust me, I will."

"You must," Elske told her.

"There is no must for a Queen," Beriel answered sharply, and this silenced them all. After a time, Beriel rose. "You may leave me, now."

Disregarding the command, Dugald said, "My Queen, I ask your blessing on my marriage."

Beriel asked, with royal displeasure, "You are wed?"

"Not wed. Promised," he answered, and looked her steadily in the eye.

"Promised," Beriel echoed him. "To whom promised?"

"I have offered and I have been accepted," Dugald said, with unconcealed happiness.

Beriel lost patience. "Name her."

"My Queen, she is Elske."

"Elske? Of course it is Elske." Beriel sounded apologetic when she said, "But, Dugald, you are to marry my sister—whichever sister you prefer—and thus join Northgate's house as close to the throne as is Sutherland's," she said. "Elske will go with my brother Aidenil to Trastad. There you must help

Aidenil, Elske, to establish a merchant bank so that he can trade, as the Trastaders do, and accumulate wealth for our royal house as well as make commercial connections in whatever cities and lands the bank does business. Var Jerrol will aid in this, Elske, for your sake. Undoubtedly, he will offer hospitality to my princely brother. You will be there to help Aidenil make our way in this new world, with your connections to the Council, and to Var Kenric's family. You will be my Ambassador to Trastad, Elske," Beriel announced, then turned to Dugald. "So you see, Elske cannot be your wife. I have need of her."

Dugald warned her, "I know you, Beriel. We have been children together, and I know how your heart is."

"Do you contravene my will? Do you seek to rule me?" she demanded.

Dugald did not shrink from her anger. "I seek to remind you to rule yourself. If you will make your two truest supporters into a meal for your pride, then your reign promises ill."

"You count yourself one of my truest men?"

"I speak of Win," Dugald said. "You have nothing to fear from Elske, Beriel."

"Have you forgotten that she is Wolfer?"

At that, Dugald laughed, then at the look on Beriel's face, answered more diplomatically, "Let us add her wild blood to our own, then, to give ours new strength."

"Dugald, you know my house. We have had new blood, my grandfathers both gave new blood to the house, and my grandmother, too, and look what it has brought—"

"Beriel, it has brought us you. I have known you

from a child, and you were ever worthy to be my Queen," Dugald answered her, and she turned from him.

She said to Elske, "I had thought you would be my voice in Trastad, and my watchdog over all of my many interests there. I thought to honor you."

Once again they kept silence, until Beriel broke it. "Leave us, Lord Dugald," she ordered. He hesitated, with a glance at Elske, but obeyed.

Beriel sat down again. Into the quiet she spoke as if her heart wept. "How can you betray me so?"

Elske knew that it was fear that dug long fingers into her neck. "My Queen, how have I done that?" she asked.

"You have allowed my Earl to give you his heart."

"How is that betrayal?" Elske asked.

"You have been a servant in Trastad, and you would marry my Earl? You have gone naked before soldiers, and all have seen you naked, and you would marry my Earl? You are a Wolfer, and you would marry my Earl?"

All of this was true. But it was not the whole truth of her, as Beriel must remember.

Beriel said now, more quietly, "Why will you not go to Trastad, where honors will be showered upon you?"

There were no words in Elske's throat waiting to be spoken.

"I know Dugald," Beriel said. "We were children together, and I know his nature. It must be you who refuses him, for he will not give you up. If you were my sister, and I forbade the match, you must obey me. If you marry him, his mother—I know her—will hate you."

Elske said, "I'm not afraid of the hatred of women."

"The men, too, his Lords, they will despise you and pity him for having such a wife. What will you do, Elske, when people do not smile upon you? For people have ever smiled on you, and been glad of you."

Elske did not speak her thoughts aloud, for she did not wish to quarrel.

Now Beriel warned her, "You'll always be a stranger where you live. In my Kingdom."

They sat across from one another at the table, like two merchants negotiating a trade. Elske answered plainly. "I have never been other than an outsider where I have lived. But my children will be born in the Kingdom."

"Your children also will be outsiders," Beriel announced.

"Are the people of the Kingdom as blind, and foolish, as the people of the Volkaric? I cannot believe that," Elske said, no longer concealing anger; and then she reminded the Queen, "I have given Dugald my word."

"Your word? What is your word next to my will?" Beriel demanded. Then she lowered her forehead down onto her folded hands, and rested there a long time. When she raised her face, she was resolute, but to what, Elske could not guess. "So you are determined to take from me the most worthy man of the Kingdom?"

"How do I take him from you by marrying him?" Elske argued, reminding Beriel, "It was one of your sisters you spoke of for his wife, not yourself."

"You cannot be such an innocent!" Beriel cried out angrily. "I know my debt to you, Elske, but you go too far with me in this. Oh, I won't forbid you. If you will marry against my will, so be it. So. You will be Northgate's Lady, and I will be sorry for it all the days of my life," Beriel promised. "And sometimes," she promised, "you will be sorry, too. For we will be parted now."

Elske had feared Beriel's death, but she did not fear to be parted from her now. Her young mistress she would have grieved for, and revenged, but this imperious and jealous Queen had no need of such service as Elske could give her.

"You have been my servant and now you will be my Earl's Lady," Beriel said, as if this thought gave her unwelcome amusement. "And who knows what you might be next, when fortune's wheel has already raised you so high."

Elske promised what she could. "You will always be my Queen. Your child and heir will always be my royal sovereign."

"And what husband must I marry to bear his children, that there will be an heir for the Kingdom?" Beriel cried.

"Why not Win?" Elske asked.

Beriel had her answer ready. "Win is one of the people and not even the firstborn son. He has nothing to give me."

Beriel had desired the throne, and been born to it, and she had earned it, too, but in the matter of her own husbanding she seemed as foolish as any other girl. "Win has no ambition more than to serve you; he will never ask more honors than those you choose to give him. He would never let himself shame you. And he has given you your brother's tongue, silenced."

Beriel listened closely to Elske's words, but still she made protest. "If he hangs? Would you wish me wed to a traitor, and a dead man?"

"No," Elske smiled. "Not if he hangs." But why should Win hang, when he was no traitor? Elske would not stand by, to watch Win die; there would be a way to save him, and she would find it.

Beriel acknowledged then, "I have spoken of marriage to Win. You should know that he refused me, for the dishonor his birth would bring to me. He will be my servant, and he will die if I need his life from him, but he refuses to be my husband and bed partner, even though he says his heart is mine, forever, and swears that he will never wed another. So, you see, even if the Priests find him innocent under the law, I may not marry Win."

Beriel rose now to return to the window where she looked out again to whatever she could see. "Even as we speak here, the Priests argue his life," she said. "I think they will decide for me. But until that question is settled, I require you with me."

"I will obey you, my Queen," Elske said.

"In that, but not in the other," Beriel said bitterly. She gave Elske no time to answer, but turned on her stick to sweep out of the room.

Elske sat for a time alone, to understand that if she wished, she might renounce Dugald and regain the Queen's favor; and to understand that she did not wish it. Also, she thought of Win. When she re-entered the hall, it was crowded with courtiers, both Lords and Ladies, several captains still wearing their light armor, and a few Priests. Servants stood along the walls. People spoke in low voices, waiting, watching the Queen. Beriel sat enthroned, lost in thought.

Elske searched for Dugald in the crowd but could not see him. She heard a woman whisper that Beriel would be crowned now, today, that there were none left to keep her from the throne, for her mother was already sent into exile in the care of Earl Sutherland. Another woman's voice answered that since this young Queen had rid the land of two evils—civil war and Wolfers—she herself was ready to bend the knee to her. And hope for the best, a third woman added, as we did when the usurper was crowned, only hope, as we must always do who are only observers in the events, we who are women. The first voice whispered that she counted that her good fortune, and the other two laughed softly.

A knocking at the great doors echoed through the hall. The company fell silent and all turned towards the sound. A steward stood before the now-opened doors to call out that the delegation of Priests awaited Beriel's pleasure. At the far end of the hall, she rose up from her throne, to stand tall and pale. "Give them entry," she commanded.

Three men in dark robes preceded one who wore a robe embroidered with colored threads, and the company parted to let them come before the young Queen. The last, most important man, had a mouth turned sternly downwards at the ends. He knelt before Beriel and his voice sounded like a bell, or a drum, reverberating through the room. "My Queen, we are prepared to give judgement."

"Rise, High Priest Ellard," Beriel commanded, and "Bring forward the prisoner," she called. Win was led in, his hands bound before him and his leather soldier's shirt stained dark. He wore the dirt of imprisonment, but his face lighted up to see Beriel, and he bowed to her before his guard escorted him up to stand before her.

Elske waited beside the dais, her hands clasped together, fingers wound around fingers. In the whole room, only Win seemed at ease, as if to face the hangman was a matter of little importance, or a joke, as if he had stood so a hundred times before. She still could not see Dugald, not among the courtiers, not among the soldiers, nor at the back of the hall or beneath the windows. She moved closer to Win, close enough to see how he watched his Queen.

Elske had moved close enough to attack the soldiers who stood beside Win, and take one of their knives in their first surprise at being so assaulted, and by a woman. With a knife, Elske could cut the rope that bound Win's hands, and also give a weapon into his hands. If Win were named traitor, then that was what she would do.

That no one might guess her intentions, she hid her hands behind her back. Something was placed into them, something with a handle, and Dugald's voice was soft in her ear. "So we are both armed. But I do not think that she will let him hang," the soft voice said. Elske grasped the knife behind her, and waited.

For a moment, Beriel lingered in front of her throne, her gown cloth-of-gold, her face as stern as the face in a painting, her bandages shining white. When she sat again, the High Priest drew his breath to speak.

All waited to hear.

303

The Priest's face was masked as a falcon's.

Elske wrapped her fingers tight around the knife she held, and considered Win's guard. The soldiers were young, and paid little attention to their prisoner, being caught up with the great events unfolding before them. Then Elske considered the rest of the company. These Lords were not even carrying swords. Elske guessed that their response to danger would be to protect their Ladies, amid shrieks and curses and rushings to safety. The captains were few, and many from the northern army; those would never attack her, nor Dugald. And Beriel, the only worthy enemy in the room, had but one good arm—besides needing a stick to walk on, for she had but one good leg. Beriel was no danger to her.

"Will you have our judgement?" the Priest asked Beriel.

"We will," she answered.

"Prisoner"—he turned to Win—"you have put yourself under the shelter of the law for your life or for your death. Do you understand this?" he asked.

"I do," Win answered, boldly.

"Then I give the law's judgement upon you." Now the Priest kept his eyes on Win, as if they were alone. Win listened to the Priest's words, but watched his Queen. "As to the accusation of treason, the law finds you not guilty, for the reason that the man—Guerric, Prince of this royal house—had usurped his sister's rightful place, and set out false rumor of her, and moreover for the reason that he had himself plotted the death of a royal Princess. Thus the man was a traitor and death his just punishment. These things are proven and determined," the Priest said.

The court sighed and clapped its palms together to signify approval. Neither Beriel nor Win responded, however. They remembered the second charge.

"As to the accusation of murder," the Priest said now. "You slew the man before many witnesses, and never sought to conceal the deed, nor deny it; however, the law finds you not guilty of murder. A soldier may not murder his enemy, or we must hang every man returned living from battle. A soldier kills but does not murder. This is the law."

Then Win did smile, and so did the Queen. He smiled for her and she smiled to fill up the room with the light of her pleasure.

Elske felt the knife being taken out of her hands so that she might clap, and be no different from her neighbors.

Beriel rose again, then. Clothed in gold she announced to all, "I will be crowned before I sleep again, for my land must not be left without its anointed ruler. I will be crowned this afternoon," she announced, and the room cheered her.

She allowed them this, then raised her hand for silence again. "There are two," she said, "and they have served me in my greatest need, at risk of all the little they had. To these two I would offer a Queen's reward. Elske," Beriel called. "Where are you, my servant Elske?"

"I am here, my Queen." Elske stepped forward to kneel down again before Beriel.

"Elske, I will ask my cousin and my Earl that will be, Lord Dugald, heir to Northgate, to husband you, and give to you the protection of his name and his lands," Beriel announced. "Dugald, this I ask of you, to take Elske for wife."

People murmured, and Elske felt their eyes on her bent neck. She thought she knew Beriel's purposes, and she hoped this would be the Queen's only revenge. And why should Beriel ask for more than that revenge?

"For all that the girl is Wolfer born, and Wolfer raised," Beriel continued, and at that the courtiers gasped softly, "I am in her debt. I ask you to pay that debt for me. Will you obey me in this, Lord Dugald?"

Dugald answered without hesitation, "My Queen, I will." This taught Elske the words to use, so when Beriel asked for her obedience also in this matter Elske said in a voice that rang as clear as his, "My Queen, I will."

Satisfied, Beriel turned to the second matter at hand. "Win," she called out, though he stood right before her. "Win, son of the innkeeper at the Ram's Head, who have been true in my service when I did not even know you served me, of you I ask more than you have already given, which has been even the offer of your life. Of you I ask also a marriage. I ask you to take the hand of your Queen," Beriel called out. "Yes, in marriage, to be her consort and her guard, advisor, husband, Prince. Will you obey me in this, Win?"

His cheeks flamed as red as his hair, almost, but Win could not, without shaming her, refuse; and so he must give his will over to hers. "My Queen, I will."

Then Beriel called for wine. Waiting, standing before her carved throne, she announced to the hall, "There remains yet one third matter of loyalty that must be settled."

"She will throw her glove down before them all," Dugald said into Elske's ear.

"And how could she do otherwise?" Elske asked softly.

Beriel accepted a golden goblet from her servant and held it out that he might pour red wine into it. The courtiers murmured uneasily, waiting for her next words. When she raised the goblet high, they fell silent.

"Today," Beriel announced in a voice that rang into every corner of the great hall, "on this day of my crowning, I offer to all of my Lords an amnesty."

Many voices breathed out sighs of relief and gratitude.

"After this day," Beriel announced, "this day of my crowning, if you serve me well I will never seek to know what you might have said or done before this day. To this I give you the word of your rightful Queen. But hear me now," she warned them. "In exchange I require your perfect obedience."

Beriel turned then, the goblet still raised, to the right, to the left, back to the front, so that she might look down on the whole assemblage and every man and woman in it. The goblet glinted in the light. She said, more solemnly but no less ringingly, "Too many have paid too great a price that I might be your Queen for any to offer me less than that perfect obedience. And I, too, have paid dearly for my throne and crown," she said. Her blue eyes looked briefly at Elske, and then Beriel made the toast herself. "May this Kingdom flourish under my rule, in all the years I am Queen."

They all echoed and answered her, "Long life to the Queen."

Elske's voice was one among many, in that well-wishing which was also a long farewell. When she could raise her voice to call "Long life to Queen Beriel," Elske must part from her mistress and companion, since Dugald was her choice. So Elske would make her own gladness after the sorrow of this farewell.

Epilogue

IN THE HISTORY of the Kingdom, these things are
told:

—How Beriel, called the Warrior Queen,
extended the borders of the Kingdom eastwards to
the sea at Pericol, and as far south as Selby. How
her armies also conquered the barren lands of the
west, obliterating the primitive tribe of the
Volkaric. In two major military campaigns, the first
against Pericol and then into the west, the second—with an army more seasoned by warfare and
experienced in success—into the south, Beriel led
her forces to victory after victory. Part of the reason for this was her weaponry, since Beriel almost
from the first possessed gunpowder. Another factor
that contributed to her military success was her
soldiers' loyalty to her. Beriel was as well a gifted
strategist and fearless general; she rode into battle
at the head of her own troops; she asked no hard-
ship of them she did not herself endure.

—How for five years after her first double victory,
over the Volkaric war bands that were preying on
the Kingdom and over a rebellious brother, Beriel's

forces went undefeated. That first, most famous, military victory was achieved without a single wound being received by a single soldier of the Kingdom.

—How for the opening years of her brief reign Beriel conquered, but at the end lost much of the territory she had taken. Nonetheless, enough remained in her control to add substantially to the increasing power and wealth of the Kingdom.

—How through Beriel, the Kingdom gained a port on the sea. Although her last years as Queen were devoted to defensive warfare, as the cities of the south fought free of her domination, she held Pericol, and built up its defenses as well as its docks. Pericol remained the basis of the Kingdom's maritime power. The Queen was among those killed in the great explosion of the magazines there, which destroyed a third of that city; she left a male heir who ascended to the throne when he had attained his twelfth year.

—How the shift from an agricultural to a mercantile economy was begun during Beriel's reign, not only as a result of the military victories and the growth of Pericol as a center for shipping and shipbuilding, but also with the discovery of copper and iron ores in the northern Kingdom. The development of these resources was the work of the Earl Northgate, and made him the most powerful man of the Kingdom, whose personal fortune exceeded even that of the royal house. At the same time, the Earl established around himself a court dedicated to learning and to civilized graces, into which any man of integrity and ability was welcomed. There were those who maintained that the merchants who flocked to trade with the Kingdom did so not so much for the profits as for the honor of being received at Northgate's court, and the pleasures of time spent there. In the annals of the time, it is sometimes referred to as the Court of Light and sometimes as the Court of Elske [*sic*]. During the long rule of this distinguished Earl, Northgate was the premier city of the Kingdom.

—How Gwyniver the Great, granddaughter of both Queen Beriel and the Earl Northgate—whose daughter had married the young King thus joining together the two great families of the Kingdom—ascended to her throne at the age of fourteen. The year of her crowning marks the beginning of the Thirty-Seven Year Peace, which extended into the sixth year after her death. Scholar, linguist, diplomat and gifted economist, Gwyniver forged a series of alliances—through marriages, through trade monopolies, through the threat of arms—among the great cities of the south as well as the emerging cities of the north, as far away as Trastad. Gwyniver is also known as the founder of the University, and as a patron of artists, musicians, minstrels, mediciners and craftsmen of all callings. During her reign the laws of the Kingdom were codified and the seasonal sitting of justices in trial instituted, as well as the profession of Speaker for the Accused. She established Pericol as the royal seat, and welcomed Ambassadors from all over the known world, thus continuing the anti-isolationist movement begun in her grandparents' day. She absorbed customs from other lands into her own government—such as guilds of craftsmen as in Celindon and the local governing Council as in Trastad. She had a reputation for wild courage, and tireless curiosity. Her citizens, from the greatest to the least, all lived without fear of want or of tyranny. In the reign of Gwyniver the Great, the Kingdom's Ambassadors were welcome wherever they journeyed, received with honor even at the court of the Emperor of the East. Under the rule of this Queen, the Kingdom enjoyed its golden age.